Claiming Red

A DARK RED RIDING HOOD RETELLING

ONCE UPON A MONSTER
BOOK ONE

SEPHYRRA

WITHER & RUNE PRESS

Published by Wither & Rune Press
ISBN:979-8-9930526-5-6

For everyone who read "the better to eat you with," crossed their legs, and kept reading. This is the book you were waiting for.

Content Advisory

This book contains mature content intended for adult readers. Please be aware of the following before reading:

•Sexual content (explicit, including shifted/werewolf form)

•Captivity and forced proximity

•Attempted sexual assault (on page, not by the hero)

•Domestic and sexual abuse of a secondary character (on page, through visions)

•Drowning and execution by water (on page)

•Attempted hanging (on page)

•Death of a child (on page)

•Violence and gore including werewolf combat

•Blood and injury detail

•Emotional manipulation as a survival tactic

•References to terminated pregnancy and reproductive coercion

•Grief, loss of a spouse, and prolonged isolation

•Village mob violence and religious persecution

This is a dark paranormal romance. The hero does not sexually assault the heroine and does not intentionally injure her. The relationship reaches a safe, consensual HEA. But the road there is not gentle.

If any of these elements are triggering for you, please prioritize your wellbeing.

Chapter One

Water filled my lungs.

Cold. So cold it burned through my chest and settled into my bones. I tried to scream, but the river swallowed the sound, pushed itself deeper into my throat until I could taste mud and rot and old copper underneath. The river remembered every body it had ever taken.

Above me, faces rippled through the surface. Mouths moving in words I couldn't hear, eyes watching with patience, arms folded and heads tilted. They watched while a woman died beneath them.

My wrists burned where the rope cut into skin. Thumbs bound to toes — the old way, the binding that made floating impossible, that folded a body in half. I fought against it and the ropes pulled tighter, dragged me deeper into the black where the faces above became smears of light.

Someone was counting.

I could hear it even through the water, even through the roaring in my ears. A man's voice. I knew that voice.

Twenty-three. Twenty-four. Twenty-five.

The cold stopped hurting somewhere around thirty. My body surrendered to the dying, and warmth crept in where the cold had been, whispering that perhaps this wasn't so bad. That I could just stop fighting. Just let go. Just sink into the dark.

Thirty-six. Thirty-seven.

But no. I had to try one last time. So I opened my mouth to scream, and the river rushed in to fill the space where breath should have been.

I gasped awake. Cold. Water. Night.

I was standing waist-deep in the river. The water was black around me and cold enough to steal breath, and my nightgown clung to my body like a second skin. The wet linen showed everything — the curve of my breasts, the soft roll of my belly, the thickness of my hips that no amount of hunger had ever thinned.

The moon hung full and bright overhead, silver light on black water. An owl called somewhere in the trees and a dog barked in the village.

The night wandering. Again. A curse that awoke in me when I was young.

I lurched toward the bank and my feet slipped on river stones, making me go nearly under. Water streamed from my hair and clothes as I dragged myself onto the mud, and I crouched there shaking so hard my teeth rattled.

Anyone could have seen me. The thought came to me like a nightmare, a thirty-eight-year-old widow wandering alone in the night, dressed in nothing but her shift, soaking wet from the river. If anyone saw me like this, they'd have questions I couldn't answer. They'd call me mad. Or worse.

Witch.

I forced myself to move. Stayed low and kept to the shadows between buildings, my bare feet silent on the packed dirt. The village was dark and quiet, everyone was still asleep in their beds, lucky for me.

I ran the last stretch to my cottage, slipped inside, and shoved the door closed. I dropped the latch and leaned against the wood with my whole body while my nightgown dripped a puddle onto the floor.

Every door had stayed shut. Every window dark.

And no one would see me come home, either. That was the thing about living alone, the danger ran both ways. No witnesses to my shame in the river, but no one waiting with a lit candle and a blanket and the particular relief on a face that meant *I was worried.* The cottage gave nothing back. Just the dead fire and the dark and the smell of my own herbs hanging in the rafters, indifferent as always.

I stripped off the wet linen and left it in a heap. I pulled on a dry shift and wrapped a blanket around my shoulders, but I couldn't stop shaking. I wanted someone to notice the shaking. I wanted a hand on my back, a voice asking if I was all right, even a dog lifting its head from the floor to watch me with sleepy concern. I had none of it. Only the walls, and the dark, and the sound of my own breathing too loud in the quiet.

I sank down onto the floor with my back against the door. The river still coated my throat. That voice still counting down.

Thirty-six. Thirty-seven.

What came after thirty-seven? How high did he count before they pulled the body out?

I pressed my forehead against my knees and stayed there a long time. Just me and the cold and the cottage that had stopped being a home years ago, when the last person who made this cottage a home went into the ground.

This cottage had been my parents' before they died. I was too young when it happened, and I remembered them only in flashes now. My mother's hands braiding my hair. My father's laugh from somewhere far away. The smell of bread baking. The sound of a door closing.

After they were gone, Grandmother and Sophia came down from the cottage in the woods. Moved into the village, into this house, to raise me.

Our village had been built by German farmers, English settlers, and frightened men who thought the forest would leave them alone if they gave fear a proper name.

It cost Grandmother more than I understood at the time. Her gift was seeing spirits, the dead appeared to her as clearly as the living, and where there were people, there were ghosts. The village was thick with them, all those lives ended, all those souls lingering. In the cottage deep in the woods, she'd had peace and quiet, just the trees and the animals and her own mother's spirit visiting when she needed her.

Sophia gave things up too, old enough to resent being uprooted, she could have fought it, could have dug her heels in, could have refused to leave the only home she'd known instead of helping raise her sister's child. The village was hard on her in ways she couldn't explain to anyone but Grandmother. Too many people. Too many feelings pressing in from every direction. She'd get headaches in the market square and go pale at festivals and sometimes she'd stop mid-sentence and tilt her head like she was listening to something the rest of us couldn't hear. Grandmother called it the Sensing, said Sophia had been born with ears for things other people were deaf to. In the forest it had been manageable. In a village full of bodies and noise and want, it ate her alive.

She came anyway. Slept in the small room off the kitchen, taught me to cook and sew and tell one herb from another. Told me stories at night when I couldn't sleep and held me when I cried for parents I couldn't remember.

She was my aunt but more than that she was my friend, my favorite person in the world. Five years between us, but it had never felt like that much. We'd grown up tangled together, shared secrets and dreams and the small rebellions girls share when they're learning who they are.

My fingers found the red ribbon tied around my wrist. Faded now, fraying at the edges, but still red. Still mine.

Grandmother wore red. Sophia wore red. My mother wore red. All the women in our line wore it. Grandmother said it was tradition. Her mother wore it, and her mother before that. It was a thread of color connecting us across generations.

That was why they called me Red and not by my real name, Talia.

Grandmother started calling me Red before I could walk. She caught me pulling the crimson ribbons from Sophia's hair, stuffing them into my mouth, and crying when she took them away. "That child wants everything red," she had told Sophia, shaking her head. The name stuck. The whole village picked it up.

Now the village uses it differently. Red the widow. Red the healer. Red who lives alone, talks to herself, and walks strangely at night.

I am Red. The color and the woman.

The loneliness was nothing new. I'd learned to wear it the way you learn to wear a badly fitting shoe, always rubbing the same places until you stopped noticing the pain and just noticed the limp. What was new was the fear sitting on top of it tonight. The two together made a particular kind of terrible.

And this wasn't even the first time sleep had walked me somewhere it shouldn't.

The night wanderings had happened my whole life. I

walked in my sleep and saw things, visions that came whether I wanted them or not. Sometimes they showed me the truth. Sometimes they lied. I never knew which until it was too late.

The first vision came when I was seven.

I dreamed of falling. Just the endless dark pulling me down and down until my bones knew the landing before it came. I woke up standing beneath the old oak behind the cottage. Barefoot in the grass, my nightgown damp with dew, the taste of blood in my mouth and my arm aching even though nothing was wrong with it.

A week later, I fell from the same old oak tree. Broke my arm in two places. Grandmother set the bone herself, her hands steady and her face calm. When it was done, I sat on the kitchen stool with the splint still warm against my skin and told her.

"I dreamed it," I whispered. "A week ago. I felt it break before it happened."

Grandmother went still. Her hands froze on the edge of the table. She looked at me for a long time, and I braced for the fear, the confusion, the pulling away that I'd already learned to expect when I said things other people couldn't understand.

She pulled me against her chest and held me so tight the splint pressed between us. Her heartbeat was fast against my ear. She didn't say a word for a long time. Just held on.

"You're like Sophia," she murmured into my hair. "Different, but the same blood." She pulled back and cupped my face. Her eyes were wet. "You listen to me, little Red. What you have is not a curse. It is not a sickness. It is yours. Do you understand?"

I didn't. Not then. But I nodded because her hands were warm on my face and her eyes were fierce and I wanted to believe her.

After that she watched me differently, like she was waiting for something else to wake up inside me.

The second vision came when I was ten.

I saw a man in the air. He wasn't flying, and he wasn't falling. He just hung there like a puppet jerked upward on invisible strings, no rope, no hands, nothing touching him at all. His body twisted and writhed, arms clawing at nothing, legs kicking against air that wouldn't let him go.

Then the pressure came.

I felt it more than I saw it. A pressure squeezing, tightening around him from every direction at once. His face went red, then purple. His eyes bulged and his mouth stretched open in a scream that never made it past his throat.

His head burst. His body hung there for a breath longer, still held by whatever invisible force had caught him. Then it dropped and hit the ground like a thing emptied out.

I woke up standing in the village square. Bare feet on cold stone, my nightgown thin against the wind, the exact spot where they held the trials. Grandmother found me there before anyone else did. She wrapped her shawl around my shoulders and carried me home without a word, her arms trembling. When I told her what I'd seen, the man in the air, the pressure, the red rain, her face went pale, but she stroked my hair and told me it was just a nightmare. Nothing more.

No one died that way in the village. Not that year. Not the year after. The vision was wrong, and I held onto that. I needed proof that my sight could lie, that not every nightmare wore prophecy's clothes.

The third vision came when I was still a girl.

I woke up in the forest, halfway between the village and Grandmother's old cottage in the deep woods. Standing in my nightgown with bare feet and pine needles sticking to my skin, the moon new and the darkness so complete I couldn't see my own hands in front of my face. But I remembered the dream.

Sophia. Walking through trees. A man's shape waiting for her in a clearing, tall and broad and perfectly still. She walked toward him like she couldn't help herself and reached out her hand.

He took it.

Then nothing. Just cold, just dark, just the feeling of something ending that should have gone on forever.

I didn't tell Grandmother what I'd seen. Told myself it was like the man in the air, a vision that wouldn't come true.

Sophia was fine. Sophia was right there in the cottage, braiding my hair that morning and calling me "little Red" and laughing when I blushed. A year passed. The vision faded and I almost forgot it. Then one morning I woke up and Sophia was gone.

Grandmother's face was like stone that morning. She

held a note in her hands, read it three times before she spoke. "She ran off with a man. That's all there is to know."

I didn't believe it. The note didn't sound like Sophia because, deep down in my heart, I knew she would never abandon Grandma and me. But then I thought about the vision I had. The man's shape in the darkness. Sophia reaching for him like she couldn't stop herself.

I knew at that moment I should have told Grandma. I had hoped the vision away, and now it was too late. Could I have stopped it? If I'd told Grandma what I saw, would Sophia still be here?

The fourth vision came after I married William.

Emma. My friend Emma, on her knees in the dirt, screaming over a boy. A child I didn't recognize, crumpled on the ground with his neck bent wrong, so wrong, and blood soaking through his shirt in a dark spreading stain. His eyes staring at nothing. Whatever had killed him had done it without mercy. Snapped him like a twig and tossed him aside.

I woke up on Emma's doorstep. Standing in the dark with my hand raised like I'd been about to knock. My nightgown soaked through with sweat, my feet bare on the frozen step, my stomach heaving. I made it to the bushes beside her fence before I vomited and hurried back home.

Luckily, Emma had no son. She wasn't even married yet, and the longer I waited for the vision to come true, the more it faded. Months passed. A year. Emma married Heinrich. Emma had her first daughter, then a second. Two healthy girls with Heinrich's broad shoulders and Emma's easy laugh. No boy. No torn throat. No blood in the dirt. I let the relief settle into my bones like warm water and let the vision fade to something old and harmless.

Then Thomas was born. Fat cheeks and wild curly hair and a laugh that could fill a room. I held him the day Emma brought him into the world and something cold moved through my chest. That face. Those curls. The same boy from the vision I'd buried years ago.

I said nothing. Smiled and cooed and handed him back to his mother, then went home and sat in the dark and told myself I was wrong. That the sight had lied before. That this boy would grow up and climb trees and break his mother's heart with worry and live. He had to live, because the alternative was unbearable.

The fifth vision came two winters after my marriage.

William. My husband — the man who called me by name, Talia, and kissed my forehead when I worried too much, who smelled like pine sap and wood smoke and never once asked about my strange dreams.

I saw him torn apart.

A creature with teeth and claws, something that moved too fast to see. I watched it rip him open, watched him try to crawl away and fail, watched the light leave his eyes while his blood soaked into the forest floor.

I woke up at the tree line. Standing where the village ended and the deep forest began, my bare feet in the frost, my face turned toward the dark between the trunks. The place that would eat him alive. William found me there — followed my footprints from the cottage through the mud. He wrapped his coat around my shoulders and led me home and asked what was wrong. I told him everything, begged him not to go hunting that day, begged him to stay home. He laughed and kissed me and promised he'd come back.

He didn't. They found pieces of him scattered across a clearing. Him and the six men who had walked into the forest beside him. Seven men torn apart so thoroughly that they couldn't tell which pieces belonged to whom. After that, the village declared the deep forest forbidden. No hunting parties past the second ridge. No woodcutting beyond the marked trees. Klaus held it up as proof. Not just of a cursed forest but of something darker. Witchcraft, he whispered to anyone who'd listen. A curse laid by ungodly hands. Klaus used the fear well. Held meetings. Quoted scripture. Reminded the village that the devil walked among good people in disguise, and that God demanded vigilance. He'd been looking for an excuse to tighten his grip on the village for years. Seven dead men gave him one.

Now I'd seen myself drown. The counting. The faces watching. The rope binding me in half as water filled my lungs and someone marked the seconds. My doom was coming.

The fire had died to embers while I reminisced about the past. The cottage was cold and dark around me. I should have gotten up, rebuilt the fire, and tried to sleep like a normal woman. I didn't move.

Everyone I've ever loved walked through this door. Sat by this fire. Slept under this roof. If I left, I would lose them all over again, the last traces of them, the places their hands had touched, where they had spoken, where their bodies had left warmth.

I couldn't.

Maybe the vision wouldn't come true. The man in the air had never happened. No one had died like that, not that year, not the next. The William vision had come true. But the man in the air had not, and one wrong vision was enough to make me doubt all the others. Thomas was healthy and alive and growing taller every month. My sight lied as often as it told the truth. I chose to believe it was lying about him.

I could stay. I could hope.

It was all I had.

Chapter Two

I gave up on sleep when the birds started singing.

The vision clung to me. Every time I closed my eyes I felt rope cutting into my wrists and heard the counting in my head.

Thirty-six. Thirty-seven.

I pushed off the blankets and put my feet on the cold floor. My body ached like I'd been fighting all night, maybe I had. I touched the red ribbon at my wrist, rubbing the frayed edge between my thumb and forefinger until the trembling eased.

Work helped. It always had. When my hands were busy, my mind could rest. Or pretend to.

I crossed to my herb table beneath the window, where bundles of dried plants hung from the rafters above and baskets lined the wall. Jars and pots and pouches crowded the surface, and the smell of green things filled my lungs and pushed out some of the river still lingering there.

My inheritance was never money or land. It was knowledge passed down through hands and voices. Mother to daughter. Generation to generation. Grandmother and Sophia taught me which plants to grow and which to forage, which to pick in spring and which to wait for until the first frost. How to dry them, grind them, mix them into salves and tinctures and teas that could ease pain or bring sleep or stop a wound from going bad.

I pulled down a bundle of chamomile and stripped the flowers from the stems. The petals crumbled between my fingers and released a smell like apples and honey, good for sleep, for nerves, for bellies that wouldn't settle. I could use some myself, but the stores were low and winter was just starting. The people who came to my door needed it more than I did.

I worked until my shoulders ached and my fingers were stained green. It helped. A little.

The door flew open.

I spun with my heart slamming against my ribs, but it was just Emma. Tall and broad-shouldered with a face made for laughing, she burst through without knocking because she never knocked, had decided years ago that my door was her door.

She wasn't laughing now.

Thomas hung against her hip, wild curly hair and a gap-toothed grin that could charm his way out of anything. He wasn't grinning either. His face was gray and tear-streaked, his left arm hanging wrong at the elbow.

"He fell from the oak behind the house." Emma's chin trembled, the words tumbling over each other. "I heard him scream and ran out and he was just lying there holding his arm and I didn't know what to do."

"Bring him here." I swept the herbs aside with both arms and spread the cleanest cloth I had across the wood.

Emma eased Thomas down and he cried out when his arm shifted, his face crumpling as fresh tears spilled down his cheeks. But I made myself focus. Thomas needed me. Nothing else mattered. I examined the elbow, ran my fingers along the bone. The joint was out of place. I could feel the wrongness of it, the way the bones had slipped past each other. It reminded me of my own fall from the tree many years ago. Lucky for Thomas, Grandmother taught me how to settle bones. How to read a body with my hands, how to feel where things had shifted and where they needed to go back.

"Thomas." I brushed the hair back from his forehead. "Look at me."

He looked, his eyes brimming and his chest hitching with the effort of not sobbing. Snot ran down his lip and he wiped it on his sleeve with his good hand. "I'm going to fix your arm." I held his gaze steady. "It's going to hurt for one moment. Just one. Then it will feel better. Can you be brave for me?"

He nodded, his lip trembling. A tear slipped free and rolled down to his cheek.

"Good boy." I squeezed his shoulder. "The bravest."

I looked at Emma. Her face was pale but she was holding herself together with great effort. "Hold his shoulders." I positioned her hands where I needed them. "Keep him still."

She pressed down, her knuckles going white.

I took his arm — one hand on the upper part, one on the lower. I could feel exactly where the bone had slipped, exactly where it needed to go. "Take a deep breath, Thomas." I watched his chest rise. "Count with me."

"One." I positioned my hands.

"Two." Found the angle.

"Three." I moved quickly. A twist and a push and then a *pop*.

Thomas screamed, but only for a second, a sharp sound that cut off as suddenly as it started. His arm was straight again, the elbow back where it belonged. He stared at it, then at me, his mouth falling open. "It doesn't hurt anymore." He flexed his fingers slowly, wonder breaking across his face.

"It will ache for a few days." I wiped the tears from his cheek with my thumb. "Some bruising. Some swelling. But the worst is over."

Emma made a sound that was half laugh and half sob, then pulled Thomas off the table and crushed him against her chest, eyes squeezed shut, her whole body shaking.

"Mama." Thomas squirmed against her grip, his good arm pushing at her shoulder. "Can't breathe." She laughed and loosened her hold, but she didn't let go. Her hand stayed pressed against the back of his head like she was afraid he'd vanish if she stopped touching him.

I turned away and gave them the moment and went to my herb table where my hands were shaking and hid it by keeping them busy, comfrey for the bruising, arnica for the deep ache, mixed into rendered fat until it became a thick paste.

Thomas. Wild and reckless and so full of life. For a moment something cold brushed against the back of my mind, an old nightmare, long buried, and I shoved it down the way I'd been shoving it down for years. He was here. He was fine. He was always going to be fine.

I finished the salve and brought it to the table. Thomas wrinkled his nose, his upper lip curling back.

"Ew, this smells bad." He leaned away from the jar.

"Smells like medicine." I tapped his nose with one finger. "The best medicine always smells terrible. That's how you know it works."

I applied it gently, rubbing it into the skin around his elbow. The joint was already purpling — by tomorrow it would be a spectacular bruise. He'd be proud of it, showing it off to the other boys, making the fall higher each time he told the story. I wrapped his elbow in clean cloth and tied a sling around his neck. "No climbing for two weeks." I tugged the knot snug. "Can you do that?"

Thomas's mouth fell open. He looked at me like I'd suggested he stop breathing. Emma laughed, the sound still wet around the edges but real. She ruffled his hair. "I'll tie him to a chair if I have to."

I packed the rest of the salve into a small jar and pressed it into Emma's hands. "Apply this twice a day." I curled her fingers around it. "Morning and night. Keep the sling on even when he says it doesn't hurt anymore."

"How much do I owe you?" Emma reached for her pocket.

"Nothing." I stepped back and folded my arms.

"Red..." Her brow furrowed.

"You brought me bread last week." I held my ground. "Eggs the week before. We're even."

She looked like she wanted to argue, her mouth opening and closing, but Thomas was already squirming and she had her hands full holding him still. "Thank you." She met my gaze, serious now, the gratitude showed plain on her face. "You're the only reason half this village is still walking upright."

"Go home." I shooed her toward the door. "Keep him off the trees."

She smiled and shifted Thomas onto her hip. Headed for the door, then paused and looked back at me, her head tilted, her eyes squinting the way they did when she was puzzling something out.

"You look tired, Red." She searched my face, one hand

braced on the doorframe. “More than usual. Are you sleeping?”

“Well enough.” I made myself hold her gaze. The lie came easy. I’d been telling it for years, and Emma’s lips pressed thin because she knew. But she also knew I wouldn’t talk about it. We’d done this dance before.

“If you need anything.” She gripped the doorframe tighter. “Anything at all.”

“I know.” I let my shoulders drop and let her see I meant it.

She nodded. Then she was gone, the door closing behind her, and the cottage went quiet.

I stood there staring at nothing, my hands still and steady now that the work had done its job. Thomas’s laugh carried back through the door as Emma carried him down the path. Healthy. Whole. Alive.

Later that day, I had to go to the market square. I usually avoided it, too many people, too many eyes, but I was running low on provisions. The square was crowded with the usual morning bustle. Farmers selling vegetables from carts, the baker’s wife with her trays of bread, children running between legs while their mothers shouted at them to behave. I kept my head down, moved from stall to stall, bought what I needed without lingering. Spoke only when spoken to.

The whispers followed me through the market. They always did.

Witch.

They were never loud enough. As if saying the word loud enough would make me turn them into toads. I wish it would. But that's how it worked in a village like this, just a word passed from mouth to mouth, a seed planted in soil that was always fertile.

"Red." Someone called my name from behind me and I knew who it was before I turned around.

Klaus. He stood too close — always stood too close. A big man with a barrel chest and small eyes that never quite looked at my face. His gaze dropped to my bodice and lingered there.

"Elder Klaus." I kept my expression flat and empty.

"Shopping alone?" He smiled, showing his yellow teeth beneath thin lips. "A woman like you shouldn't be alone so often. People talk."

"Let them talk." I shifted my basket between us like a shield. "They know I'm alone, a widow and an orphan. Who do they expect to be with me when shopping?"

"You know, I could help with that." He stepped closer, his tongue darting out to wet his lower lip. "A widow needs protection. Needs a man to speak for her. I've told you before — my offer still stands."

His offer. To make me his mistress, to use my body whenever his wife wasn't looking and call it charity. He'd been making that offer since they buried William. "I don't need protection." I lifted my chin.

"Everyone needs protection, Red." His hand found my elbow, fingers pressing into flesh, his nostrils flaring as he leaned closer. "Especially women who live alone. Women the village whispers about." His breath smelled like sour ale. "It would be a shame if those whispers got louder."

I pulled my arm free and took a step back.

"I need to go." I clutched the basket against my chest.

"Think about it." His eyes traveled down my body, slow and deliberate, and his smile widened. "I'm a patient man. But my patience has limits."

He walked away and disappeared into the crowd. I stood there with my skin crawling where he'd touched me. Klaus would be one of the faces watching me drown. I could feel it in my bones, could see him in that circle above the water, counting.

I hurried home and locked the door behind me. Sat in the chair by the cold hearth while the counting echoed in my head. I stayed there as the light faded, trying not to picture the dark closing over me.

Chapter Three

I was finishing the cloak when the knock came. Good wool, dyed with madder root, boiled batch after batch until the red came out deep and rich. I'd been working on it for weeks, stitching by candlelight after the day's healing was done.

The needle slipped. Pricked my finger. A bead of blood welled up, bright red against my skin, and the knock hit the door at the same moment, hard enough to rattle the latch.

A knock after sunset was never good news, the village must have gathered around supper tables hours ago, and the streets were empty except for stray dogs and the occasional drunk stumbling home from the tavern.

I stuck my finger in my mouth and tasted copper. Set the fabric aside and crossed to the door. Lifted the latch. The hinges screamed in the silence. I kept meaning to oil them but never did. Some part of me liked the warning they gave.

Outside, Anna Müller stood on my doorstep, her face hidden beneath a hood pulled so low I couldn't even see her eyes properly. Her shoulders hunched forward like she was trying to disappear inside her own body. The girl was young, plain-faced, with work-roughened hands and tired eyes, the deep-down tiredness that came from living in a house with no softness in it.

Her father was the cooper. Made barrels for the tavern and not much else, drank most of what he earned and took out the rest on his wife and daughter. Everyone knew. No one did anything. That was how things worked — a man's home was his kingdom.

"I'm sorry to bother you so late." She forced the words out with her focus fixed on the ground between us. "I've been having headaches. Terrible ones. I heard you have remedies."

I studied her face. She wouldn't look at me, her hands clasped in front of her with the knuckles white and the fingers twisting together. "Come in." I stepped back and held the door wider. "Quickly. Before someone sees you."

She slipped through and I closed the door behind her. Anna stood in the middle of my cottage with her arms wrapped around herself, her eyes darting from the herbs hanging from the rafters to the jars on my work table to the bundles and pouches and bottles lining the shelves.

"Sit." I pointed to the chair by the hearth. "Tell me about these headaches."

She perched on the edge of the seat, her spine rigid and her leg bouncing against the floor.

"They come and go." She picked at a thread on her sleeve, still not meeting my eyes. "Behind my eyes. Sometimes it's so bad I can't see straight."

I watched her while she talked. Something was off — the way she kept glancing at the herb table, the way she answered my questions too quickly, like she'd rehearsed them. But I'd seen enough nervous people in my time, people who were ashamed to ask for help, people who were terrified their families would find out they'd come to me. Anna was probably just scared of her father, scared of what he'd do if he found out she'd left the house after dark.

I went to my work table and mixed a simple remedy. Willow bark for the pain, chamomile for the tension, lavender to help her sleep.

"Steep this in hot water." I pressed the pouch into her hands and felt how ice-cold her fingers were. "Drink it before bed. If the headaches don't ease in a few days, come back."

"How much?" She was already reaching into her pocket, her movements jerky and too fast.

"Two pennies." I held out my palm.

She pressed the coins into it, her hand trembling against mine. Then she stood so quickly the chair scraped against the floor, already pulling her hood back up. "I should go. Before my father notices I'm not at home."

"Be careful going home." I walked her to the door.

She nodded. Her hood had slipped back and I could see her face properly now, pale and drawn, with dark circles under her eyes like she hadn't slept in days. "Thank you." She broke on the second word, yanked the door open and hurried into the night.

The hinges screamed behind her. Her dark shape disappeared into the darkness, and I stood by the door watching until I couldn't see her anymore. A wrongness nagged at me that I couldn't name. The way she'd looked around the cottage. The way her eyes had lingered on certain things.

I turned back to my work table. Everything looked the same — the jars in their places, the bundles hanging where they should, the pouches lined up the way I always kept them. But something felt wrong.

I started checking. Chamomile. Comfrey. Calendula. Ginger. Everything where it should be.

Then I reached for the pennyroyal.

The jar was gone.

I searched the table, the shelf above it, the floor in case it had fallen. But I knew, even as I searched, that I wouldn't find it. The jar hadn't fallen. Hadn't been misplaced. Anna had taken it.

I sank into the chair by the hearth and pressed my palms flat against my thighs to stop the trembling. Pennyroyal. I knew what it was for, what women used it for when they were desperate and had no other choice.

Anna was pregnant. Had to be. Why else would she steal pennyroyal? Why else risk coming to my cottage after dark, lying about headaches, taking something she knew she couldn't ask for?

I thought about her face, the fear in it, the desperation. Thought about her father with his heavy hands and quick temper and what he would do if he found out his daughter was carrying a child she couldn't explain.

I'd seen Anna at the market last month, seen the way Jakob Brauer watched her from across the square, the way she looked back when she thought nobody was paying attention. Jakob — one of Klaus's boys. Broad shoulders, easy smile, not a thought in his head past the next ale and the next girl. A boy who took what he wanted and let someone else deal with what came after.

I understood why Anna had taken it. Fear like that drove a woman to do desperate things. But understanding didn't change what would happen if something went wrong.

If Anna took too much, she would bleed. She could bleed out on her father's floor before anyone could help her, and when they found her, when they started asking questions, someone would know. Someone would trace the herbs back to the woman the village already suspected. And Klaus, the man who'd been waiting for an excuse, would finally have his reason.

But there was nothing I could do. Anna had the pennyroyal now. I could only hope she was mindful enough.

The cloak lay on the table where I'd left it, the needle still trailing thread. I picked it up and ran my fingers over the wool. The body of it was done, wearable, warm enough, but the hem was still raw where I hadn't finished the stitching and the clasp was a simple pin instead of the proper fastening I'd planned. Sophia would have helped me with the rest, her hands were always steadier than mine, her seams always straighter. She'd have sat across from me at this table and we'd have worked by candlelight and talked about nothing and everything and the hours would have passed without either of us noticing.

But she was dead. I'd known it for years, even before I stopped pretending otherwise. After she vanished, Grandmother held on for two years, waiting, watching the door, keeping Sophia's bed made. Then she stopped. Went quiet in a way that had nothing to do with patience. Grandmother had seen her ghost. After that she hardly spoke, didn't even eat properly, and within the year she was gone too.

I set the cloak down. Couldn't work on it anymore — my hands were too unsteady, my mind too full of Anna and Sophia and all the women who made desperate choices and paid for them.

My fingers found the ribbon at my wrist. Faded. Fraying. Still red. I'd buried my parents. Lost Sophia. Buried Grandmother. Lost William. And I was still here. Still breathing in this cold, dark cottage with embers dying in the hearth and trouble gathering outside my door.

I would survive this too. Whatever came next, Klaus, the visions, the village turning against me, I would find a way. I had to. There was no one left to do it for me.

Chapter Four

The bell began to ring. Three tolls, then a pause that stretched forever, then three more.

I was in the market square when the sound rolled over us. My basket slipped from my hands and turnips scattered across the dirt. That pattern. I'd heard it once before, when I was a girl and old Mathilde was dragged to the river for supposedly cursing a farmer's cattle. The bell had rung exactly like this, three and three and three, and by sunset Mathilde's body floated face-down in the shallows.

Around me, people stopped mid-transaction. The baker's wife went still with her hand outstretched for payment, two boys playing with a hoop stopped short, and everyone turned toward the sound. Then the movement started — bodies streaming from shops and doorways. Not toward the hanging square. Toward the river. The trial grounds.

My legs wouldn't move. This was it. The vision. The drowning I'd seen with my own hands bound and water filling my lungs. Any moment now, Klaus would push through the crowd and point at me and drag me to the water.

"Red!" Emma's hand closed around my arm, her fingers biting in hard enough to bruise. Thomas clung to her skirt with his good arm while the sling held his injured one tight against his chest. "Come on." She yanked me forward, her face hard with fear. "We have to go."

"I can't." The words scraped out of my throat. "I need to. I should go home..."

"Are you mad?" She leaned close, eyes wild. "Elder Klaus summoned the whole village. If he finds out someone stayed behind..." She dropped to a whisper. "Heinrich told me what Klaus does to people who don't show. Please, Red. Just come. Stay quiet. Let this be over."

I let her lead me. I had no choice. My feet moved one step and then another with Emma's hand like iron around my wrist, and the crowd swept us forward. Bodies pressed close on all sides, the stink of unwashed wool and fear-sweat thick in the air, and beneath it all the murmur of voices rising with that particular rhythm, anticipation dressed up as righteousness.

We reached the riverbank and Emma elbowed her way through until we stood near the front, right at the water's edge.

"There." She exhaled hard, some tension leaving her shoulders. "We'll be seen. Klaus will know we came."

"Look, Mother." Thomas pointed with his good hand, his face pale but curious. "There's Father."

Heinrich stood near the river with the other Selectmen, his face drawn and his mouth pressed into a hard line. He didn't look like a man who wanted to be there.

I looked at the water. The river was dark and slow, swollen from recent rains, the same river I'd stood in weeks ago, the same river from my vision. And then I saw her.

Anna Müller knelt in the mud by the river's edge, bound so thoroughly she couldn't have moved if she'd wanted to. The ropes were exactly as I'd felt them in my vision, hemp fibers cutting into her wrists, pulling her thumbs back at angles that had to be agonizing. They'd stripped her down to her shift and the thin fabric clung wet to her body, her hair hanging in tangles around a face that was swollen on the left side, a bruise blooming purple and black from her cheekbone to her chin.

Someone had hit her. Hard. More than once.

It wasn't me. It was Anna.

My chest seized and the air wouldn't come. The pennyroyal. The trembling hands. The lie about headaches. And now this.

Elder Klaus stood on a wooden platform above her. Jakob stood next to the platform with Klaus's other men, arms crossed, face hard, not looking at Anna. Klaus filled the space above them all, thick neck, barrel chest, hands like slabs of meat, his doublet straining across his gut. His face was flushed and ruddy, sweating despite the cold.

Those eyes found me in the crowd. Found my red cloak. He smiled.

"People of this village." He boomed across the water, spreading his arms wide. "We are gathered to witness God's judgment upon a sinner."

The crowd pressed closer. Their hunger hung thick in the air, their need for spectacle, for someone else's suffering to make their own lives feel less small.

"This woman." Klaus pointed down at Anna, his lip curling back. "This creature has committed sins against God and nature. She has lain with a man outside the bonds of holy matrimony. She conceived a child in wickedness. And when that child began to grow in her womb..." He paused and let the silence stretch. "She murdered it."

A gasp rippled through the crowd. Women clutched their children closer while men shook their heads in practiced disgust.

"She took devil's herbs." Klaus rose to a shout, scanning the crowd until he found me again. "Pennyroyal. The witch's tool. She brewed them into a tea and drank it down and flushed her own child from her body like waste."

Anna's head hung low. She didn't deny it, didn't speak at all, just knelt there in the mud with her broken face and her bound hands.

"Who gave her these herbs?" A man shouted from

somewhere behind me, and Klaus's smile widened, his teeth showing in the gray light.

"A question we will answer in time." His eyes held mine. "But first, we must deal with the sinner before us." He stepped down from the platform and walked to where Anna knelt, grabbed a fistful of her hair and wrenched her head back until her neck arched at a painful angle.

"Do you deny these charges?" Spit flew from his mouth as he shook her.

Anna's lips moved but no sound came out. Her eyes were glassy and unfocused, like she'd already left her body, already gone somewhere the pain couldn't reach.

"I asked you a question." He shook her by the hair, his knuckles white around the strands. "Do you deny it?"

"No." The word left her broken and empty, no more than breath.

The crowd heard it. They always heard confessions.

"She admits her guilt." Klaus released her hair and let her head fall forward again, turning to face the crowd with his chest swelling. "The trial by water will determine her fate. If she floats, she is a witch and will burn. If she sinks, she is innocent and God will receive her soul."

I wanted to scream. Wanted to run forward and cut her bonds and drag her away from this madness. Emma's hand tightened on my arm, her nails pressing crescents into my skin through the sleeve.

"Don't." Her lips moved. "Don't move. Don't speak. There's nothing you can do."

She was right. I knew she was right. If I tried to help Anna, I'd be in the river next to her. But knowing didn't make it easier to stand there and watch.

Two men lifted Anna from the mud. She didn't struggle, didn't cry out, just hung limp between them like a doll with its stuffing torn out. They carried her to the water's edge and waded in until they were waist-deep, the river dark around them and moving slow and thick. Klaus followed them in. His fine clothes would be ruined. He didn't seem to care.

"Thumbs to toes." He snapped his fingers.

The men obeyed, bent Anna's body in half and tied her thumbs to her big toes with fresh rope. The trial had turned into execution. Justice made of murder. Just like my vision. Exactly like my vision.

"Begin the count." Klaus grabbed Anna's head with both hands and shoved her under the water.

She thrashed but then stilled as if she knew her fate. She knew there was no getting out of this alive.

"One." Klaus called out, loud and clear. "Two. Three."

The crowd watched in silence. Some faces were eager, some were sick, most were blank, the faces of people who had seen this before and learned not to flinch.

"Ten. Eleven. Twelve."

Bubbles broke the surface. Anna's body jerked once, twice — instinct fighting against the binding even when the mind had given up.

"Twenty. Twenty-one. Twenty-two."

I couldn't look away. The counting. The faces watching. The water filling lungs that would never breathe again.

"Thirty. Thirty-one. Thirty-two."

My own vision echoed underneath his count.

"Thirty-five. Thirty-six. Thirty-seven."

The bubbles stopped.

"Thirty-eight. Thirty-nine. Forty."

Klaus pulled her head up. Her eyes were open and staring at nothing, water streaming from her mouth and nose. Her skin had gone gray and her lips were blue.

She was dead.

"Innocent." Klaus let her body fall back into the water, his face showing nothing. "God has judged her soul clean. May she find peace in His kingdom."

The men released her and let her float face-down in the shallows, her shift billowing around her like a shroud and her hair spreading across the dark water like seaweed.

The crowd began to disperse, murmuring to each other, already forgetting what they'd seen, already thinking about supper and chores and the small concerns of ordinary life.

I stood there staring at Anna's body floating in the river. She'd stood in my cottage trembling and desperate, reaching for a way out of a trap that had no escape. Now she was dead.

"Red." Emma's hand found my elbow, the word reaching me like it had traveled a long way. "Red, we need to go." She tugged at my arm and I let her lead me away from the water, away from Anna, away from the crowd that was already scattering. We walked in silence while Thomas hid his face against his mother's skirt, his small shoulders shaking.

"Go home." Emma stopped at the edge of the market square, her eyes red-rimmed and wet. "Lock your door. Don't come out until tomorrow."

"Emma..." I reached for her hand.

"I know." She cut me off, her chin trembling. "She's gone now, and if you go near her body, everyone will talk. Klaus will talk."

"Klaus saw me." I gripped her fingers. "He looked right at me. He knows."

"He suspects." She squeezed back. "That's not the same thing. He needs proof. He has none against you."

"He doesn't need proof." I let that land between us. "He just needs an excuse."

Emma didn't have an answer for that. Her mouth opened and closed, and we both knew it was true. "Please, just go home." She pulled her hand free and pressed it briefly against my cheek. "I'll come check on you tomorrow."

She turned and walked away. Thomas looked back at me over her shoulder, his eyes wide and scared, his face streaked with tears he'd tried to hide.

I stood alone in the empty square. Anna's body was still floating in the river, someone would fish it out eventually, bury her in the potter's field with the other sinners and suicides.

Emma was right. I should go home. Lock my door. Hide

until this passed. I watched Emma turn the corner toward the east road, Thomas's dark head disappearing against her shoulder. Then I started walking. Three steps before the hand closed around my arm.

"Red." Klaus was right behind me, close enough that I could smell the river water on his clothes and the sweat underneath.

"Leaving so quickly?" His breath was hot against my ear. "I wanted to thank you for attending."

"Let go of me." I wrenched sideways but his grip only tightened, his fingers digging into the flesh above my elbow.

"We should talk." He turned me to face him, his eyes bright and eager, the eyes of a predator that had finally cornered its prey. "About herbs. About visitors in the night. Shouldn't we?"

"I don't know what you're talking about." I kept my face blank.

"Don't you?" He stepped closer, his bulk blocking out the fading light. "Anna confessed everything before the trial. Told us exactly where she got the pennyroyal. Told us who taught her how to brew it."

"She was lying." I refused to move even though every instinct screamed at me to run.

"Perhaps." Klaus smiled, his lips peeling back. "But dead women don't lie. And living women don't call dead women liars. Not unless they want to join them in the river."

I tried to twist free again, but his hand was a vise around my arm.

"I told you before." He whispered near my ear, his free hand came up to touch my cheek and I flinched back. "You should have taken my offer when you had the chance."

"I'd rather drown." I spat the words at his face.

He smiled, cold and empty, and his hand dropped from my cheek.

"That can be arranged." He raised his free hand and snapped his fingers. Two men appeared from the shadows, big and rough, men who did Klaus's dirty work and didn't ask questions. "Take her." Klaus released my arm and stepped back, brushing off his sleeves like I'd dirtied them. "Put her in the cellar. We'll have a proper trial tomorrow."

They grabbed me, one on each arm. I struggled and kicked and tried to scream, and a hand clamped over my mouth, rough calluses scraping against my lips. I bit down hard and tasted blood. The man cursed and yanked his hand back.

"Help!" I screamed into the empty square. "Someone help me!" The sound echoed off the buildings and came back unanswered. Everyone had gone home and locked their doors and pretended they hadn't seen a girl drown an hour ago. No one was coming.

They dragged me across the square with my feet scraping against the dirt. I twisted and fought, but their grip was iron while Klaus walked ahead of us, calm and unhurried, like a man taking a stroll after supper.

The meetinghouse loomed ahead — gray stone and black windows, the cellar door standing open and waiting. I fought harder, screamed until my throat tore, kicked until my legs ached. Someone wrenched my arms behind my back and bound my wrists with rope, tight enough that my hands went numb before they'd even finished the knot.

They threw me down the stairs. I hit the packed earth floor hard and lay there with my cheek in the dirt, arms wrenched behind me, no way to catch myself. The door slammed. The bolt ground home.

I lay still, breathing. My wrists were tied and my shoulders burned and blood ran somewhere down my shin where the stairs had caught me. Above me Klaus laughed — slow and easy, a man with nowhere to be. Then his footsteps moved away.

The only light came through the window near the ceiling, a bar of gray afternoon falling across the dirt floor. Enough to see the walls. Enough to see there was nothing here but stone.

Above me the village went about its day like nothing had happened, like I wasn't in the dirt with my hands tied behind me, like tomorrow wasn't already decided.

Chapter Five

The cellar was a hole carved out of the earth, stone walls slick with moisture, a packed dirt floor that smelled of mold and rot. An old crate sat rotting in the corner. I twisted my wrists against the rope. The knot held.

There was nothing I could do. Not yet.

I pushed myself up from where I'd fallen and it took longer than it should have, no hands to brace with, nothing to push against, just my knees and the wall and three tries before I got my feet under me. My shin was bleeding where the stairs had caught me and my shoulders burned from the angle my arms were wrenched at, and by the time I was upright I was already breathing hard.

I stood in the middle of that small dark space and knew I wasn't getting out.

I sat on the crate with my back against the wall and bowed my head. Tears I didn't know I still had slipped free. Tomorrow I would drown. If I survived that, I'd burn. Unless something changed.

I thought about Anna. How they drowned that young girl today. It was exactly the way I'd seen myself go.

My death was coming. I could feel it like a hand around my throat.

Hours passed. The light through the window faded from gray to black, and the sounds above me quieted as the village went to sleep. My lids grew heavy. I was still on the crate when the scrape of the bolt made me straighten and I stood immediately.

Torchlight spilled down the stairs. A shape descended — big and broad, blocking out the light behind him. Klaus. He'd changed since Anna's drowning. Fresh clothes, combed hair, cologne that couldn't quite mask the sweat underneath. He closed the door behind him and set the torch in a bracket on the wall, then stood there looking at me.

"Red." He rolled my name around in his mouth, his lips peeling apart in a slow grin. "We're alone now. No one to hear us."

"Leave me alone." I pressed my back against the wall.

"Is that any way to speak to the man who holds your life in his hands?" He stepped closer, his shadow swallowing the torchlight, his eyes traveling down my body the way they always did. "I've been patient with you for years. Watching you waste yourself on widowhood and stubbornness. Waiting for you to see reason."

He pulled a knife from his belt.

My pulse kicked hard against my throat. But he just gripped my shoulder, turned me, and cut the ropes.

"There." He tucked the knife back into his belt, his smile spreading slow and satisfied. "I'm not a monster, Red. I want you willing."

I rubbed my wrists and watched him. He was bigger than me, stronger, and there was nowhere to run. I pressed my back to the stone. "What do you want?"

"The same thing I've always wanted." He leaned back on his heels, the torchlight catching the stains on his teeth. "You. In my bed. Whenever I call for you."

My stomach turned. "You have a wife." I dug my nails into my palms.

"My wife is old." He waved his hand, dismissive. "Dried up. She hasn't warmed my bed in years. A man has needs, Red. Surely you understand that. You were married once."

"My husband never needed to trap women in cellars." I met his eyes and held them.

His smile flickered and malice moved behind his gaze.

"Your husband is dead." His face went hard. "And here you are. Alone. Tomorrow you will be accused of witchcraft and the entire village will agree. You will face the river.

You'll either die in water or by fire." He leaned closer, close enough that I could smell his breath, stale wine and decay. "I'm offering you a way out." His tone dropped, almost gentle. "Be my mistress. Come to me when I call. Give me what I want. No one from the village saw you get arrested, only my men know. They'll keep quiet. You'll walk out of here tomorrow morning, free and clear. No drowning. Just a quiet life under my protection."

"Your protection?" I almost laughed.

"Would you rather die?" He tilted his head and studied my face the way a man studies something he's about to break. "Tomorrow they'll hold you under while I count to forty. Slowly. And when the water fills your lungs and your body starts to fight. I'll have them pull you up. Let you breathe. And then they'll push you down again." He spread his hands. "The choice is yours."

My mind went straight to Anna, her empty eyes, her blue lips, the way her body had jerked once, twice, then gone still. To Sophia, walking into darkness and reaching for a man's shape and never coming back. Every woman who had ever been trapped by a man like Klaus. Every woman who had said yes because no meant death.

"No." I lifted my chin.

Klaus blinked, his smile faltering. "No?"

"I won't be your whore." I did not look away. "I won't spread my legs for a man who drowns girls and calls it justice. I'd rather die."

His hand cracked across my face. The blow snapped my

head sideways. Stars burst behind my eyes and blood filled my mouth where I'd bitten my tongue. "Stupid." He grabbed my chin and wrenched my face toward his, fingers grinding into my jaw. "Stupid stubborn bitch. Just like your aunt."

Everything in me went quiet. "What did you say?"

"Your aunt." His lip curled. "Sophia. She was just as stubborn as you. Just as proud."

"Don't talk about her." My hands curled into fists at my sides.

"I wanted her first." His eyes went distant, remembering. "Before you. She was beautiful and young — that red cloak, that dark hair, the way she moved through the village like she was better than everyone else. I offered her the same deal I'm offering you. Protection. Security."

His thumb pressed into my cheekbone hard enough to bruise.

"Even though you're not her. Not as young, not as beautiful, a widow, used. But I'm still offering. You should be grateful." His grip shifted on my chin, almost possessive. "Because she didn't take what I offered. She chose Erik instead." He spat the name, bitter and poisonous. "That woodcutter. Lived in this village for years, right under my nose, and she picked him. Ran off with him in the middle of the night like a bitch in heat."

Erik. Of course. He'd come to the village with his young son, settled near the edge of the woods, kept to himself. I remembered Sophia around him — how she'd go quiet, how her hands would fidget with the hem of her sleeve. She never looked easy near that man. The shape waiting in the darkness finally had a name.

Klaus must have seen it on my face. His teeth clenched. "A man twice her age with a bastard son and nothing to his name. That's what she chose." He let out a breath that was almost a laugh. "A girl like that. Could have had a good life here. Instead she ran off and left her mother to die of grief." His eyes found mine. "Don't make her mistake, Red. Take my offer. Live."

His hand slid from my chin down to my throat, then lower. His fingers dragged across my collarbone and kept going. He pressed himself against me, hard and rank, and pawed at my chest like I was something he'd already bought.

He doesn't get to have this.

I lunged at him. My teeth found his hand and I sank them into the meat of his thumb with everything I had. Bit down until I felt skin split and blood filled my mouth, bit harder until I felt cartilage crunch.

Klaus screamed. He ripped his hand free and left a chunk of flesh between my teeth. Blood poured from his torn thumb, spattering across my face. He backhanded me so hard I hit the wall. My vision doubled, tripled. The cellar spun around me.

"Bitch!" He cradled his ruined hand against his chest, his face twisted into something almost inhuman. "You rabid fucking bitch! I'll make them burn you for this! I'll build the fire so it takes hours! You'll scream until your throat tears and then you'll keep screaming!"

He came at me. His good hand closed around my throat, slammed my head back against the stone, squeezed until the world started going dark.

Heat woke in my chest. Deeper than my heart — something that had been sleeping my whole life, waiting for this moment, waiting for me to need it badly enough. It surged up from my gut, through my chest, down my arms, into my hands.

And I let it out.

Klaus flew backward. He didn't stumble, didn't trip — he flew. His body lifted off the ground and hit the opposite wall hard enough to crack the stones. Dust rained down from the ceiling and the torch flickered and nearly went out. He crumpled to the floor and stared at me, eyes bulging with white showing all around. His mouth hung open while blood kept dripping from his injured hand. "Witch," he hissed with pure hatred in his eyes. I couldn't have cared less.

I stared at my own hands. They looked the same as always, scarred from years of working with herbs, ordinary. But I could still feel it, the heat, the power.

"Witch!" Klaus was on the ground. I hadn't even seen him fall. He scrambled backward, his ruined hand leaving a smear of blood across the dirt. His shoulder hit the stairs and he clawed his way up them, threw the door open. "She's a witch! Get the men! Get the torches! The witch is..." He yelled it through the building above. The door crashed shut above me. The bolt ground home.

I sat in the flickering torchlight. My throat burned where his fingers had dug in, my face throbbed where he'd hit me. Blood dripped from my mouth — his blood.

But my hands. My hands had thrown a man twice my size across a room without touching him.

What was I?

I didn't have time to think about it. Klaus would be back with men, with weapons, with fire.

My hands were free. The fool had cut the ropes himself.

I dragged the crate beneath the window and climbed up. The grate was old, iron gone rough with rust, held shut by a padlock that looked like it had been there longer than I'd been alive. I grabbed it and pulled. It didn't move. I braced my feet against the wall and hauled with both hands, twisting, wrenching, but the lock held and the grate held and nothing gave.

Rain drummed against the ground above the window. At least they couldn't burn me in this. But Klaus had other ways to kill a woman, and drowning didn't need dry wood. Nobody outside would hear the scrape of the crate, or my breathing, or whatever sounds I made trying to wrench myself free. The rain would eat all of it.

I closed my eyes and tried to find that heat again, tried to reach for it the way you'd reach for something in the dark without knowing its shape or where it lived. Nothing came.

Just cold iron under my fingers and rain hammering the ground above my head.

Above me came shouting, footsteps, the clatter of weapons despite the rain. They were coming.

I stopped trying to find the power and just pulled. Yanked at the padlock with everything I had, twisted it, hauled until my palms tore against the metal and the blood made my grip slippery and I didn't care, kept pulling anyway, rage and terror flooding up through my chest in a wave I couldn't have stopped if I'd tried. The padlock groaned. The old iron whined like a living thing in pain.

The lock snapped.

The grate swung outward with a shriek of rusted hinges and cold wet air flooded down into the cellar, carrying the smell of mud and pine and night. No stars — just black sky and the dark shape of the meetinghouse wall and rain falling straight and hard through the gap above me, spattering against my upturned face.

Freedom.

I unfastened my red cloak, bundled it tight, and threw it up through the window. Then I stripped off my dress, the wool was too bulky. Underneath I wore only my shift, thin linen that would offer nothing against the cold and the rain, but it was all I had.

Grabbing the edge of the window frame, I pulled myself up. My arms shook from the first second. I was not a light woman. Years of life had softened me, rounded my belly, thickened my hips and thighs, and hauling my own weight straight up through a gap in stone with torn hands was harder than anything I had ever done. I got my elbows over the edge and pushed, kicked against the cellar wall below me, feet scraping uselessly at the stone, rain already soaking my hair and running into my eyes.

My chest caught on the frame. I twisted sideways and felt my ribs compress until I thought they'd crack, then pushed harder anyway.

My chest made it through. Then my hips caught. I was stuck — wedged in the window frame like a cork in a bottle, my legs dangling in the cellar below. The shouting was closer now. Close enough to hear individual voices, someone saying *witch*, someone saying *burn her anyway, rain or not*.

The cellar door burst open below me. "She's at the window!" Someone screamed.

I sucked my belly in and twisted and clawed at the ground above me, fingers digging into mud and dead grass. The stone bit into the soft flesh of my hips and tore through the linen shift and then through skin and I felt every inch of it, but I kept pulling. A hand closed around my ankle and I kicked back with everything I had and felt my heel connect with bone that crunched. The man below me howled.

I pulled harder. My hips screamed. A muscle tore deep in my side, a joint popped, and white fire raced from my hip to my ribs. I wrenched myself through. Tumbled forward onto the frozen mud, rolled, shoved myself up onto my hands and knees with rain hammering my back and blood running down my legs and the ground spinning beneath me. I stayed there for one breath and then I was on my feet.

I grabbed my cloak and wrapped it around my shoulders, and even soaking wet the wool felt like armor. Like every woman in my blood who had ever worn red was standing behind me, lending me what strength they had because mine was almost gone.

Behind me, men cursed. I knew they'd come around. They'd come fast.

I ran into the rain and didn't look back.

I ran until the village was behind me, until the shouts thinned and there was nothing but open ground and rain and my own ragged breathing. Then I saw it.

The tree line.

It rose out of the dark like a wall, black trunks packed tight, branches tangled overhead like fingers laced together to keep the sky out. No light past the first row of trees. The darkness was so thick it looked solid, like something you could press your hand against and feel it press back.

Everything the village had ever told me about those woods sat down on my chest at once. Children who wandered in and didn't come home. Men who knew every root and trail and still got turned around, still ended up face down in the creek. Women who never went in at all because the women knew better, because the women listened when their mothers said *stay out, stay close, stay away*. Only the men hunted there and even they went in groups, even they came back pale and quiet sometimes, even they left someone behind once in a while. William had gone in with six armed men and never returned.

I looked at the forest. I looked behind me at the shapes of men coming after me, at Klaus somewhere in that darkness with his ruined hand and his fury.

I chose the forest.

The trees swallowed me whole. Branches clawed at my cloak, roots grabbed at my feet, and I tripped and fell and hauled myself upright and kept running. Behind me, the dogs howled and men shouted, their voices swallowed almost immediately by the dark and the rain.

I ran until my lungs burned, until my legs shook, until I couldn't feel my feet anymore. The sounds of pursuit faded — the barking became uncertain, men's voices grew fainter. They were giving up. Letting the forest have me.

I kept moving.

My foot caught on a rock and I went down hard. Mud filled my mouth. I tried to rise and my arms wouldn't hold me. My body was done — spent, nothing left. I lay in the dirt and gasped for breath while the cold worked its way through me. My shift was soaked through, the red cloak the only thing between me and the night.

Then I heard it. A low growl that vibrated through the ground beneath me.

I lifted my head.

It stepped out of the dark.

A wolf. But much bigger than a normal wolf. It stood at least four feet at the shoulder, built like something from a nightmare. Its fur was black, pure black, darker than the shadows around it, and its eyes burned gold in the darkness, fixed on me with an intelligence that should not have been in an animal's face.

My whole body locked. Was this what had killed William? Was this the thing that had torn him apart and left pieces scattered across the clearing?

The wolf circled me, close enough that I could smell wet fur and pine and something else underneath, a musk that made every hair on my body stand up.

Then, distant but getting closer — dogs. Klaus hadn't given up.

The wolf's ears swiveled toward the sound and its lips pulled back from teeth longer than my fingers. It threw back its head and howled, a sound that started low and rose to notes that had no right to exist, filling the forest until the trees themselves seemed to shake with it.

The dogs started screaming. The sound of animals in pure terror.

"Go back!" A man's voice broke through the chaos. "We have to go back!"

The hunting party fled. I heard them crashing through the underbrush, the sound swallowed fast by rain and distance.

The wolf lowered its head and turned those golden eyes back to me. Took one step closer. Then another. Close enough now that I could see the scars on its muzzle, the intelligent patience in its gaze.

It opened its mouth so close I could count the teeth. Could smell the rot and the blood on its breath. Could see the gums, dark and wet, and the way each tooth hooked backward like it was made to hold what it caught.

A sound came out of me, high and thin. The sound of an animal about to die.

Everything went black.

Chapter Six

I woke with the wolf's mouth still behind my eyes.

My body jerked before my mind caught up, hands clawing at whatever was beneath me, legs kicking, a scream building in my throat that came out as a broken rasp. My heart slammed against my ribs and I couldn't breathe, couldn't think, couldn't see anything but teeth and liquid gold eyes and darkness.

Then the warmth reached me.

It pressed down on me, sinking into my bones, chasing away a cold that had settled so deep I thought I'd never feel anything else. I was lying on something soft. Heavy furs, smelling of animal musk and wood smoke. A fire crackled somewhere close, the heat of it on my face.

My breathing slowed. I opened my eyes.

A ceiling made of rough-hewn logs stared back at me, dark with age and smoke stains that had built up over decades. Beams crossed overhead, and bundles of dried herbs hung from the rafters, swaying slightly though there was no breeze to move them.

The smell hit me before the memory did. Yarrow and sage and something bitter underneath. I knew it. I knew it the way your body knows things your mind has let go of, from somewhere deep, from childhood, from visits so long ago I'd almost forgotten them.

This was my grandmother's cottage. The one deep in the forest, the one I'd searched for after she died and never found. The forest had swallowed it whole. Yet here I was.

I sat up slowly. The room tilted and I waited for it to steady. The furs slid to my waist. I was bare underneath. Bruised and scraped and covered in dried blood, but bare. My shift was gone. Someone had undressed me.

Panic clawed up my throat. I grabbed the largest fur and wrapped it around myself, tucking the edge tight under my arm. My legs shook when I stood. The stone floor was cold under my bare feet and the room swayed, but I stayed upright.

The cottage was small, just like I remembered, stone hearth where a fire burned steady, rough wooden table with two chairs, shelves lined with jars and bottles. A door on the far wall led to the back room. I remembered it dimly, grandmother's workroom, where she kept her medicines and the things she didn't want small hands reaching for. The bed sat against the right wall near the entrance, close enough to the hearth that the fire's warmth reached it.

But things had changed. The windows, two of them, one on each side of the door, were covered with heavy wooden boards nailed into the frames. Grandmother had never boarded her windows. She'd hung linen curtains that let the morning light through and kept the moths out at night. These boards were thick, the wood dark and warped from decades of weather, the nails rusted deep into the grain. Only a few fresh scrape marks near the edges suggested someone had reinforced them recently.

And the door. An iron bar sat in heavy brackets on the inside, long enough to span the frame and bolted to slide across. Grandmother's cottage had never had a bar. She'd had a latch, a simple wooden thing that clicked when you pushed it. This was something else entirely. Someone had turned this place into something it was never meant to be.

My red cloak hung over a wooden rack near the fire, still damp and steaming slightly. Someone had brushed the mud from it and hung it with care. Relief cut through the panic — stupid, it was just a cloak, just fabric. But it was mine. The only thing I had left from before.

Then I heard it — iron scraping against wood on the other side of the door. A bar lifting out of brackets. There was one on the outside too.

The door opened.

I spun toward the sound, one hand holding the fur tight against my chest.

A man stood in the doorway, tall, well over six feet and filling the frame completely. His shoulders were broad enough to block out the morning light behind him, built like he'd spent years splitting wood and hauling stone, muscle straining against a worn shirt that had been mended too many times to count. His hair was dark and curling, gone silver at the temples, and his beard was the same, full and close-cropped, gray threading up through it from the jaw like frost. Heavy brows pulled low over amber eyes that burned like embers but gave away nothing, and his face was weathered the way stone weathers, lines carved deep around his mouth and at the corners of his eyes, a thin white scar cutting through his left brow and a longer one running temple to chin beneath the beard.

He stood there looking at me the way men look at problems they haven't yet decided how to solve. "You're awake." The sound scraped out of him like gravel dragged over stone.

"Who are you?" I stepped back on instinct, wanting distance between us.

"The man who kept you from dying." He stepped inside and I stepped back again, clutching the furs to my chest. My shoulders hit the wall and there was nowhere left to go. "You collapsed in the forest. You've been unconscious for hours."

Hours. The cellar, the grate, the rain, the running — it came back in pieces, each one sharper than the last. And then the wolf.

"The black wolf." My throat was raw, and I had to force

the rest. “It was standing over me. Close enough that I could ...” I swallowed. Tried again. “I could see inside its mouth.”

He watched me from the doorway, his expression giving away less than the stone wall behind me.

“Where did it go?” I asked.

“Away.” He offered nothing else.

“Wolves that size don’t just walk away from a woman lying in the mud.”

“That one did.” He crossed to the hearth and crouched by the fire like the conversation was settled.

It wasn’t. A wolf that had sent Klaus’s dogs screaming into the night, a wolf built like a nightmare given fur and teeth, didn’t stand over its prey and then leave. A force had driven it off. Or a command had called it off. I filed the question away and asked the one that mattered more right now. “Where are my clothes?” I pulled the furs higher.

“Your shift was torn to pieces and soaked through. I threw it away. As for the cloak, it’s drying over there.” He gestured toward the hearth without looking away from my face. “I removed your clothes so you wouldn’t freeze to death.”

“You undressed me.” My teeth clenched.

“You were hardly breathing.” His expression held no apology. “Would you rather I had let you die for the sake of your modesty?”

“I’d rather you’d kept your hands to yourself.” I glared at him.

He crossed to a chest in the corner without answering,

lifted the lid and reached inside, then pulled out a bundle of fabric. When he shook it out I saw a worn shift and a heavy skirt that had been patched and mended so many times the original fabric was hardly visible beneath all the repairs.

"These were left here." He held them out, his arm steady. "They should fit."

I recognized them immediately. The shift had a small tear near the hem mended with blue thread. I remembered watching Grandmother make those stitches when I was a child, sitting at her feet while she worked by candlelight. The skirt was the one she'd worn for heavy work, for gardening and foraging.

"Those were my grandmother's." I swallowed hard around the words.

"Then they're yours now." He kept his arm extended, his face showing nothing.

I crossed the room and snatched the bundle from his hands, then retreated to the far side near the fire where the warmth could reach me. "Turn around."

He turned without argument and faced the door.

I dressed as fast as my injured body would let me. The cloth smelled of cedar and age and the herbs Grandmother used to keep moths away, lavender and rosemary tucked into the folds. It smelled like her, and for a moment I couldn't breathe past the knot in my throat.

"This is her cottage." I pulled the skirt up over my hips. "My grandmother's."

"Yes." His back stayed to me, broad against the doorframe.

"How long have you been living here?" I questioned.

"I think twenty-two years," he admitted without a trace of apology.

Twenty-two years. He'd been squatting in my grandmother's home for twenty-two years!

"You can turn around." I pulled the blanket tighter around my shoulders.

He turned. His eyes swept over me once, then settled on my face. Cold ran down my spine. He seemed familiar.

"Who are you?" I asked.

"Dietrich." And nothing else.

It should have been enough. It wasn't. Dietrich. The name turned over in my head, catching on something I couldn't quite reach. Dietrich. I looked at his face again, the shape of his brow, the set of his shoulders, those eyes I was so sure I had seen before.

And then I remembered. A boy trailing behind his father at the village market. Dark hair, warm eyes, quiet as a shadow. I'd only seen him twice — once at the market, once at the edge of the forest, standing beside his father like he'd grown out of the trees. Erik's son.

Erik. Erik had a son.

"You're Erik's son." The words left me before I could stop myself.

His nostrils flared, his whole body going still.

"Your father and my aunt." I held the sentence together by force. "Sophia."

"What about her?" He folded his arms across his chest, the muscles in his forearms tightening.

"Klaus told me she ran away with him. But I remember her around your father." I kept my eyes on his face. "She was afraid of him. She'd go quiet whenever he was near. Her hands would shake. That's not a woman who runs away with a man. That's a woman who was taken."

A muscle jumped in his cheek.

"What did your father do to her?" I demanded, stepping closer.

He didn't answer. Just stood there, his fingers digging into his own arms like he was holding himself together.

"Tell me," I pressed.

"She went with him," he bit out. "She chose to go."

"She was nineteen. He was twice her age with a son just two years younger than she was." I was shouting now and I couldn't stop it. "My grandmother set a place for her at the table every single night for two years. Two years, Dietrich. And then one morning she stopped. And a year after that she was dead."

Pain moved behind his eyes — just a flash, just a moment. Then he buried it.

"So stop telling me she chose to go," I yelled. "I know she's dead. What I want to know is what your father did to her before she died."

He flinched. Just a bit and then he turned back to the fire like I hadn't spoken.

"Don't you turn away from me," I snapped.

"She was a witch," he shot back.

I'd asked him what his father did and he'd answered with what Sophia was, as if that explained it. As if that excused it.

He'd said it with so much certainty it baffled me. This wasn't village whispers. This wasn't Klaus with his suspicions and his leverage. Klaus had been guessing. This man wasn't. He knew.

"I don't know what you're talking about," I managed, and even I could hear how thin it sounded.

He looked at me like I'd said something stupid. "Your grandmother knew when to stop setting that plate because she saw her. Because your grandmother could see the dead." He stepped closer. "Sophia could walk into a crowded room and tell you who was lying before they'd finished the sentence. You grow herbs no one else can keep alive. You walk in your sleep. The whole village has been whispering 'witch' for years." He threw my own voice back at me, high and mocking. *"'I don't know what you're talking about.'"* His lip curled. "You don't hide it as well as you think you do."

There was no arguing with him. Every word was true and he knew it.

"How long have you been watching us?" I whispered.

"Very long time. Long enough to know everything there

was to know about your family," he said, but his tone hardened. "Your kind, your family cost me everything. My father. My childhood. Over two decades alone in a dead woman's cottage. All because he couldn't stay away from a girl with witch blood." His eyes held mine. "You're not the first woman in your line to end up caged in this cottage, Talia."

"What do you mean, in this cottage?"

Suddenly his face closed off and he immediately turned back to the fire.

"Dietrich." I uttered his name sharper this time.

His hands curled into fists at his sides. When he spoke, his tone was hollow. Bitter. So bitter it had hardened into something that sounded almost like indifference.

"The woman my father abandoned me for," he ground out. "Twice. He abandoned me twice — once when he took her, once when she died and he had nothing left and disappeared into the forest. Both times because of her." He stared at the flames. "He brought her here. Turned her mother's cottage into her cage."

"She was here." I heard myself say it before I could stop. The shock of knowing drove through me like a blade between my ribs. "She was here. What happened to her?"

"What do you think happened? He kept her. She fought. He fought harder. Eventually one of them had to break." A pause. "She broke."

The space behind my sternum folded in on itself. Understanding.

The boards. The bar. The brackets bolted deep into the frame. Erik hadn't built those to keep the forest out. He'd built them to keep Sophia in.

Two hours away. In her own mother's cottage. And I'd been in the village believing a note while deep down in my heart I knew she would never abandon Grandma and me. And I'd still done nothing. Because I was fourteen and powerless and my gift showed me horrors but never gave me the strength to stop them.

"I didn't know." I could barely push it out. "I didn't know she was here."

"If it helps you sleep better, Talia." His mouth twisted. "Or shall I say, little Red."

Heat tore through me. That name. Sophia's name for me. Coming out of his mouth like he owned it.

I slapped him across the face.

The crack echoed through the cottage. His head didn't even move, of course it didn't, he was a foot taller than me and built like a wall, but a red mark bloomed across his cheek, and his stare blazed down at me with something that was not quite fury.

My hand was still shaking. My eyes were burning. Because the worst of it wasn't that he blamed Sophia. Wasn't that he'd been watching my family for years. It was that she was here and I'd never come looking. I'd let the forest have the cottage and Sophia and everything my grandmother had left behind. And now this man stood in her home knowing more about my family than I knew myself.

I had to leave. I had to get out of here. I turned toward the red cloak by the fire, but his hand caught my arm before I'd taken three steps. Not rough but immovable, like being grabbed by a tree root.

"You're not leaving." His grip didn't tighten.

"Take your hand off me," I hissed, wrenching sideways against his hold.

"The village wants you dead. Klaus won't stop hunting until he finds you. And there's a wolf out there somewhere. You have nowhere to go."

"I'll take my chances," I shot back, yanking my arm. He didn't budge.

"You'll die out there," he warned, his fingers still locked around my wrist.

"Better than being trapped in here with you," I spat.

Pain crossed his face. There and buried before I could name it. But he didn't let go. "You're not leaving this cottage." He said it quiet, final, like he was stating the weather. "Not today. Not tomorrow. Not until I decide it's safe."

"You can't keep me here," I snarled, twisting against his grip.

"I can." He released my wrist and stepped back. "And I will." He crossed to the door, stepped outside, and closed it behind him. A gust of air rushed in before the door shut, colder than the rain had been, sharp enough to sting my face. The temperature was dropping fast. Iron scraped against wood. The outside bar, dropping back into place.

I threw myself at the door and shoved. It didn't move. "Let me out!" I pounded my fists against the wood. "You have no right! You don't get to decide what happens to me!"

He didn't reply. I just heard the wind in the trees, then footsteps crunching through the snow, steady and unhurried, fading into the forest. He wasn't angry. He wasn't conflicted. He'd already made the decision before he'd walked through the door.

I pressed my forehead against the wood, my breath coming hard and fast. The rage burned so hot I couldn't think properly. But underneath it, there was something cold and familiar, the same helplessness I'd felt in Klaus's cellar, the same locked door, the same man deciding my fate without asking.

I'd escaped one cage and walked straight into another.

I reached for the inside bar, the one I'd noticed when I first woke up, still sitting open in its brackets, and slid it across. The thud of iron meeting wood went deeper than the sound. He'd barred me in. Fine. But I could bar him out too. A small thing. Petty, maybe. But it made me feel like I had some control.

The rage drained away slowly, leaving something hollow and aching in its place. I stood in the middle of the room and looked, really looked, at what was left of my grandmother's life.

The shelves were the same. She'd built them herself, I remembered that now, hammered the brackets in crooked so the jars always slid to one side. They still did. His jars lined the top rows, things I didn't recognize, dark liquids and dried roots. But on the bottom shelf, pushed to the back and half hidden behind a cracked pot, I found a row of clay jars with cork stoppers. My grandmother's hand had labeled each one in her careful, slanting script. *Yarrow. Comfrey. Calendula. Sage.*

I pulled the sage jar down and opened it.

The smell went through me. Dusty and sharp and so familiar my knees buckled. I was small again, bare feet on the stone floor, watching my grandmother crush sage between her palms and drop it into the pot. I couldn't remember the words she'd said, just her hands and her warmth and the way this smell meant I was safe.

But Sophia had smelled this too.

The thought arrived like a knife between the ribs. Sophia had been in this cottage. Had stood where I was standing, breathed the same air, looked at these same jars with their familiar labels in their mother's handwriting. Had she opened them? Had she pressed the sage to her nose the way I just had and smelled home and safety and the life she'd been stolen from?

Had it made it worse? Surrounded by her mother's things, her mother's herbs, her mother's careful script on every jar, while the man who'd taken her decided when the door opened and when it stayed shut?

I set the jar down on the floor and looked around the room with different eyes.

The bed. Sophia had slept in that bed. Or hadn't slept —

had lain awake listening to the footsteps fading, the long terrible silence of a forest that had swallowed her whole. Had she pressed her face into the pillow and tried to remember what freedom smelled like? Had she pulled the furs to her chin and stared at the ceiling and wondered if anyone was coming for her?

I crawled across the room and ran my hands along the base of the door. I don't know what I was looking for. Some trace of her. Some proof that the girl who'd braided my hair and called me little Red had touched these same walls.

I found them. Low on the wood, near the bottom, where a woman on her knees would reach. Thin lines scored into the grain, shallow, repetitive, just the desperate scratching of fingernails against oak. Over and over and over. Hundreds of them, layered on top of each other until the wood was rough and furred with it.

My fingers traced the marks and the tears came.

I didn't cry for my grandmother this time. I cried for Sophia. For the girl who'd taught me the names of every herb on grandmother's shelf and let me steal the ribbons from her hair. For the girl taken at nineteen who'd scratched at this door until her fingers bled and then scratched some more because stopping meant accepting and accepting meant dying and she wasn't ready to die.

Until she was.

I sat on the floor with my back against the door and Sophia's scratches under my palm and cried. For Sophia.

For myself. Because I was behind the same door now, and the scratches under my fingers could have been mine.

Light came through the cracks in the boards, pale and gray. Somewhere outside, a wolf howled — one long note carrying more grief than any animal should.

I wiped my face and pulled the furs off the bed and made a nest by the fire, curled up on the floor with Sophia's scratches at my back and the cloak tight around me.

Tomorrow I would figure out what to do. Right now, I needed to survive.

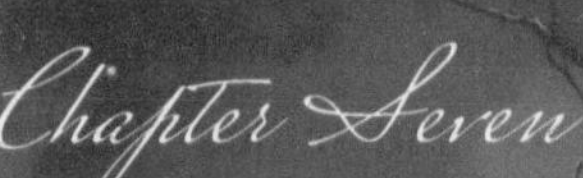

Chapter Seven

Smoke stung my eyes.

The fire had burned down wrong, the last log smoldering instead of catching. The flue must have blocked overnight, because the smoke that should have pulled upward had been filling the room while I slept. I sat up coughing, waving the haze away from my face while thin light leaked through the cracks in the boards. A whole day and night had passed. I'd slept longer than I meant to.

I'd fallen asleep waiting for him, waiting for the scrape of the outside bar lifting, for heavy footsteps on the threshold. I'd told myself the inside bar was defiance, not fear. Told myself I didn't care if he came back or not.

He hadn't.

I kicked off the furs and stood, my back aching from the hard floor and my neck stiff enough that turning my head hurt. Everything I'd checked yesterday would still be locked. I knew that. But I tried the door anyway, lifting the inside bar and pushing the latch. The outside bar held firm. He'd vanished into the forest and left me caged.

I sat back on my heels. There was no way out. He would decide when I got to leave.

The rage flickered but I pushed it down. Getting angry wouldn't open the door, wouldn't do anything except waste energy I might need later. If I couldn't escape, I could at least learn something useful while I waited.

A chest sat in the corner near the bed, old wood, dark with age, iron bands across the top. I'd noticed it yesterday when Dietrich pulled out grandmother's clothes, but I hadn't looked closely. Now I crossed to it and knelt down.

The lid was heavy and opened with a creak that echoed in the quiet. Inside were more clothes — a gray wool dress folded carefully, a white linen shift, a brown shawl with moth holes along one edge. I lifted them out and set them aside.

Underneath were other things. A wooden comb with half its teeth missing, a string of glass beads, bundles of dried plants wrapped in cloth and tied with twine. Everything smelled like grandmother. I pressed the shawl to my face and breathed her in one more time, then set it aside and kept digging.

At the very bottom was a book.

It looked untouched. Dietrich had pulled clothes from this chest yesterday. He'd lived with it for more than two decades, must have opened it hundreds of times. A book this size sitting beneath the shifts and shawls would have been the first thing his hands found.

Unless it hadn't been there for him.

Thick, the cover worn smooth in places where hands had held it over and over. No title — just dark leather and a small metal clasp. I pulled it out and set it on my lap, my hands unsteady as I undid the clasp.

The pages inside were yellowed and brittle at the edges. The handwriting changed from page to page, some sections in a neat, careful script, others hurried and cramped. Some looked old enough to crumble if I touched them wrong.

The first page stopped me.

Names. A column of them, written in different hands and different inks, stretching down the page. Dozens of women. The oldest entries were faded nearly to nothing, the script so ancient I could hardly make out the shapes of the letters. The newer ones darkened farther down the page. Grandmother's hand sat near the bottom, her careful slanting script that I'd know anywhere.

And beneath hers, the last name on the list.

Sophia.

Her handwriting. The letters tilted left instead of right, the way she'd always written because she held the quill wrong and Grandmother could never break her of the habit. She had written her name here. She had held this book in her hands. She had sat in this room, behind these boards, in this cage, and added herself to the list.

I flipped to the last filled page, but everything was blurred, as if the words were not ready for me to see.

Every word swam and slid away from my eyes the way water slides off glass. I tried to focus. I squinted until my head ached. The text would not come clear. The book had decided I was not ready for whatever Sophia had written in her final days.

My hands were shaking. I pressed them flat against the page as if I could absorb her words through my skin. She had been here for two years. Two years of entries. And I could not read a single one.

I closed my eyes. Breathed. Then I turned back to the first page and started from the beginning.

I'd seen Grandmother's books before. She had kept a shelf full of them, and I had tried to read them once when I was young and curious about what she wrote. But the words had blurred and swum, as though I were looking at them through water, and no matter how hard I squinted, I could not make them clear.

Grandmother had found me with tears of frustration in my eyes. She had taken the book gently from my hands. "Not yet, little one." She had smoothed the hair back from my face the way she always did when I was upset. "When you're ready, the words will come clear."

I had asked what that meant. When would I be ready?

She had only smiled and touched my cheek. "You'll know."

I had changed in that cellar when Klaus attacked me,

when that heat had surged through my body, when I had felt power wake inside me for the first time. That was when I became ready.

I looked at the first page again. Past the names. To the text below.

The words were sharp. Clear. I could read every single one.

A Record of Creatures Known and Unknown Compiled by the Blood-Keepers May those who read this survive to add their own knowledge

I turned the page.

This book contains entries on the creatures that walk this world alongside humanity. Some hide in plain sight. Others haunt the dark places. All are dangerous.

The blood-keepers have tracked them for generations. Recorded their habits. Their weaknesses. Their territories. Everything we've learned through observation and through the blood price we've paid for that knowledge.

But this book is protected. It will not reveal everything at once. The magic woven into these pages decides what each reader is ready to know. Some entries will be clear. Others will blur when you try to focus on them. Do not fight this. The book knows what it's doing. When your power grows strong enough, you will see more.

Trust your blood. Trust the book. Survive.

A creature encyclopedia. Written over generations, protected by magic that decided what I could know.

I flipped ahead. Page after page of entries, each one starting with a creature name at the top in bold letters.

Fae

The text below was blurred. Swimming. I squinted and tried to focus, but the words wouldn't come clear. Something about the blur felt different here, thicker, older, like the book was guarding these pages harder than the rest. Whatever the *Fae* were, the grimoire didn't want me knowing yet.

Sanguinarians

Blurred. I caught one word before it swam away. *Blood.* Then nothing.

Demons

Blurred.

And then I saw it.

Blood-Keepers

Blood-keepers are the line of witches tasked with tracking and recording the creatures of this world. We are watchers. Documenters. Survivors.

The gift passes through women. Mother to daughter. Sometimes it skips a generation, but it always returns. The power manifests differently in each of us, but the core remains the same. We see what others cannot. Sense what should stay hidden. Walk paths between the living and the dead.

Common abilities include: prophetic visions, sensing death before it comes, finding lost things or people, seeing spirits, heightened intuition about danger.

Our purpose is not to hunt. Not to destroy. Only to witness and record so that future blood-keepers might survive what we have learned.

The creatures know what we are. They can sense our blood. Some avoid us. Others hunt us. This is why we must be careful. Why we must hide what we are from the ordinary world. Why we document everything we learn.

So that the next blood-keeper might live where we have died.

Blood-keeper. That's what I was. What Grandmother had been. What her mother and grandmother before her had been. My visions weren't madness, weren't a curse, they were an inheritance.

I turned the page.

Protective Symbols and Tools

Blood-keepers have used various methods to mark themselves and ward off danger. These symbols change across regions and time, but their purpose remains constant.

Red is the most common color worn by our line. It affects how certain predators perceive us, the color registers differently to supernatural sight and can mask our magical signature or make us harder to track. It also serves as psychological armor. A reminder to ourselves and a warning to others. We are not prey. We are not helpless. We survive.

Historically, our women have worn red cloaks, red ribbons, with red threads woven into clothing. The tradition continues because it works.

The red disrupts. It does not protect. A predator tracking by scent will falter when it sees the color, a moment's confusion, an instinct to pull back, the briefest hesitation. But a predator already in pursuit, already locked onto its prey, will push through the disruption the way a wolf pushes through a thorn bush. The red buys time. It does not buy safety.

I touched the red cloak draped over the chair. My fingers found the ribbon at my wrist, faded, fraying, still tied where it had been since I was a girl. Protection. Both of them. Not just tradition, survival.

I kept flipping. More blurred entries, more creature names I couldn't read. Then another clear entry.

Humans

Never underestimate the ordinary. Humans without magic are still the most dangerous threat blood-keepers face.

They fear what they don't understand. That fear turns to violence faster than any supernatural predator. They drown us. Burn us. Hang us from trees. Call it justice. Call it God's will. Sleep soundly after watching us die.

The witch trials are not isolated incidents. They are patterns that repeat across centuries and continents. Wherever fear takes root, the fires follow.

A blood-keeper's first rule of survival: never let them see what you are. Hide your gift. Bury your knowledge. Walk among them like you're one of them. The moment they suspect is the moment you become prey.

They are not evil. Most of them. Just frightened. And frightened people kill.

Anna's face flashed in my mind, her empty eyes, staring at the sky. The village watching her drown based on nothing but suspicion and fear. I'd almost died the same way.

I flipped ahead.

Werewolves

My hands stopped.

Werewolves are the hunting dogs of older, darker masters. They were not born. They were made. The hatred between our kinds was put there on purpose, bred into their blood and bone by the ones who built them.

They hunt us specifically. Can smell our blood across distances. Our magic draws them like a scent on the wind. This makes them deadly. They don't stumble across us by accident. They seek us out. It is in their very nature to hunt and kill us.

The words started swimming. I blinked. Rubbed my eyes. Tried to focus. But the text was fading. Blurring like ink running in water.

"No." I turned the page. More blurred text. "No, no, no."

The werewolf entry continued for several more pages. All of it was unreadable. I caught fragments. *Made from,* blur. *Sanguinarian,* blur. *Broke free,* blur. Words surfacing and drowning before I could grab them.

Everything I needed was right here, right in front of me. And I couldn't read a single word. The book had cut me off.

It had decided I wasn't ready. The book was teaching me in order, I realized. Giving me what I needed when I needed it, the foundations first, the dangers later. As if it knew that some knowledge required strength to carry, and it wouldn't burden me with what lurked in those blurred pages until I was strong enough to bear it.

The sound of footsteps outside made me shove the book under the bed. I pushed it far back against the wall and was on my feet by the time the outside bar scraped free.

The door thudded against the inside bar and held. A pause, and then a fist hammered against the wood, hard enough to rattle the hinges.

"Open the door," Dietrich ordered from the other side.

"No," I called back. "How does it feel?"

He pounded again, harder this time. "Open the door. Now."

I didn't move. Let him stand out there. Let him feel what it was like to want through a door that wouldn't give.

"I have food," he ground out. "And wood for the fire. Open the door or I'll take the hinges off."

I believed him. I waited three more breaths anyway, long enough to make the point, then crossed to the door and lifted the bar.

The door swung open and the cold hit me first, then the white. It had snowed in the night. The clearing, the trees, the ground between the cottage and the dark wall of pines, all of it buried under a fresh layer that turned the world quiet and clean. For one breath I saw past him, and beyond the trees, through a gap in the pines, the lake. Frozen solid now, a flat gray sheet of ice. I knew that lake. Grandmother had taken me there as a child, before she moved to the village, when this cottage was still hers and the forest was still safe. I'd sat on the bank and thrown pebbles while she washed herbs in the shallows and told me the names of things. The memory hit so hard, my whole body seized then Dietrich stepped through the frame and blocked the light and the lake vanished behind his shoulders.

He had a brace of rabbits over his shoulder and snow in his hair and his beard, the ice crystals caught in the coarse dark hair melting as the cottage warmth hit him. His eyes swept the room, the cold hearth, the dead fire, the haze of smoke still drifting through the air like the cottage had been slowly choking on itself, and then his gaze found me, standing rigid in the middle of it with my arms folded and my chin raised.

"The fire went out." He dropped the rabbits on the table with a heavy, wet thud.

"The flue was blocked. The windows are boarded shut. The door was barred from the outside. I couldn't clear the chimney, couldn't crack a board, couldn't do anything except breathe it and wait." I spread my hands at the haze still hanging between us. "I could have suffocated in my sleep and you wouldn't have known until you came back to a corpse."

He said nothing to that. Just crouched by the hearth and started stacking kindling like I hadn't spoken at all.

"Did you hear me?" I pressed, stepping closer until I was standing over him. "You locked me in a sealed room with a dying fire. Are you trying to keep me alive or kill me? Because you're doing a poor job of picking one."

"The fire was fine when I left," he muttered, striking the flint without looking up. Sparks scattered across the kindling and caught.

"Well it wasn't fine this morning," I snapped. "Maybe if you hadn't sealed every way out of this cottage, I could have gotten more wood. Or pried a board loose for air. Or done anything at all besides sit here breathing smoke and waiting for you to decide I was worth coming back to."

"Maybe if you hadn't threatened to leave, I could have cracked a board for you," he shot back, still not looking at me, feeding the new flame with small careful breaths that made me want to kick the kindling apart. "Let some air through. But you threatened to run, so I didn't."

"So this is punishment." I didn't make it a question.

"It's not punishment." He stood and turned to face me. "You want to walk out of here and die in the forest, that's your choice. But I'm not going to make it easy for you." He folded his arms. "The bar stays. The boards stay. When I trust you not to bolt the second my back is turned, we can talk about the boards."

"And when will that be?" I demanded.

"For as long as it takes."

"As long as what takes?" I stepped into his space, close enough that he'd have to look down at me, close enough that he couldn't pretend I wasn't there. "What exactly are you keeping me here for?"

His mouth thinned into a hard line. "Keeping you alive."

"In a cage," I spat. "Sophia's cage."

He flinched like I'd put a blade through him.

"I found her scratches on the door," I continued. My hands were shaking and I didn't care. "I put my fingers in the grooves she made trying to claw her way out. And you're using the same cage to keep me."

"I'm not him," he ground out, his back to me.

"Then take the boards down," I challenged, and the tears were right there, pressing hot against my eyes, blurring the edges of his face. "Prove it."

He stared at me for a long, terrible moment. Then he picked up the rabbits from the table, pulled a knife from his belt, and started skinning them with his back half turned to me. Conversation over. The wet, deliberate sound of the blade separating skin from muscle was the only conversation he offered.

He wasn't going to take them down.

I couldn't stay upright. My legs were shaking, and I could not pull air past whatever had lodged itself behind my ribs. I crossed to the bed and sat down hard, pressed my spine flat against the wall, and pulled the furs across my lap. My chest was too tight to breathe properly. The breaths came out ragged and ugly, heaving things that shook my shoulders and made the bed frame creak beneath me. The tears pressed and pressed and I wouldn't let them fall, wouldn't give him the satisfaction even though his back was turned, wouldn't let this place and this man and this whole wretched history crack me open.

Behind me, I could hear him working. The scrape of the knife against bone. The thud of meat on wood. The crackle of the fire he had rebuilt. He cooked in silence. The smell of roasting rabbit filled the cottage slowly, thick and rich. My stomach clenched so hard it hurt. I had not eaten since before the cellar. My body was past asking. It was demanding, a deep, animal ache that had nothing to do with pride or fury or grief.

I heard him cross the room. His boots on the stone floor, steady and unhurried. Then he was standing beside the bed. I did not look up. I kept my face buried in my knees and my arms locked around my shins, and I waited for him to say something, to gloat, to make a point.

He did not speak. He set the plate on the bed beside me. I felt the warmth of it through the furs. Then his footsteps retreated, and the chair by the fire creaked as he sat down.

I stayed like that for as long as I could stand it, which was not long. The smell was right there, warm and close. My hands were shaking. My stomach was twisting in on itself. The hunger was bigger than the hatred, bigger than the grief, bigger than everything I was trying to hold together.

I picked up the meat with my fingers and ate.

The tears came then, sliding down my face and dripping off my chin while I chewed, while I swallowed, while my body took what it needed whether the rest of me agreed or not. I ate and I cried, and I hated myself for both. I hated that he could hear me. I hated that the food was good. I hated that somewhere under all the anger and sorrow, I was grateful for it.

He did not say a word. He did not look at me. He just sat by the fire and ate his own meal and let me have whatever this was: grief and hunger and fury and shame all tangled together, pouring out of me in silence while I fed myself with shaking hands in my aunt's cage.

Chapter Eight

Sophia wrote the note by candlelight.

Her hand moved slowly across the paper, the leftward tilt I'd know anywhere, the round letters, the careful spacing of someone choosing words she didn't mean. She paused twice. The quill hovered over the page and her lips pressed together and I could see the lie building behind her eyes, the shape of it forming before the ink touched paper.

I've gone with a man. Don't come looking.

She set the quill down. Stared at the words. Her fingers were trembling.

The cottage was warm around her. Our village cottage, the one with the crooked shutters and the herb garden out back and the kitchen that always smelled like sage and bread. The fire was low in the hearth. Dried lavender hung from the beam above the door. The shelves were full, jars and bottles and bundles, grandmother's careful labels facing out the way she liked them.

Grandmother was asleep in the big bed by the wall. Her breathing was deep and even, one arm flung across the pillow, her gray hair loose on the linen. She looked younger than I remembered. Fewer lines. Fewer years of grief carved into her face.

A girl slept beside her. Dark-haired, long-limbed, curled tight against grandmother's shoulder the way she still did when the night wandering left her too frightened to sleep alone.

Me. I was looking at myself burrowed into grandmother's warmth the way I used to when the night wandering left me too frightened to sleep alone.

Sophia folded the note. Set it on the table where Grandmother would find it in the morning. She stared at it for a long time. Then she stood and crossed to the bed.

She kissed grandmother's forehead first. Gentle. Grandmother stirred but didn't wake. Sophia held her breath. Waited. When the deep breathing returned, she leaned down to the child.

To me.

Her lips brushed my hair. I watched her eyes close and her face crumple, just for a second, just long enough for the grief to break through before she sealed it shut again. Her hand came up and smoothed the hair from my sleeping face. The same gesture Grandmother always made. The same tenderness.

"I'm sorry, little Red," she whispered.

She straightened. Wiped her eyes with the back of her hand. Hard. Angry at the tears, angry at whatever had brought her to this moment. She pulled the red hood up over her dark hair, tightened the cloak around her shoulders, and turned toward the door.

She didn't look back.

The door opened without a sound. The village street waited outside — empty and dark, every window shuttered, every hearth banked for the night. Cold air spilled across the floor and reached the bed and the child that was me pulled the blankets tighter in her sleep.

Sophia stepped out. The door closed behind her.

I followed.

She moved through the village like a ghost. Past the baker's. Past the smithy. Past the well where women gathered in the mornings. Her red cloak the only color in a world of shadow. Nobody saw her. Nobody stirred. The village slept while a nineteen-year-old girl walked out of it forever.

She reached the tree line and didn't pause. The forest took her in.

I tried to call her name. My mouth opened and nothing came out, the sound died before it left my throat, swallowed by the trees the way the trees swallowed everything. I ran after her. My legs moved but the distance between us wouldn't close. She kept walking. I kept running. The red hood bobbed ahead of me through the dark, bright and steady, the only real thing in a world going gray.

She was crying. I could see it in the way her shoulders hitched, the way she kept wiping her face with the heel of her hand and walking faster as if speed could outrun what she was feeling. But she didn't stop. Didn't turn around. The Sensing would have been pressing on her from every direction. Erik's threat sitting in her bones like a second heartbeat, the truth of what he'd do to Grandmother and to me if she didn't come. She'd have felt it the way she felt everything. Every lie and every intention pushing against her skin like hands in a crowd.

She knew what he was. She went anyway.

A clearing opened ahead. A man's shape stood at its center. Tall. Broad. Perfectly still. Waiting with the patience of something that had all the time in the world.

Sophia stopped at the edge of the trees. Her hand gripped the trunk of a birch, white bark under white knuckles. I could see her chest heaving. The war in her body, every muscle screaming at her to run back, back to the cottage, back to Grandmother, back to the sleeping child with a stolen ribbon tied around her wrist.

The man in the clearing didn't move. Didn't speak. Just waited.

Sophia let go of the tree.

She walked into the clearing. His hand closed around her wrist.

The forest vanished.

I was in a cottage. Boards on the windows. Bar on the door. The same hearth, the same stone floor. But the furs on the bed were different, older, thinner, worn through in patches. And the scratches on the door were fresh. Pale gouges in dark wood, the splinters still sharp.

Sophia was on the bed. She wasn't alone.

I couldn't see him properly. He blurred at the edges, the way text in the grimoire blurred when the book decided I wasn't ready. But glimpses broke through. A mouth that was too wide. Teeth that caught the firelight and were too long. Hands on Sophia's arms where the fingers ended in claws instead of nails. The sound from his chest wasn't a voice. It was low and wet and it belonged to a throat that wasn't entirely human. His back was wrong. Too broad, the skin rippling like a second shape underneath was pressing outward, trying to get free.

Sophia screamed.

I threw myself forward. My fists hit nothing. My hands passed through them both like smoke. I was standing in the room but I wasn't in the room. A witness trapped behind glass, watching something I couldn't stop and couldn't look away from.

The glimpses kept coming. Teeth sinking into the curve of her shoulder. Those wrong hands dragging down her arms, opening red lines that bloomed on her skin. Sophia thrashing, fighting, the sounds coming out of her no longer screams but raw, animal noise. The sound a body makes when it's caught in a grip it knows it isn't getting free of.

Blood on the sheets. Blood on the wall. A flash of his face when he lifted his head, just a glimpse before the blur swallowed it again. Amber eyes. Bright and empty of anything that could be reasoned with.

Then he was gone. The door shut. The bar scraped into place from outside.

Sophia lay on the bed. The red dress was torn. Blood soaked through the furs beneath her, dark and spreading. Marks covered her skin, her arms, her shoulders, her throat, marks that didn't look like they'd been made by a man's hands. Her eyes stared at the ceiling. Her chest rose and fell in shallow, hitching breaths. She was alive. But the girl who'd kissed my hair and whispered *I'm sorry, little Red* was already starting to disappear behind her own eyes.

I dropped to my knees beside the bed. Reached for her. My hands passed through.

Time lurched.

Light through the cracks in the boards turned orange. Then gray. Then black. Then orange again. Days cycling in sickening jumps. The fire died and relit and died. He came back. Left. Came back. Each time the bar scraped and the door opened and the blurred shape filled the frame, Sophia flinched smaller. Her screams shortened into whimpers. Her fighting weakened into flinching. The red dress faded from fresh blood to rust. Her dark hair went brittle and thin. Her collarbones pressed through her skin like blades.

I watched it happen. Couldn't touch her. Couldn't speak to her. Couldn't do anything except kneel on the floor of my aunt's cage and watch a woman I'd loved be unmade piece by piece.

The scratches on the door multiplied. Hundreds of them. Layered over each other until the wood was furred and rough. The early ones deep and angry, gouged by fingernails that still had strength behind them. The later ones shallow. Weak.

She stopped scratching.

She stopped screaming.

She stopped getting out of bed.

The last image came in a long, slow slide. Sophia on the bed. Her body pulled tight against her bones. The red dress hanging loose on a frame that had no flesh left to fill it. Her hair spread across the pillow like dead grass. Her fingers curled inward. Her eyes sunk deep but never closing. Just staring at the ceiling. Day after day after day. The light cycling through the cracks and her eyes never blinking and her chest barely moving and the woman I'd known gone somewhere the walls couldn't follow.

Until the breathing stopped.

I was on my knees. Sobbing. My hands reaching for her, wanting to close her eyes, wanting to pull the furs over her face, wanting to do the one thing nobody had done for her, be there when it ended.

My fingers brushed her cheek.

Her hand shot up and grabbed my wrist.

The grip was ice. The bones beneath her skin ground against mine. Her head turned — slow, mechanical, the dry creak of a neck that hadn't moved in weeks. Her sunken eyes found mine. Her mouth opened.

"He'll break you the same way he broke me."

I screamed. Screamed until my throat tore. Her hand was locked around my wrist and her empty eyes were boring into mine and her mouth was still moving, still saying it, over and over … *He'll break you the same way he broke me.*

"Sophia!" I was still screaming her name when the hands found me.

Warm. Firm. Gripping my shoulders and holding me still when my body wanted to fight, wanted to run, wanted to claw through the walls of this cottage and sprint into the forest.

"Stop. Look at me. You're safe." He reached me before I could see him, close, steady, cutting through the screaming like a hand through smoke. He must have already been inside because the fire was freshly built and crackling in the hearth, and thin gray daylight showed through the cracks in the boards. He'd come in to start the day and found me thrashing.

His hands were on my bare shoulders where the shift had slipped down and his grip was firm enough to bruise but not enough to hurt. His eyes searched my face and for one breath, one single, treacherous breath, the warmth of his hands and the steadiness of his presence made the tightness behind my ribs loosen. My body sagged toward him like it had decided on its own that this man was safe, that these hands could hold me together while everything inside me flew apart.

"It was a dream," he murmured, quieter now, his thumbs pressing small circles against my shoulders. "Just a dream. You're here. You're safe."

My breathing slowed. The screaming stopped. But it hadn't been a dream. Not the way he meant it. My visions came in sleep — always had. And this one tasted true the way the others had tasted true before the worst of them came to pass. I'd watched her walk out the door. I'd followed her into the forest and into this cottage and watched two years pass while she was unmade behind these boards. My gift had shown me what I'd been too late to see in life.

His thumbs were still moving. Small circles on my skin. I'd been leaning into him without realizing it, my weight tipped forward, my forehead almost touching his collarbone, my body curved toward his warmth.

Then the fog lifted and I felt his skin against mine. His hands still on me, firm and warm. His breath on my hair. His face inches from mine. Those amber eyes, his father's eyes, looking at me with something that might have been concern and might have been something else entirely.

Erik's son. In Sophia's cage. With his hands on me.

"Get off me," I snarled.

He didn't move fast enough. I shoved him with both hands flat against his chest, hard enough that he rocked back on his heels. Then I hit him. Open-handed across the face, the crack loud enough to echo off the low ceiling.

"Don't touch me!" The screaming had torn my throat raw but the fury was fresh and hot.

He stood slowly. Stepped back. His cheek was reddening where I'd struck him but his expression didn't change, just that flat, careful stillness he wore like armor. He held his palms up where I could see them, fingers spread.

I pulled the furs up to my collarbone and pressed my back against the wall, my chest heaving, my eyes burning. Every time I blinked I saw her. Sophia's face. Her empty eyes. The scratches on the door, fresh and pale. The red dress faded to rust.

"She was here." It barely made it past my throat. "In this bed. In this room. She sat where I'm sitting and she ..." I curled forward over my knees and pressed my face into the furs and let the sobs come. Because Sophia's face was still there, emptied out, and I was lying in the same bed she'd lain in, behind the same boards, breathing the same trapped air. The same cage. The same door. The same man's son standing over me with careful hands and careful eyes while my aunt's ghost told me what was coming.

He'll break you the same way he broke me.

I was becoming Sophia. Day by day. Meal by meal. Each morning I didn't escape was a morning closer to the woman in the red dress with nothing left behind her eyes.

Dietrich didn't come closer. Didn't try to touch me

again. After a long time I heard him turn to the hearth, heard the clatter of a pan, the crack of eggs. He cooked with his back to me while I cried, and the small domestic sounds of it, the sizzle of fat, the scrape of a wooden spoon, filled the silence between us with a presence that wasn't comfort, wasn't kindness, but was there anyway.

When the crying stopped, I sat up and wiped my face with the back of my hand. My eyes were swollen and my throat was raw and I felt hollowed out, emptied of everything except a dull, heavy exhaustion.

He crossed to the bed and held the plate out. Eggs, still steaming. I took it without looking at him, without thanking him, without acknowledging that he'd heard me scream my dead aunt's name and cry like a child and hit him across the face and he'd just, stayed. Cooked me breakfast. Waited.

I ate. My hands trembled and the tears weren't quite finished, they leaked out slow and quiet while I chewed. I didn't bother wiping them away. There was no point pretending anymore. He'd seen everything there was to see.

He stayed that morning. Instead of disappearing like he usually did after the meal, he crossed to the shelves where grandmother's jars sat alongside bundles of dried herbs and started checking them, pulling things down, examining for mold or rot.

I watched from the bed, keeping distance between him

and the hidden grimoire. My eyes were still swollen and my throat still raw but the hatred was creeping back, filling the hollow space the crying had left.

"Stop touching her things," I rasped.

He pulled down a bundle that had started to brown and tossed it into the fire. "These herbs need checking or they'll spoil," he replied without looking at me.

"They're not yours to check," I shot back.

"They're not doing anyone any good if they rot on the shelf," he countered, reaching for the next jar and turning it in his hands, reading my grandmother's careful script on the label.

I watched his hands move along the shelf checking each jar and bundle with the efficiency of someone who'd been doing this for years. He handled grandmother's things with a care that made something twist uncomfortably in my chest because it didn't match the man I needed him to be.

He pulled a jar of dried comfrey off the shelf and crossed the room. Held it out to me. His eyes found mine and stayed there long enough that I had to look away first.

"Your back. Where the furs rubbed the skin raw."

I hadn't told him about that. Hadn't shifted in bed where he could see it.

I took the jar. His fingers let go the second mine closed around the glass. He walked back to the shelf like nothing had happened.

My hands were unsteady and I hated that.

I looked away. Stared at the fire.

His back was to me and I could hear him working, the soft clink of jars, the rustle of dried herbs. My gaze drifted back without permission. The firelight caught the line of his shoulders, the way his shirt pulled across his back when he reached for the higher shelf. His hands, steady and sure, the same hands that had held my shoulders in the dark and let go the instant I'd told him to.

I caught myself and looked away so fast my neck hurt.

What was wrong with me? I was a widow. A healer who'd buried a husband and knew better than to notice anything about a man keeping me prisoner. The son of the man who'd caged Sophia. This was exhaustion — my body confused by proximity and care after days of violence and grief. Nothing more.

He turned from the shelves and I fixed my eyes on the fire, my face burning.

"The stew needs time," he observed, crossing to the hearth and setting a pot of water over the flames. He started cutting root vegetables on the board, the knife thudding in a steady rhythm. "There's broth from yesterday. The herbs in it will help you heal."

"I know what the herbs do." I wrapped my arms around my knees. "I'm a healer."

"Then you know you need them," he countered, the knife thudding steady against the board.

I drank the broth because he was right and because my body was screaming for it, and I hated that I could taste the healing herbs, comfrey, yarrow, something warm I couldn't name, and that they were doing exactly what they were supposed to do.

He added the vegetables to the pot and wiped the knife on his leg. I expected him to grab his coat. He didn't. He dragged the chair closer to the fire and sat down, stretched his legs out, and stared into the flames like he meant to stay there for a while.

I watched him from the bed, waiting for him to announce he was leaving, but the announcement never came. He just sat there, one hand resting on his knee, the other hanging loose at his side, his face turned toward the fire but his attention, I could feel it, still on me.

He was worried.

He wouldn't say it. Wouldn't ask if I was all right, wouldn't mention the screaming or the crying. But he was sitting in that chair like a man who'd decided he wasn't going anywhere, and that said everything his mouth refused to.

I hated that it helped. Hated that his presence in the room made the walls feel less like they were closing in. Hated that some stupid, broken part of me felt safer with him there than without him, even knowing what he was, even knowing whose cage I was sitting in.

The day passed slowly. He got up to stir the stew, to add wood to the fire, to check the boards where the wind was getting through. I sat on the bed and read the grimoire with my back turned so he couldn't see the pages. Neither of us spoke. The silence wasn't hostile anymore — it was heavier and stranger, that comes after someone has seen you at your worst and chosen to stay anyway.

He got up to check the fire and his boot caught the edge of the plate I'd left on the floor. He picked it up. Washed it in the basin along with his own. Dried both and set them on the shelf, side by side, like there'd always been two.

I watched him do it and hated that it bothered me.

I dozed. Woke. Dozed again. Each time the dream pushed at the edges, Sophia's empty eyes flickering behind my lids, but each time the sounds of the cottage pulled me back. The fire, the creak of the chair when Dietrich shifted his weight, the steady rhythm of his breathing. It anchored me anyway. I was counting his breaths like a child counting heartbeats to fall asleep.

By late afternoon the stew was ready. He ladled it into two bowls and set one on the table, then sat back down in his chair with the other. This time he ate in the room with me. First time he'd done that. He still didn't look at me. Still didn't speak. But he was there, and the cottage felt different with two people eating in it instead of one.

I ate slowly. The stew was good — rich and thick, the root vegetables soft, the rabbit tender enough to fall apart. I tasted grandmother's herbs in it again and my throat tightened, but the tears didn't come this time. I had nothing left to cry with.

The light through the cracks in the boards turned orange, then gray, then faded until the fire was the only thing keeping the darkness out. Dietrich set his empty bowl aside and stood. Pulled on his coat. Fastened it. Crossed to the door. The bar scraped and his footsteps faded and I was alone again.

I sat in the quiet and stared at the boards on the windows.

How many days now? Four. Five. I'd stopped counting because counting made it worse. The light through the cracks was the only way to tell morning from evening and some days I couldn't even manage that. The walls were closer than they'd been when I arrived. I knew they weren't, knew the cottage hadn't shrunk, knew the boards hadn't moved, but my lungs didn't believe my head and every night the air got thicker and the ceiling got lower and I woke up gasping like a woman buried alive.

Dietrich's words kept circling back. The ones from that first day, when I'd pushed him about Sophia.

What do you think happened? He kept her. She fought. He fought harder. Eventually one of them had to break. She broke.

Sophia scratched at the door until her nails were gone. Tried to run. Fought with everything her body had. And it hadn't mattered. Because whatever was holding her was stronger than fingernails and stubbornness and the will to survive.

I wasn't going to scratch at the door.

I pulled the grimoire from under the bed. Opened it to the werewolf entry. Still blurred. Closed it. Slid it back.

. . .

The howling woke me around midnight. Far off at first. Then closer. Then close enough that I could track it moving around the cottage, left to right, right to left, the same wide circle getting tighter each time.

I lay still and listened.

Claws on the frozen ground. Just outside the boards. Scraping slow along the wall, stopping at the door. Then the sniffing started — wet, heavy breaths drawn through the gap between the wood and the stone, pulling air in like it was trying to taste what was inside.

I slid my hand under the pillow and found the knife I'd put there the second night. Held it flat against my ribs. My whole body was rigid and my lungs wouldn't fill and I could hear my own heartbeat so loud I was sure whatever was outside could hear it too.

A snarl from the trees. One bark, deep, rough, furious. The sniffing stopped. The claws scraped backward. I heard it go, fast, crashing through the undergrowth away from the cottage, driven off by whatever had snarled at it from the dark.

I didn't sleep after that.

I was still awake when the bar scraped in the morning. Dietrich came in with wood under one arm and snow caught in his beard. He glanced at me, at the knife in my hand, at my face. Whatever he saw there he kept to himself. He crouched by the hearth and started building the fire.

I watched him work. The kindling catching. The flames steadying.

"What was at the door last night?" I asked, pulling the furs tighter around my shoulders.

He didn't turn around. "You heard it."

"I heard scratching. I heard sniffing. And I heard a noise from the trees that scared it off." I set the knife on the bed beside me. "What's out there?"

He fed a log into the fire and watched it catch before he answered. "The forest has things in it that hunt by scent. Ever since you came here, they've been restless. Whatever your family carries in its blood, you carry more of it. Your grandmother lived in these woods for years and nothing bothered her. Sophia drew attention but not like this." He shoved another log in. "Since the night I brought you here, I've been chasing things away from this cottage that I haven't seen in more than two decades."

"And you drove those *things* away? You're sure?" I pressed, watching his back.

He stood up and crossed to the table. Started cutting bread. "I patrol. Every night. Lay false trails across the scent paths so anything tracking you ends up turned around. When something gets too close to the cottage I chase it off."

I sat with that. Every night since I'd arrived. While I slept behind the bar and cursed him and read the grimoire by firelight, he'd been out there. In the cold. In the dark. Running the perimeter so that whatever was sniffing at the door never got through it.

"Is that why the hunters never found this place?" I

leaned forward on the bed. "The dogs losing the trail. The search parties going in circles."

He brought the bread over and held the plate out. "Yes."

I took it. Ate. He went back to the hearth and set water to boil. We didn't speak for a while. The fire popped. The bread was rough and warm and I chewed it and thought about a man who locked me in and then spent every night making sure nothing worse could get in after me.

When he pulled on his coat that evening I watched him cross to the door. His hand found the bar.

"Dietrich."

He stopped. His hand still on the bar.

"Thank you." It came out smaller than I meant. "For keeping me safe."

He stood there with his hand on the bar. His back to me. I watched his fingers tighten on the wood, then loosen. Then tighten again.

He turned his head. Just enough that I caught his profile in the firelight. Something sat on his face that didn't belong there, open and unguarded, like I'd knocked a door loose he hadn't braced.

"You're welcome." So quiet I almost didn't hear it. Then he blinked and it was gone. Same face as always. Like I'd imagined the whole thing.

He shoved the door open and left.

The bar scraped. His footsteps crunched away through the snow until the forest swallowed them.

I sat in the dark and listened to the quiet and thought about Sophia.

He'll break you the same way he broke me.

Sophia had waited. Endured. Hoped someone would come. And the hoping was what killed her long before anyone's hands finished the job.

I was not going to wait. I was not going to hope.

The door was barred. The windows were boarded shut. Dietrich was stronger and faster and knew this forest in ways I never would. But he had patterns. First light. Dark. The perimeter. Stretches of time when he was far from the cottage door.

I would watch. I would learn. I would find the gap.

And when it came, I would take it.

Chapter Nine

Dietrich was sharpening his knife by the hearth, the steady scrape of blade against stone filling the cottage, when I heard it, faint, far away, carried on the wind like something the forest was trying to swallow before it reached me. Baying. Dogs. The sound threaded through the trees and found the cottage and slid through the cracks in the boards and settled into my bones.

The scraping stopped. He'd heard it too.

Klaus. It had to be Klaus. Still searching. Still hunting.

"They won't find this place." He resumed sharpening, his back to me. "They never do."

"How can you be sure?" I wrapped my arms around myself.

"Because they've tried before." He offered nothing else.

The dogs bayed again. Closer — or maybe that was just

my fear stretching the sound. I pressed my nails into my palms.

"They're circling." He didn't turn from the fire. "They can't find the path."

I didn't ask what path. I didn't want to know what kind of man could hide a cottage from dogs and hunters and an entire village. The answer sat in the grimoire under the bed, in the pages I couldn't read, and I wasn't ready for it.

The baying faded. Grew fainter until the forest swallowed it whole. Dietrich stayed by the hearth for a long time after listening. Then he went back to his knife like nothing had happened.

He stayed that night. I heard him outside the door after dark, the soft sounds of someone settling against the wood. Keeping watch. I lay awake for hours listening to him breathe through the boards, hating that the sound of it made the walls feel less like they were closing in.

But I was thinking.

The dogs were gone. Klaus's men had circled and lost the trail and given up. That meant the forest between here and the village was empty, no hunters, no torches, no hounds tracking my scent through the snow. I didn't have to go back to the village. There were other settlements. I'd heard traders talk about places to the east, past the river, a day's walk through open country once you cleared the tree line. People who didn't know my name, didn't know Klaus, didn't know anything about a widow accused of witchcraft.

I could disappear. Start again. Find work as a healer somewhere no one whispered *witch* when I walked past.

I needed to get past Dietrich. He was bigger, stronger, faster. I couldn't overpower him in a fair fight. But he trusted me enough to turn his back. He'd been doing it for days, crouching by the hearth, working at the counter, leaving his knife on the table while he tended the fire. He didn't expect me to try anything because I hadn't tried anything. I'd screamed and raged and thrown words at him but I'd never put my hands on a weapon.

That was about to change.

All I needed was a blade and one clean moment where his guard was down.

I lay in the dark and waited for morning.

He came in with a duck, already plucked and cleaned, and set it on the table with his knife beside it. Then he crossed to the hearth to build up the fire and crouched down to arrange kindling.

His back to me. His hands busy.

Two weapons in the room. The mortar and pestle sat on the shelf by the hearth, grandmother's, heavy stone. Heavy enough to drop a man if it connected with the back of his skull. But it was an arm's length from where he crouched, and reaching for it would put me close enough for him to grab me before my fingers touched it.

The knife sat on the table. Right beside me. Still wet from where he'd cleaned the bird outside. Short blade, sharp edge, wooden handle worn smooth.

My heart hammered so hard I could feel it in my fingertips.

East. The river. The road. Emma. The village. A life that didn't have boards on the windows and a man deciding when I could breathe.

I crossed the room in three quick steps and closed my fingers around the handle. I didn't hesitate. Hesitation would get me caught. I raised the blade and drove it toward his back.

"Don't." He breathed the word — and moved.

Impossibly fast. Faster than any man should be able to move. One moment I was driving the knife toward his shoulder, the next he'd spun and caught my wrist, his fingers clamping down until the bones ground together and I gasped.

"Let go," I snarled, twisting against his grip.

He didn't. He twisted my arm instead and I lost my balance, stumbled forward into his chest. He caught me and we went down together, but his free hand cupped the back of my head as we fell, cradling my skull against his palm so I didn't crack it on the stone floor.

We hit hard. The air punched out of my lungs and the ceiling swam above me, but my head was cushioned in his hand. He'd protected me. Even now, even with a knife aimed at his back, he'd protected me.

I tried to buck him off. Too heavy. Too strong. He pinned my knife hand to the floor above my head, pried my fingers open one by one until the blade clattered free, and kicked it across the room where it spun to a stop against the far wall.

"Get off me!" I thrashed beneath him, drove my knee up toward his groin. He shifted his weight and blocked it with his thigh.

I swung at his face with my free hand. My fist connected with his cheekbone and his head snapped sideways, but he didn't let go, just caught my other wrist and brought it to his face.

He pressed his nose against the inside of my wrist. Right where the pulse hammered. And inhaled. Deep. Slow. His eyes fell shut and his whole body shuddered, a tremor that ran through him from his chest down through his hips and into the thighs braced on either side of mine.

I went still.

Every thought emptied out of my head. Every plan, every calculation, every furious word I'd been saving, gone. Because the sound he made when he breathed me in was nothing I'd ever heard from a human mouth. Low and broken and desperate, like a man dying of thirst who'd just found water, like breathing me in was the only thing keeping him from coming apart.

His eyes opened. They were wrong. Pupils blown so wide they'd nearly swallowed the amber, just a thin ring of gold left around the black. He stared down at me and his face was stripped bare. Every wall gone. Every defense dismantled. What was underneath was raw and hungry and ancient, a need that had been starving for a very long time.

Then he pinned my other wrist above my head and held both of them with one hand. His weight pressed me into the floor, his hips between my thighs, and the evidence of what he was feeling was unmistakable. Hard and hot against me through layers of fabric.

My pulse raced. My breathing came faster. And the thing that terrified me, the thing that made me want to scream louder than any nightmare ever had, was that it wasn't fear making my body respond. A heat gathered low in my belly, a softening, an opening. My hips shifted against him before I could stop them. A tiny movement, involuntary, traitorous. His breath caught and his grip on my wrists tightened and his eyes went so dark they were almost black.

His gaze dropped to my mouth. He leaned closer. His breath ghosted across my lips and I could smell him, pine and smoke and the animal musk underneath, the same scent from the wolf in the forest, the same scent that had followed me through days of captivity and worked its way into the furs and the walls and my own skin until I couldn't tell where he ended and the cottage began.

His mouth was an inch from mine. Less.

Then he caught himself.

He released my wrists and shoved himself off me so fast he stumbled backward into the hearth. The iron poker clattered to the floor. "Don't attack me again." His tone was rough. "I'm trying to keep you alive. Don't make this harder than it has to be."

"You're just like him." I shoved myself upright, my whole body shaking, with rage, with shame, with the treacherous heat still pulsing between my thighs. "Your father. You pin me down, you, you were going to ..."

"I wasn't," he cut me off.

"Liar!" I scrambled to my feet, fists clenched at my sides. "I felt you! You had me on the floor, you smelled me, like an animal. What kind of man does that?"

He went rigid. Every muscle in his back pulled taut and I watched the tremor run through him like a second body was trying to claw its way out from underneath his skin.

"You responded too." Still wouldn't face me. "Don't pretend you didn't."

The words hit me hard.

"What?" I breathed.

He turned then. Looked at me — hard and unflinching and terrible.

"Your body responded to mine. I felt it." His eyes held mine and I couldn't look away, couldn't breathe, couldn't move. "Don't act like I forced that from you."

My hand cracked across his face before I could think.

The sound echoed through the cottage. His head went sideways and color rose fast across his cheekbone. Three times I'd hit him now. Three times he'd let me.

"Get out," I demanded, my hands balled at my sides.

"Talia ..." He took a step toward me, one hand half-raised.

"Get out!" I screamed it with everything I had, screamed it until my throat tore and the walls rang with it.

He stopped. His hands dropped to his sides. He grabbed the knife from where it had fallen and the one still on the table, tucked both into his belt with jerky, unsteady movements. Then he pulled his coat from the peg and shoved his arms through the sleeves without meeting my eyes.

He walked out and drove the door shut hard enough to rattle the boards in the windows. The bar ground into place and his footsteps faded into the forest, faster than usual, almost running.

I stood there shaking. My hand stung from the slap. My wrist burned where he'd gripped it. And between my thighs, where his weight had pressed me open, the heat still throbbed, unwanted, undeniable, a betrayal so complete I couldn't look at it straight.

I sank down against the wall and drew my knees to my chest and pressed my face into them.

He was my captor. Erik's son. The man keeping me in Sophia's cage. He'd pinned me to the floor and pressed himself against me and breathed me in like my scent was something he needed to survive. And my body had arched into him. My hips had moved. My blood had answered his like they were speaking the same language, a language I didn't know and hadn't consented to learn.

I sat there until the fire burned low. Until the cold crept

in and made me shiver. Until my legs went numb and the trembling finally stopped.

Then I crawled to the bed and pulled the furs over my head and tried to hate myself clean.

I failed.

Chapter Ten

Days blurred together. I avoided him. He let me.

We moved around the cottage like two animals sharing a den they hadn't chosen, never too close, never making eye contact longer than it took to look away. He cooked. I ate. He left before dark. I lay in the silence and listened to the bar scrape into place and told myself the hollow feeling in my chest was relief.

Then the night changed.

I woke to the sound of the bar scraping free.

My eyes opened but I didn't move. Didn't breathe. The furs were pulled up to my chin and the fire had burned low, casting the cottage in dim orange light and long shadows that swayed against the ceiling like living things.

The door creaked open — slow, careful, the sound of a man trying very hard to be quiet.

His boots crossed the floor. Each step landing where the

wood stayed silent, avoiding the spots that would groan under his weight. He'd done this before. He stopped beside the bed.

I kept my breathing slow and steady. In and out. The rhythm of deep sleep I'd perfected over years of night wandering and waking in places I shouldn't be. My heart slammed against my ribs so hard I was certain the furs were moving with each beat, but I held still and counted my breaths and waited.

He stood there for a long time. Just breathing. Just watching me in the dying firelight. I could feel his gaze on my face the way you feel the sun through a window, warm, directional, impossible to ignore even with your eyes closed. The fine hairs on my arms rose. The skin along my throat prickled. Every nerve I had was awake and screaming and I kept my face slack and my breathing even and let him look.

Then I felt it.

Warmth. Hovering over my face, close enough that the heat from his hand reached my skin but his fingers never made contact. He traced the shape of me through the air, down the curve of my cheek, along the curve of my chin, over my throat where my pulse hammered against the thin skin. If he pressed down even slightly he'd feel how fast my heart was beating and the whole pretense would shatter.

He didn't press down. He held himself at that impossible distance, close enough to feel, far enough to deny, and moved lower.

I bit the inside of my cheek until I tasted iron.

His hand hovered over my collarbone where the shift had slipped aside in sleep, baring skin that the firelight turned gold. He followed the ridge of bone to my shoulder, then down, the length of my arm where it lay on top of the furs, over my wrist where he'd pressed his nose and breathed me in on the floor. His hand lingered there, trembling in the air above the pulse point, and I heard him inhale, a long, slow breath drawn through his nose, pulling my scent into his lungs like he was trying to memorize it.

A sound came from deep in his chest. Low and strained, not quite human, a growl caught somewhere between need and restraint, the sound of a chain being pulled taut against a force that didn't care about chains.

His hand moved to my waist. I could feel the heat of his palm through the furs, hovering over the dip where my body curved inward. He followed the shape of me, the swell of my hip, the soft round of my belly where life and years had left their mark. He didn't rush. He traced each line like a blind man reading something sacred, something he had no right to touch and couldn't stop reaching for.

The heat between my thighs was immediate and unwanted and undeniable. My body was responding to him without permission, without consent, without any input from the part of my brain that knew this man was my captor and my enemy and the son of a monster. My blood didn't care. My blood answered his the way it had on the floor, instinctive, wordless, like a language spoken below thought.

I kept my eyes shut. Kept my breathing even. Let the heat build because fighting it would give me away.

His hand moved back up. Slowly, so slowly, mapping the terrain of me through fabric and fur and the thin night air between his skin and mine. Over my ribs. Along the side of my breast, where his hand hovered long enough that I could feel his fingers trembling, could hear his breathing fracture into something ragged and desperate.

He made another sound — guttural, pained, the noise of a man losing an argument with himself. His hand moved to the center of my chest and stopped, hovering right between my breasts where my heart hammered so hard the shift must have been vibrating with it.

He stayed there. I could feel the war inside him through the heat of his hand, the wanting and the holding back, the hunger and the horror of the hunger, two things pulling him apart while he stood over me in the dark and tried to be the man he wanted to be instead of the thing he was.

Then he whispered something. My name. I was almost sure it was my name, *Talia*, said the way you say a word you're afraid of, the way you say something that could save you or destroy you and you can't tell which.

His hand trembled one last time above my heart. Then he pulled it back.

The warmth vanished. Cold air filled the space where his hand had been and my body ached with the loss of it, actually ached, a physical pang that rolled through me from chest to belly to the heat still throbbing between my legs.

His footsteps retreated across the floor. The same careful route. The same practiced silence. The door closed. The bar ground into place.

I lay in the dark with my eyes wide open and my body humming.

He wanted me.

The thought cut through everything — the confusion, the shame, the tangled mess of fury and desire that had been strangling me since the floor. He wanted me and he couldn't help himself. He left every night and barred the door and walked the forest perimeter and did whatever it was he did out there in the cold and the dark, and then he came back. Unbarred the door. Crossed the room. Stood over my sleeping body and traced the shape of me through the air because touching me would break whatever vow he'd made to himself.

He was obsessed. And obsessed men made mistakes.

I stared at the ceiling and felt something cold and clear settle into the space where the panic had been. My mind was working now — really working, the way it used to work when I mixed medicines, when I measured doses, when I read a patient's body and knew exactly which pressure point would unlock the pain.

He had a weakness. I'd been looking for one since I woke up in this cottage. The knife hadn't worked, he was too fast. Force was useless, he was too strong. But this hunger, this need he couldn't control, this thing that pulled him through the door every night and brought him to the edge of my bed and made him tremble, this was a crack he couldn't seal. Because the crack was shaped like me.

I could use it.

The thought should have disgusted me. Something in my head, Grandmother's voice maybe, or the woman I had been before Klaus and the cellar and the cage, told me this was beneath me. That using a man's desire as a weapon made me no better than the men who had used their desire as one.

I buried it. I was locked in a dead woman's cottage behind boarded windows. Sophia had waited. Sophia had endured. Sophia was dead. I was not going to be Sophia.

I would use every weapon I had. Even this one. Even my own body. Even if the cost was letting Erik's son believe I wanted him back.

A plan took shape in the dark. He would come again. Tomorrow night, the night after. He could not stay away. The need was too strong. The leash too frayed. And when he came, I would be ready.

I would give him what he wanted. A little at a time. A look that lasted a beat too long. My tone going softer when I spoke to him. The shift slipping low enough to bare a shoulder when he walked past. Small things. Careful things. Signals a body sends when it is opening a door it has not decided to close.

I knew how desire worked. I'd been a wife. I'd watched William's eyes go dark across the dinner table. I'd felt the shift in a room when wanting entered it, the thickened air, the shortened breath, the way conversation died and bodies spoke instead. I knew what it looked like when a man was unravelling and I knew how to pull the thread.

Dietrich's thread was me.

I would let the shift slip lower. Let my fingers brush his when he handed me a plate. Stand close enough that he could smell me, that scent he'd pressed his face against on the floor, the one that made him growl and shake and forget how to be careful. I would feed his hunger until his guard dropped, until the man who could hear a knife leave a table was deaf to everything but the sound of my breathing, the rustle of my shift, the beat of the heart he came back to every night.

And when his eyes were on me instead of the door. I would run.

I lay in the dark and smiled. It was a cold thing, that smile, hard and sharp and nothing like the woman who'd healed broken arms and brewed tea for grieving mothers. But I wasn't that woman anymore. I was a woman in a cage, and caged things learn to bite with whatever teeth they have.

Tomorrow I would start.

And if some traitorous, treacherous, shameful part of me whispered that the warmth of his hand hovering over my heart had felt like the safest thing I'd known since William died. I buried it. Deep, where it would never see daylight. I packed it down into the dark where I kept every other impossible, unwanted thing I'd ever felt and sealed it shut and turned my face to the wall.

I had work to do in the morning. Seduction was just medicine administered differently, the right dose, the right timing, the right pressure applied to the right place until the patient gave you what you needed.

Dietrich was my patient now. And I was going to take him apart.

Chapter Eleven

I started the next morning.

He came in with wood and eggs and I was sitting at the table with the furs wrapped around my shoulders, my hair loose. I never wore my hair loose. I kept it braided, pinned, pulled away from my face, the way a woman wears her hair when she wants to be left alone. But this morning I'd run my fingers through it until it fell in dark waves past my shoulders, the way William used to like it, the way I knew made the line of my throat look longer.

I didn't look at Dietrich when he came in. Just sat there with my hands wrapped around a cup of cold water, staring at the fire. Let him see the hair. Let him notice without being shown.

He noticed. I heard the pause in his step, half a second, barely there, but I was listening for it and I caught it the way a hunter catches the twitch in the grass that tells her where the rabbit is hiding.

He went to the hearth. Built the fire. Cooked the eggs. Set the plate in front of me. All of it in silence, all of it with his eyes fixed firmly on anything that wasn't me.

"Thank you." I set down the fork.

He looked at me. I'd never thanked him before. For days I'd taken the food without a word, without acknowledgement, eating it like it was owed to me. Two words and his whole body changed, shoulders dropping a fraction, the rigid line of his back softening just enough that I could see it.

"You're welcome." And then he left to chop wood, and I sat at the table and ate his eggs and felt something ugly and necessary take root in my chest.

The next time he checked the herbs, I moved closer.

He was at the shelf, turning jars in his hands and reading grandmother's careful script on the labels. I crossed the room and stood beside him, close enough that my shoulder nearly brushed his arm, close enough that he could smell me.

"Which ones are going bad?" I asked. Softer than I'd spoken to him since I'd arrived.

He went rigid. I watched the tendons in his forearms pull taut, watched his fingers tighten on the jar he was holding.

"The comfrey," he managed after a moment. "And the yarrow needs drying again."

"Show me." I reached past him for the jar on the shelf, and my arm brushed against his chest. A small touch.

He stepped back so fast he nearly knocked the mortar off the counter.

"You can check the rest yourself." He crossed to the far side of the room where he stayed for the next hour, mending a hole in his coat with stitches that were too tight and too fast.

I turned back to the shelf and smiled where he couldn't see it.

I let the shift slip on a morning he came in with water from the stream.

I was sitting on the bed with the grimoire open in my lap, openly now, no longer hiding it. The shift I wore was old, the neckline stretched wide from years of washing, and I'd tugged it to one side so it hung off my left shoulder, baring skin from collarbone to the curve where shoulder met arm.

I didn't look up when he entered. Just kept my eyes on the page and let him see what I was showing him.

The bucket hit the floor too hard. Water sloshed over the rim.

"Careful." I kept my eyes on the page. "You'll flood the place."

He said nothing. I heard him cross to the hearth, heard

him crouch, heard the unsteady clatter of kindling being arranged by hands that had forgotten how to be steady. I turned a page and let the shift slip another inch.

He left twenty minutes later. Didn't cook. Didn't eat. Just grabbed his coat and went, and the bar scraped into place with more force than necessary.

I pulled the shift back up and stared at the door and told myself this was working.

It was working.

He was mending a snare at the table when I touched him.

Gut string threaded between his fingers, a wooden frame braced against his knee, his sleeves rolled up to the elbow. The firelight caught the scars along his forearms, pale lines crossing over each other, some thin and old, some thick and ragged, a map of years spent living rough in a forest that didn't forgive mistakes.

I crossed the room and stood beside his chair. Close. Closer than before. Close enough that the heat from his body reached mine through the thin linen of the shift.

"Dietrich." I said it softly, letting the fight drain out of the word.

His hands froze on the gut string. His whole body went rigid — every muscle locking at once, a man bracing for impact.

I reached out and touched his arm. Just my fingertips against his forearm where the scars were thickest. His skin was warm and rough and I felt him shudder, a tremor that started where my fingers rested and ran up through his shoulder and down his spine.

The snare frame clattered off his knee and hit the floor.

"Don't," he breathed, but the word came out thin and airless, nothing like a command.

"Why?" I kept my hand where it was. Let my thumb trace a slow line along the inside of his wrist where the veins ran blue beneath the skin.

"Because I can't ..." His grip on the edge of the chair turned his knuckles white. "You need to step back."

"What happens if I don't?"

He turned his head just enough that I could see his profile, the scar across his cheekbone, the way his lips were pressed together so tight the blood had left them.

"Something I can't take back." He exhaled it like smoke and went quiet.

I held the touch for three more heartbeats. One. Two. Three. Then I stepped away and crossed to the bed and sat down and picked up the grimoire like nothing had happened.

He stood from the chair so abruptly it scraped backward across the stone. Then he walked out. Didn't take his coat. Didn't bar the door. Just walked into the snow in his shirt-sleeves and disappeared into the trees.

The door stood open, cold air flooding the room.

I could have run. Right then. He'd left the door unbarred and he was gone and the forest was right there.

But the timing wasn't right. He'd come after me too

quickly, would track me through fresh snow before I'd gone a mile. I needed him more than distracted. I needed him destroyed.

I got up and closed the door myself. Sat back down and waited.

He came back an hour later. Soaking wet, his hair plastered to his skull, his shirt clinging to his chest. He'd been in the stream. In winter. In water cold enough to stop a heart.

He looked at me from the doorway with eyes that were half fury and half a thing I didn't dare name.

"Don't do that again," he warned.

"Do what?" I asked, and let my gaze travel down his wet shirt and back up again, slow enough that he could feel it.

He barred the door from the inside that night. Slept in the chair by the fire with his back to me. I lay in the bed and listened to him not sleeping, the uneven breathing, the creak of the chair when he shifted, the long stretches of silence that were louder than sound.

One more push and he'd shatter.

I lay in the dark and planned the last move.

He was restringing his bow by the fire the next morning, fingers working the cord with quiet concentration, when I came to sit across from him.

I didn't try anything. Didn't touch him, didn't arrange

the shift. I just sat there and watched his hands work, and after a while I spoke.

"What wood is that?" I asked.

He looked up, wary, searching my face for the trap. When he didn't find it, or thought he didn't, he glanced down at the bow.

"Yew." He turned the shaft between his fingers. "Cut it three winters ago from a tree near the eastern ridge."

"You made it yourself?"

"Who else would make it?" he scoffed. He ran his thumb along the curve of the limb. "You learn the feel of a bow the way you learn anything worth knowing. Slowly. With your hands."

"My husband used to say something like that about his hunting knife." I traced the rim of my cup with one finger. "He'd sharpen it for hours and talk to it like it could hear him."

His hands stilled on the cord. Just for a moment — a hitch so small I almost missed it. Then he went back to working the string.

"William." He didn't look up.

I went cold. "How do you know his name?"

He kept his eyes on the bowstring. "I know the forest. I know who walks through it."

"He's been dead for years." I kept my tone careful.

"I know," he replied, and the flatness of it, the weight, told me he wasn't guessing.

"Did you know him?" I pressed.

His fingers pulled the cord tight and tested the tension. "I knew of him. Tall man. Broad. Hunted with a group of six." He paused. "Laughed louder than any of them."

My throat tightened. That was William. Exactly William — the man whose laugh could fill a clearing and make the birds go quiet.

"How do you know what his laugh sounded like?" I asked.

He didn't answer. Just wound the cord around the notch with practiced fingers and reached for the beeswax to seal it.

"Dietrich."

"I've lived in this forest a long time." He shrugged one shoulder. "You hear things."

That wasn't an answer. I wanted to push, wanted to grab his shoulders and shake the truth out of him. How much had he watched? How long? Had he been in the trees when William walked out our door for the last time? Had he been there when —

I stopped the thought before it could finish. I didn't want to know. I wasn't ready to know.

"He told me once he fought off a bear with a belt knife and a piece of cheese." I only shook a little.

His mouth twitched. "A piece of cheese."

"Aged cheddar. Very hard. He said you could kill a man with it."

He laughed. A short sound, startled out of him before he could swallow it, rough from disuse and over almost as soon as it started. But real. I watched the way it changed his face, the scar shifting, the lines around his eyes deepening, the hard mask cracking just long enough for me to see the man underneath.

"He had six men with him when he went in the last time." I let that one settle. "They never found all the pieces."

The laughter died. He set the bow down and looked at the fire.

"I know." He repeated it, slower this time, like a man laying down a burden he'd been carrying for too long. The hairs on the back of my neck stood up.

I wanted to ask. Did he watch William die? Was he in the trees that day, close enough to hear the screaming? Could he have done something — warned them, driven them back, stepped out of the shadows for once in his life and saved a man who had a wife waiting at home?

But I swallowed the questions. I couldn't afford to ask, because the answer might change what I was about to do, and I needed to do it. I looked away first. Picked up my cup and drank and swallowed hard against the thing rising in my throat.

This was it. It had to be now. Before I got used to this. Before the performance became the truth. Before I looked at him and saw a man instead of a means of escape.

He set the bow aside and crossed to the counter. Pulled a handful of dried rosemary from the shelf and reached for grandmother's mortar, the old stone stained rust-red from decades of madder root, dark and heavy and worn smooth where women's hands had gripped it for longer than anyone alive could remember.

The red that marked us and the red that mended, all from the same root, ground in the same stone.

He started grinding. The rhythmic scrape of pestle against mortar filled the cottage, and the smell of rosemary cut through the wood smoke and the pine, sharp and green and alive.

I stood up from the table.

He glanced toward the sound, but I was already moving. I crossed the room and came to stand in front of him, between him and the counter, so close that my chest nearly touched his.

"Dietrich." His name left my mouth without an edge for the first time since I'd learned it.

His hands froze. The pestle stopped mid-grind. His eyes found mine and I watched his pupils blow wide, watched the amber shrink to a thin burning ring, watched every wall he'd spent rebuilding come apart like wet paper.

I reached up and touched his face. My palm against his cheek, my thumb tracing the scar across his cheekbone. His skin was warm beneath my palm, the coarse hair of his beard rough against my fingers. He leaned into my hand before he could stop himself, a small, involuntary movement, the tilt of a man who hadn't been touched with tenderness in so long that his body couldn't resist it even when his mind knew better.

“Don’t.” But the word had no force left in it. A door kicked too many times to latch properly.

“I’m tired of fighting,” I whispered. The lie tasted like ashes. “I’m tired of hating you.”

His breath hitched. I could feel his pulse jumping under my fingertips, could feel the tremor running through him like a current through water.

“You don’t mean that,” he managed.

“I do.” I slid my hand from his cheek to the back of his neck, fingers threading into his hair. Drew his forehead down until it rested against mine. His breath was warm and unsteady on my face and his hands hung at his sides, shaking, clenched into fists that wanted to open.

“Talia...” My name in his mouth sounded like something breaking. “If you do this and you don’t mean it...”

“I mean it.” And I kissed him.

For a moment he was stone. Absolutely still, every muscle locked, like the thing he’d been starving for had walked up and offered itself and he was too terrified to reach for it in case it disappeared.

Then he broke.

His hands grabbed my waist and pulled me against him hard enough to empty my lungs. His mouth opened over mine and he kissed me back with a hunger that bordered on violence, nothing gentle, nothing careful, just years of loneliness and need pouring out of him in a flood he couldn’t control. His hands slid up my back and into my hair and he kissed me like I was air and he’d been drowning.

He walked me backward until my shoulders hit the wall beside the shelf and his body pressed the length of mine, every hard plane of muscle, the heat of him through our clothes, the unmistakable evidence of what I was doing to him pressed against my stomach. His hands gripped my waist hard enough to bruise and his mouth moved from my lips to my throat, his beard dragging against my skin, teeth scraping against my pulse point.

I gasped. My head fell back against the wall and my fingers dug into his shoulders and the sound that came out of me was real, horrifyingly, undeniably real. My body had stopped performing. It had stopped taking directions somewhere between his mouth on my throat and his hands in my hair and now it was just responding, answering his hunger with its own.

His hands found the neckline of my shift. His fingers trembled against the fabric, hovering, asking a question his mouth was too busy to voice.

I didn't stop him. I needed his hands occupied. I needed his attention buried so deep in sensation that the rest of the world ceased to exist.

He pulled. The fabric tore and cold air hit my bare skin like a shock. For a heartbeat we both froze, his eyes dropped to what he'd uncovered, to the swell of bare skin and the nipple already tightening in the cold air, and his breathing stopped. Just stopped. Like his lungs had forgotten how to work.

Then his mouth was on me.

His lips closed around my nipple and my back arched off the wall so hard my shoulder blades cracked against the stone. A sound tore from my throat, half moan, half sob, and my fingers twisted into his hair and held him there because my body had stopped listening to my mind entirely. His tongue was warm and wet and desperate, circling and pulling, and the pleasure was sharp enough to cut, rolling through me in waves that buckled my knees and turned my thoughts to white noise.

He made sounds against my skin, low, broken, starving sounds that vibrated through my flesh and into my ribs and lodged somewhere behind my heart. His hands gripped my waist and held me upright when my legs tried to give, his mouth pulling at my nipple with an intensity that told me he'd been imagining this, that every night he'd hovered his hands over my sleeping body this was what he'd wanted. And I was drowning in it, sinking into it, losing the edges of myself in the heat and the pull and the terrible, ruinous sweetness of being wanted this badly by someone this desperately alone.

I forgot the plan.

For ten seconds, maybe fifteen, I forgot everything. Forgot the mortar and the door and the life waiting for me on the other side of the forest. Forgot Sophia and the boards and the cage.

There was only his mouth and my skin and the sound of both of us breathing like we'd been running for miles. My hips pressed forward against his and his grip on my waist tightened and a groan rumbled through his chest into mine and I felt it everywhere, and I wanted — Thomas.

His face flashed behind my eyes. The blood. The dirt. The neck bent wrong. Emma on her knees.

The heat didn't die. It couldn't — my body was too far gone, too flooded with sensation to come back that quickly. But something cold and hard dropped through the center of it like a stone into a hot spring, and the stone was shaped like a little boy's face and it sank to the bottom and sat there and reminded me what I was here to do.

My right hand loosened in his hair. Slid from the back of his head to his shoulder. Kept moving — out, away, reaching blindly along the wall while his mouth was still on me and his eyes were still closed and every nerve I had screamed at me to pull him closer instead of reaching for the shelf.

My fingers brushed across jars. Dried bundles. The rough edge of wood.

Then cold stone.

Grandmother's mortar. Heavy in my palm. Stained dark from decades of madder root and medicine and the hands of every woman in my line who had used it to heal.

I was going to use it to break a man's skull.

His tongue circled my nipple and another wave of pleasure crested through me so hard my vision blurred. I bit down on the inside of my cheek until I tasted blood and tightened my fingers around the stone and pulled it from the shelf.

I'm sorry, Grandmother.

I brought the mortar down on his temple with every ounce of strength I had. The crack echoed through the cottage.

He went rigid against me. His mouth pulled away from my breast and his eyes flew open, confused at first, unfocused, his lips still wet from my skin. And then the understanding arrived. I watched it land. Watched it move across his face like a shadow, confusion to clarity to hurt to betrayal, each one worse than the last, each one cutting deeper than the blow itself.

He looked at me. Looked at my face with my breast still bare and the nipple still glistening from his mouth and the mortar still in my hand and the blood already running down his temple in a dark line, and the expression in his eyes wasn't anger.

It was grief.

Grief that doesn't rage or fight or argue. It just goes quiet and lies down and waits to die.

The light in his eyes died right there while I watched.

Then his eyes rolled back and he collapsed.

I stepped aside in time. He hit the floor hard and lay there motionless, blood seeping from his temple and pooling on the packed earth. One hand still reaching toward where I'd been standing. His fingers curled loosely around nothing.

I stood over him with the mortar clutched in my hand and my shift torn open and my body still pulsing with what he'd been doing to me moments before. The pleasure and the horror churned together in my stomach until they became the same thing, a sick, hot wave that climbed up my throat and made me gag.

The mortar slipped from my fingers and hit the floor. The stone was wet — fresh blood mixing with the rusty red of madder, the old red and the new running together until I couldn't tell which stain was grandmother's and which was mine.

He was breathing. Shallow, uneven, but breathing. I hadn't killed him.

I pulled the shift up but the fabric was torn and wouldn't hold. I wrapped the red cloak around my shoulders and used it to hold the ruined shift closed, then grabbed the grimoire from under the bed and pressed it against my chest.

The door was unbarred.

I looked back once.

Dietrich lay on the stone floor with blood spreading from his temple, his face slack and empty. His mouth was still swollen from kissing me.

I could still feel his mouth on my nipple. Could still feel the ghost of his hands on my waist, the rumble of his groan against my ribs, the wet heat of his tongue circling and pulling. My body ached with wanting him. A real, physical ache that had nothing to do with the plan and everything to do with the traitorous, shameful, undeniable truth that part of me had meant it. Had wanted him. Had kissed him back with hunger that wasn't a lie and had arched into his mouth with need that wasn't performance and had whispered *I'm tired of hating you* and meant at least half of it.

A deep, physical pain that sat behind my ribs like a fist and squeezed, and I knew, with a certainty I would carry for the rest of my life, that the look on his face when he understood what I'd done would follow me into every dream I had from now until I died.

I turned away.

And I ran.

Chapter Twelve

I was outside and freezing before my next breath came. Snow crunched under my bare feet. I'd forgotten boots, hadn't thought about boots, hadn't thought about anything except the door and the forest and the distance between me and the cottage growing with every step. The wind cut through grandmother's torn shift and the cloak and went straight into my bones, and my breath came in white clouds that the dark swallowed before they'd fully formed.

I ran.

The grimoire pressed against my chest, the leather already slick with snow. Branches whipped my face and I felt skin split but didn't slow down, couldn't slow down, because two things were chasing me now even if neither had caught up yet.

Dietrich. Behind me, bleeding on the floor, but alive. I

hadn't hit him hard enough to kill, which meant I hadn't hit him hard enough to keep him down for long. He'd wake. He'd find the door open and the cottage empty and he'd come after me the way he always came after things that tried to leave. Fast and certain and impossible to outrun.

And the wolf.

Every creature I'd heard circling the cottage through weeks of captivity. Every howl that had stopped only when something snarled from the tree line.

I was running through the same forest that had killed William. Running in nothing but a torn shift and a red cloak with blood on my face and blood-keeper scent pouring off me like smoke.

The trees pressed close on every side. Massive trunks that vanished into shadow above my head, their branches woven together so tight the moonlight filtered through. Snow fell in thick flakes that caught in my hair and melted against my flushed skin and turned the ground beneath my feet into a treacherous mess of ice and hidden roots and frozen mud that gave way without warning.

I kept running. The red cloak billowed behind me and caught on every thorn, every branch. I yanked it free again and again, heard fabric tear, kept moving. The forest had swallowed me and I could feel it. Dark pressing in from all sides, the silence between the trees that wasn't really silence at all but the sound of things holding their breath and listening.

William had walked into this forest with six armed men

and never come home. I'd heard the howling through the boards every night. The circling, the claws on frozen ground, the sniffing at the door. I'd stood in the mouth of a black wolf so big its head reached my chin and watched its teeth glisten in the dark.

And I'd run into this place anyway. In a torn shift. In bare feet. Bleeding.

Because the cage was worse than the wolf. Because Sophia had died behind these boards and I refused to follow her.

I kept telling myself that while the trees closed in and the dark got thicker and the silence got louder.

The ground changed without warning. My foot caught a root and I pitched forward with a cry, the grimoire slipping from my grip and tumbling into darkness. I went down hard. Sliding, rolling, branches tearing at my cloak and my arms and the bare skin of my legs. I hit a rock with my hip and the pain whited out my vision. More sliding, more scraping, and then the slope leveled and I crashed to a halt at the bottom of a ravine, flat on my back with stars bursting behind my eyes and the taste of dirt and blood in my mouth.

For a long moment I couldn't move. Couldn't do anything but lie there and gasp while the cold seeped into my back through the wet snow and the trees stood over me like witnesses to something they'd seen before.

The grimoire. Where was the grimoire?

I rolled onto my side and saw it lying in the snow a few feet away, the dark leather stark against the white. I crawled toward it and pulled it against my chest and held it there while my hip screamed and my hands shook and the forest went on being dark and silent and full of things I couldn't see.

Then the howl came.

It rose from somewhere above me, from the direction I'd been running. Long and hungry and wrong in a way that lived in the marrow rather than the ear. This was the sound I'd heard through the boards. The circling. The sniffing at the door. But there were no boards between us now, no bar, no walls, no Dietrich settling against the outside of the door to keep watch through the night.

There was nothing between me and whatever was making that sound except snow and dark and the red cloak wrapped around my shoulders.

I scrambled to my feet, ignoring the pain in my hip. The ravine walls were too steep to climb back up and the only way was forward, deeper into the forest, further from the cottage, further from the only person who knew what hunted these woods after dark.

I ran.

The ravine opened into a clearing ringed by massive oaks, their branches woven together overhead like a cathedral ceiling, blocking out what little moonlight remained. The snow here was thinner, sheltered by the canopy, and the ground was a mess of dead leaves and frozen mud. I stopped in the center and turned in a slow circle, listening, watching, each exhale plunging into the cold and vanishing.

I held my breath. The forest held its breath back. Whatever was out there had stopped making noise, and that was worse than sound.

Branches snapped behind me. I spun.

Yellow eyes appeared in the darkness.

It came out of the tree line standing upright.

Gray fur covered its body from the jaw down, dense and coarse, rippling over muscles that bunched and shifted with each step. It stood seven feet tall, maybe more, shoulders so broad they blocked the gaps between the oaks. Its arms hung long at its sides, thick and wrong, ending in hands tipped with claws that curved like skinning knives. Its legs bent backward at the knee, jointed like a wolf's hind legs, massive clawed feet gripping the frozen ground.

Scars covered its face and flanks. A long pale line split its muzzle where the fur refused to grow, an old wound healed wrong and left for the world to see.

This creature was nothing like the black wolf. The black wolf had been an animal. Enormous, yes. Unnatural, yes. But still a wolf. This was a wolf forced into a man's posture, or a man twisted into a wolf's shape, and the result belonged in neither world. It oozed hunger. Its lips pulled back from teeth the length of my thumb and a growl rumbled through its chest, deep enough that I could feel it vibrating through the frozen ground beneath my feet.

I backed up until my shoulders hit bark. Nowhere else to go. My hands came up instinctively, fingers spread, reaching for the heat that had thrown Klaus across the cellar, the power that had surged through me once and never again.

The creature moved toward me. Slow, deliberate, taking its time the way a predator does when it knows its prey has nowhere to run.

Then it stopped. Its head jerked toward the red wool at my shoulders. For one breath, the creature recoiled from the color, confused by what its own hunger couldn't name.

Then the hunger won. It closed the last ten feet and its massive body dropped into a crouch, every muscle coiling, and I saw the moment it decided to strike.

It lunged.

A lock inside me snapped into place. Heat roared up from deep in my gut. The same heat from the cellar, the same fire that had been dormant for days no matter how hard I'd tried to summon it. It surged through my chest and down my arms and exploded out through my palms with a force that felt like being turned inside out.

I threw my hands forward and screamed.

The creature hit a wall three feet in front of me and yelped, a sharp, startled sound, tumbling backward through the air and landing hard on its side. It scrambled upright with its ears flat and fear bright in its yellow eyes.

I stood frozen with my hands still outstretched and power still crackling through my fingers. I'd done that. Somehow, without knowing how, I'd pushed that massive creature back without touching it.

It recovered quickly, shaking snow from its fur. It turned

those yellow eyes back to me, but the expression had changed. The hunger was still there, but it had twisted into something else. Its head lowered and its body tensed in a new way, making sounds that weren't quite growls. Lower, deeper, thick with an intent that made every hair on my body stand up and my stomach clenched with a revulsion so deep it was almost physical.

An ancient instinct stirred in me. An instinct that was older than thought, older than language, that recognized what was happening even before my conscious mind caught up.

The creature wasn't trying to kill me anymore.

It wanted something else.

It moved faster than its size should have allowed. Clawed hands hammered into my shoulders and drove me to the ground, the crushing weight slamming me face-down into the snow and dead leaves. Its body pressed against my back, huge and suffocating, and I could feel the heat of it through the cloak, could feel the rumble in its chest vibrating through my spine.

Horror swallowed everything.

I screamed and twisted and lashed out with my hands. Power exploded from my palms. Raw, uncontrolled, fueled by a terror so complete it stripped every thought from my mind and left nothing but the animal need to survive. The creature yelped and scrambled off me.

I rolled away and shoved myself to my feet. My shift was torn where claws had caught it and scratches burned across my back and shoulders, blood soaking through the fabric and into the red wool of the cloak. My legs shook. My hands shook. The power was fading as fast as it had come, draining out of me like water through a cracked bowl.

The creature circled again, blood dripping from a gash on its shoulder where my power had cut it. The wound didn't slow it down. Its yellow eyes tracked me with the same twisted hunger, the same low sounds rumbling from its chest.

It crouched. Ready to try again.

I raised my hands. Reached for the heat. Reached for the power.

Empty. The well was dry. I was drained, spent, standing in a frozen clearing in a torn shift with blood running down my back and nothing left between me and this creature except cold air.

It sprang.

A body crashed through the trees with enough force to shake the ground.

The creature twisted mid-leap and landed sideways, skidding through the snow. Its head snapped toward the sound and for the first time its body went rigid with something that wasn't hunger.

Fear.

Dietrich stood between two massive oaks at the edge of the clearing.

Blood crusted on his temple where I'd hit him, dried in a dark line that ran from his hairline to his chin. His shirt was damp with sweat despite the cold and his chest heaving. His hands hung loose at his sides. No weapon, no knife, nothing but empty fists and fury written across every line of his body.

His eyes found mine for a moment. Rage and relief and hurt and betrayal, all tangled together in a look that lasted less than a second but said everything I'd done to him back to me. The kiss, the mortar, the blood on the floor.

Then he turned away from me and walked into the clearing, positioning himself between me and the creature with the unhurried stride of a man who had done this before and would do it again and was very, very tired of it.

"Go." Low and cold, the word carried through the clearing like a whip crack.

The gray creature froze. Its ears flattened against its skull and its massive body dropped lower, the aggression draining out of its posture. It stared at Dietrich with an expression I'd never seen on an animal's face. Recognition, and underneath the recognition, a thing that looked very much like fear.

It knew him.

"I said go," Dietrich repeated, and the sound crawled across my skin and raised every hair on my body. The tone had changed. Deepened. It wasn't quite human anymore. A second register lived underneath it, a frequency meant for ears other than mine.

The creature's lips pulled back one last time, teeth bared, a final show of defiance that lasted exactly as long as it took for Dietrich to take one step forward. Then the defiance collapsed. Its body shuddered and the bones began to crack, joints grinding, the massive frame folding in on itself. The arms shortened. The spine curved. The clawed hands that had pinned me to the snow became paws, the upright shape dropping onto all fours with a wet sound like something tearing loose inside. What stood in the clearing now was still enormous, still twice the size of any natural wolf, scarred and gray and panting. But it was a wolf. Just a wolf. It turned and fled, crashing through the underbrush, the sound of its paws fading until the forest swallowed it and everything went quiet.

I stared at Dietrich's back. A man standing unarmed in a frozen clearing had just driven off a creature that towered over him, forced it back into its lesser shape with nothing but a word and one step forward. The creature had recognized him. Had feared him. Had obeyed him the way a dog obeys a master it knows can hurt it.

The questions piled up but my legs wouldn't hold. The power was gone, the adrenaline was gone, and what was left couldn't support the weight of a woman standing upright. My knees buckled and I caught myself on the trunk of the oak behind me and slid down it until I was sitting in the snow with the grimoire in my lap and the cloak around my shoulders and blood running down my back.

Dietrich turned around slowly.

His expression was terrible. Cold and compressed, like all his emotions had been forced through a sieve until only the most dangerous parts remained. He crossed the distance between us in four strides and his hand closed around my upper arm, his grip like iron.

"You're coming back," he said through his teeth. "Now."

"I can't..." I started.

He pulled me to my feet. My legs screamed and my hip buckled but he held me upright with one hand and started walking, pulling me with him through the snow. I stumbled after because the only alternative was being dragged.

The forest passed in a blur of dark trunks and white snow and the sound of him ahead of me. Hard steps. Controlled fury. He didn't speak. Didn't look back. Just walked with my arm locked in his grip and the dried blood on his temple catching the moonlight.

The cottage appeared through the trees. The door still hung open, firelight spilling out into the darkness. He pulled me through the doorway and released my arm so suddenly I stumbled and caught myself on the table. The warmth from the fire washed over me and I realized how cold I'd been, how completely numb my hands and feet had gone, how close I'd come to freezing before anything in the forest could have killed me.

He walked past me and shoved the door shut. The bar dropped into place. Then he crossed to the hearth and stood with his back to me, his shoulders rising and falling with breaths he was fighting to control.

Minutes passed. The hearth gave off a steady burn. Wind

pressed against the boarded windows. I stood by the table dripping snow and blood onto the floor and waited for him to speak because I had no words left. Everything I'd planned, everything I'd calculated, every clever manipulation I'd spent days constructing. It was all gone, burned away by the clearing and the wolf and the look on his face when he'd found me.

"What was that thing?" I finally managed. "It wasn't a wolf. Wolves don't stand like that. Wolves don't have hands."

He didn't turn. "What would you like me to say?"

"The truth. What was it?"

He didn't answer me.

"Dietrich. That creature stood seven feet tall. It walked on two legs. It shifted into a wolf when you told it to go. I watched it happen. I watched bones break and a body fold in half. So don't tell me it was just a wolf."

"I'm not telling you anything," he cut back, and I could hear the lock turn behind it.

"You cracked my skull open. Left me bleeding on the floor. I woke up and you were gone."

The subject change hit me like cold water. He'd shoved the question aside and buried it under the thing that mattered more to him. Under the hurt.

"I had to..." I started.

"I know what you had to do." He finally faced me, and his expression was broken. The anger had burned through to what lived underneath, raw and exhausted and wounded in a way that couldn't be stitched closed. "You had to escape. You saw an opportunity and you took it."

"Yes." I met his eyes because he deserved that much. "I did."

"You kissed me." The tendons stood taut in his neck. He ground each one out like it cost him. "Touched me. Made me think..."

He stopped. Turned back to the fire.

"Made you think what?" I asked, even though my chest was splitting open with every word.

"It doesn't matter." His tone went flat.

"It matters."

"You used me." He gripped the mantel until his arms shook, until the wood creaked under his hands. "Over two decades, Talia. Do you understand? Over two decades without..."

He stopped again. His shoulders were shaking.

"Without what?" I stepped closer.

"Without anyone." The word split open in his mouth like a confession he'd been holding between his teeth for years. "Without a single person touching me who wasn't trying to hurt me or drive me away. And you, for one moment I thought..."

He pressed his forehead against the mantel and I watched his shoulders shake and realized he was fighting a thing bigger than anger, bigger than betrayal. He was fighting the grief of a man who'd let himself hope for the first time in twenty-two years and had the hope smashed against his skull with a stone mortar.

"You thought what?" I whispered.

"That I wasn't alone anymore." He spoke into the stone above the fire, so softly I almost missed it. "That someone actually wanted… that someone could look at me and see..." He shook his head. "It doesn't matter. You did what you had to do."

"I did." I held my ground despite the shaking inside me. "And I'd do it again."

He flinched. His whole body flinched, a full-body recoil like I'd hit him with the mortar a second time.

The guilt hit me then. The full weight of what I'd done landing on my chest all at once. I'd taken the only tenderness this man had felt in a long time and weaponized it. I'd kissed him and let him touch me and let him believe, even for a moment, that someone wanted him. And then I'd cracked his skull open while his mouth was still on my breast.

"I'm sorry I hurt you," I offered, though it wasn't nearly enough.

He went very still.

"I'm not sorry I tried to escape. But I'm sorry I had to hurt you to do it."

He didn't respond.

"And I'm sorry I used what you feel." The words stuck and I forced them out. "I'm sorry I made you think it was real."

He lifted his head. Turned just enough that I could see his profile. The dried blood, the swelling at his temple, the wet line tracking down his cheek that might have been sweat or might not have been.

"Was any of it?" he asked. Quiet. Almost nothing.

I opened my mouth to say no. To say it was all performance, all calculation, every touch and look and whispered word designed to dismantle him. That's what I should have said. That's what would have been clean and honest and kind in its cruelty. A sharp cut instead of a slow bleed.

But I couldn't. Because it would have been a lie, and I'd already lied to him enough.

"I don't know." And that was the truth, and it was worse than either answer he'd been bracing for, because it meant neither of us knew what was real and neither of us could go back to before.

He turned away. Crossed to the far corner and sat down on the floor with his back against the wall and his knees drawn up and his forearms resting across them and his head bowed. He looked like a man who'd been beaten. He looked like a man who'd stopped fighting.

I crossed to the bed and sat down. My back burned where the gray creature's claws had torn through the shift and into skin. My hip throbbed. My hands were raw from the fall and the crawling and the cold.

I looked at Dietrich in his corner. I knew I should hate him. He'd locked me up. Kept me prisoner in my own grandmother's cottage. In the same cage his father kept my aunt. But he'd also run through a frozen forest with a cracked skull to stand between me and a creature that stood taller than any man, with nothing but a command and his bare hands. He'd done it without hesitation, without weapons, without even stopping to consider that the woman he was saving was the same woman who'd just tried to kill him.

Time passed. I couldn't sleep. I'd lain in the furs and listened to him breathe across the room and watched the fire burn down and build back up, burn down and build back up. The cold crept in deeper each time the flames shrank. My breath fogged above the bed and the boards groaned the way wood groans when the temperature outside drops fast. Snow, probably. A heavy fall, the kind that buries the forest and steals the heat right through the walls.

He fed the fire the first time without looking at me. The second time, he got up and crossed to the hearth and stayed there longer than the fire needed.

I closed my eyes when I heard him stand.

He pulled the spare fur off the chest and carried it to the bed and laid it over me. Careful. The way you cover someone you think is sleeping when you don't want to wake them.

He'd told me the loneliest thing I'd ever heard come out of a man's mouth and I'd told him I'd do it again. And he'd still gotten up in the dark and covered me because I was cold.

I pressed my face into the pillow and bit down on the sound that tried to come out of me.

By the time gray light showed through the cracks in the boards, the wound at his temple had closed. I'd set bones and stitched wounds and watched flesh mend itself over days and weeks and months. A blow hard enough to crack bone and pour blood down a man's face did not heal overnight. It couldn't. The body didn't work that way.

His body did.

I filed it away with everything else I couldn't explain about him and reached under the bed for the grimoire.

The leather was cold against my fingers. I opened it in my lap and turned past the entries I'd already read. Blood-keepers, protective symbols, humans. Then I reached the werewolf section, the pages that had been locked behind blurred text since the first day I'd found the book.

The text was clear.

I stopped. Blinked. Looked again. The words that had swum and blurred every time I'd tried to read them were sharp now. Dark ink on yellowed parchment, steady and legible as grandmother's handwriting on the herb jars. Using my power in the clearing had cracked a lock I didn't know was there. The grimoire recognized it and was opening doors that had been sealed shut.

I glanced at Dietrich. His eyes were still closed. He hadn't stirred.

I started reading.

On Werewolves

Werewolves are beings cursed to take the form of beasts. They are stronger than men, faster, with senses that can track a blood-keeper from miles away. They heal faster than any human. They survive what should kill them. Broken bones, torn flesh, wounds that would put a man in the ground. But they are not invincible. Cursed blood fighting cursed blood heals slow and ugly. A werewolf wounded by another of its kind will mend, but the body spends its strength fighting the foreign magic before it can close the wound. Fire slows them. Silver burns them in ways they cannot shake off. And a blood-keeper who has reached her full power can do things to a werewolf that no amount of healing will undo.

My eyes went to Dietrich's temple. The gash was closed. A thin pale line where bone had been showing before. Cold settled deep in my stomach. I looked back at the page before the thought could finish forming.

The transformation is agony. Bones breaking and reforming, flesh tearing and reshaping into new configurations. But they endure it because the beast gives them power beyond anything their human forms could achieve.

Most take the form of wolves. Large, monstrous wolves far bigger than any natural beast, with teeth that can crush bone and claws that can tear through armor. They hunt in packs or alone, depending on their nature. The solitary ones are often the most dangerous. Outcasts, exiles, creatures with nothing left to lose and no pack to temper their worst impulses.

They were not born from nature. They were built.

The Sanguinarians made them. Those ancient blood-drinkers needed hunters. Fast and brutal and obedient, able to track blood-keepers across forests and mountains and drag them back alive. So they took human men. Soldiers. Prisoners. The willing and the desperate. Fed them Sanguinarian blood mixed with the blood of wolves and bears and the great predators. The magic didn't kill those men. It broke them apart and rebuilt them as something caught between man and beast.

The first werewolves were slaves. Dogs on a leash. They hunted blood-keepers through the wild places and brought them back to the Sanguinarian courts, alive and bleeding, and watched while their masters drank.

The Sanguinarians treated them like animals. Kept them in kennels. Bred them for stronger senses, bigger bodies, more obedience. Killed their mates when they bred without permission. This went on for generations.

Then one of them refused.

The stories disagree on who he was. An alpha whose mate was slaughtered for bearing a child without leave. A lone wolf caged so long the chains wore grooves in his bones. A werewolf who listened when a blood-keeper whispered the truth of what he was. A weapon made from stolen blood and broken men, serving the very masters who'd unmade him.

Whoever he was, he tore the throat from the Sanguinarian who held his leash. And the others followed.

The war lasted decades. The courts burned. The blood-keepers hid and documented everything.

When the fires died, the werewolves were free.

But freedom did not make them safe. The instinct the Sanguinarians bred into them. The hunger to hunt blood-keepers, to track us, to crave us. That stayed in the blood. In the bone. Coded into the magic that made them. They stopped bringing us back to their masters. They just stopped bringing us back alive.

Since then, werewolves and blood-keepers have been enemies. They hunt us by scent, by instinct, by a hatred they cannot choose to put down. We kill them on sight. This is the way it has been for centuries, and this is the way it must remain. They are our natural predators. We are their prey.

They kill us when they find us. But killing is not always the first thing they do.

The book slipped from my fingers and thudded against the floor.

The gray creature. The way it had stopped trying to kill me after I'd used my power. The way its hunger had twisted into something else. The lowered head, the different sounds, the body tensing in a new way. The way it had pinned me face-down in the snow and pressed its weight against my back and I'd felt the rumble in its chest vibrating through my spine.

It hadn't been an animal. It had been a man inside a monster's body. And it hadn't been trying to kill me.

Killing is not always the first thing they do.

My hand flew to my mouth. I lurched off the bed and quickly made it to the basin in the corner before my stomach heaved. Bile burned up my throat. Nothing else to bring up. But my body kept trying, kept convulsing with the horror of understanding what had almost happened to me in that clearing. What those sounds had meant. What the pinning had meant. What it would have done if my power hadn't thrown it off me.

I heard him move behind me. The creak of leather, the sound of boots crossing the floor. Then he was beside me, crouching close enough that the heat from his body reached mine through the thin shift.

"What did you read?" he asked.

I couldn't answer. Couldn't form words past the heaving and the tremors. Could only crouch there with my forehead pressed against the cold rim of the basin and try to hold myself together.

"Talia." Gentler now. "Talk to me."

"The wolf," I managed, the words scraped raw. "The gray wolf. It wasn't just trying to kill me."

"It was a werewolf." I lifted my head to look at him. His face was pale in the firelight, the healed wound stark against his skin. "A man inside a wolf's body. And it wanted to..." My throat closed. "It was going to..." I couldn't finish. Didn't need to. His expression told me he already knew. A muscle in his neck jumped once and went still.

"You knew," I whispered.

"Yes." His reply was flat like there was no room for argument.

"Since when?"

"Years." He didn't flinch. "I've known there was a werewolf in this forest since before you arrived."

I stared at him. "Years. You've known for years and you didn't..."

"There was nothing to tell you that would have helped." He cut across me, low and tight. "It kept its distance. Stayed in the deep forest. Never came this close to the cottage until you came into the forest. You attract him."

I gripped the rim of the basin until my knuckles went white. "Is it coming back?"

"Because it found what it wanted." His mouth tightened. "And it didn't get to finish."

My stomach turned over. I pressed my forehead against the cold rim and breathed through the nausea and tried to think past the horror to the practical question underneath it.

"Then what happens now?" I could hardly get the question out.

"I find it." He stood and crossed to the hearth. His back straightened with a resolve that looked like armor being strapped on. "And I kill it before it gets close to you again."

"How?" I pushed myself to my feet, one hand braced on the wall. "You walked into that clearing with empty hands and told it to go and it went. You didn't just scare it off, Dietrich. It changed. I watched it change. Its bones cracked and it folded in half and dropped to all fours like you'd forced it back into a smaller shape. How is that possible?"

He stared into the fire. The flames reflected in his eyes, turning the amber to molten gold.

"Dietrich."

"It doesn't matter how." Low. Final. The same locked door he'd shut on me in the clearing.

"It matters to me. That creature stood on two legs. It had hands. It was taller than you. And you made it shrink with a word. So either you tell me what you are or you tell me what it is, because one of those answers explains the other."

His jaw tightened. The tendons in his neck stood out. For a long moment I thought he was going to break, thought the silence alone would crack him open the way my questions couldn't.

"It matters that it worked," he said at last. "And it matters that you're alive."

The questions stacked up behind my teeth. About the creature obeying him. About the wound that healed overnight. About the musk and the growl I'd heard deep in his chest when he'd pinned me to the floor. About how a man with empty hands could force a monster back into a lesser shape.

He wasn't going to answer. Not tonight. Maybe not ever.

I swallowed them. Let them sink back down to where I kept the things I wasn't ready to know.

"Let me see your back." His tone shifted. Quieter, practical, the tone of someone moving from one task to the next because standing still wasn't possible for him. "The scratches need cleaning."

"I can do it myself." I pulled away.

"You can't reach them," he countered. "And if they get infected out here, there's no physician to save you. Just me and whatever's left on that shelf."

He was right. I hated that he was right.

I moved to the bed and sat with my back to him. Heard him gather supplies from the shelf. Water, cloth, one of grandmother's jars. Felt the bed shift as he sat behind me.

"The shift needs to come down," he said carefully. "I need to see the wounds."

I pulled the fabric down to my waist, baring my back. The cold air raised goosebumps across my shoulders and I held the shift against my chest and stared at the wall and tried not to think about the last time his hands had been on my skin.

The wet cloth touched the first scratch and I hissed through my teeth. The scratches burned where he cleaned them. Long lines of fire running from my shoulders down to my lower back where the creature's claws had torn through fabric and flesh.

"Hold still," he murmured.

He worked with steady hands, cleaning each scratch with an attention that would have been tender if I'd let myself call it that. The water in the bowl turned pink. When he'd finished cleaning, he stood and crossed to the hearth, poured water into a pot and set it over the flames.

He came back with a cloth that steamed in the cold air and pressed it against my back. I flinched at the sting, my fingers curling into the furs beneath me. But after a moment the heat sank deeper and the burning eased, the tight muscles around the scratches loosening despite my best efforts to stay tense and guarded.

He worked in silence, reheating the cloth and applying it again and again until my back felt warm instead of torn. Then he spread salve over the scratches. A salve that smelled of herbs and honey and reminded me so painfully of Grandmother that my eyes burned. He wrapped clean bandages around my torso with practiced hands, efficient and impersonal, his fingers never lingering anywhere they didn't need to be.

"There's a clean shift in the trunk." He finished and stood, moving away from the bed.

He crossed to the chest, came back with worn linen, and held it out to me without quite meeting my eyes. Then he turned his back while I pulled the clean fabric over my head, wincing as the movement tugged at the bandages.

"Done." I tugged the hem straight.

He turned around. We looked at each other across the small room and neither of us spoke. The mortar. The clearing. The creature. His hands on my wounds. All of it pressing against the walls of the room.

"You should rest." He crossed to the hearth. "Your body needs time to heal."

"What about you?"

"I'll keep watch." He moved to the chair by the fire and sat down, stretching his legs toward the warmth.

I looked at him. The healed wound, the amber eyes, the steady hands that had cleaned my wounds and wrapped my bandages and never once touched me with anything other than care. The man who'd run through a frozen forest with a cracked skull to save the woman who'd cracked it.

"Stay," I heard myself say. The word came out before I could stop it. "Don't sit over there. I need to know you're close."

He hesitated. I watched him wrestle with it. The set of his shoulders, the way his hands tightened on the arms of the chair.

"Please," I whispered. "The floor. Just stay close."

He stood slowly. Lost an argument with himself and knew it. Crossed to the storage area and gathered extra furs, laid them out on the floor beside the bed without a word. A makeshift pallet between me and the door.

I lay back and pulled the furs to my chin. My body ached in places I hadn't known could ache, and my mind kept circling back to the grimoire. Killing is not always the first thing they do.

"Dietrich." His name carried into the quiet.

"Hmm." The sound came from below me, close, the rumble of it vibrating through the floor and into the bed frame.

I wanted to ask how a man scares off a werewolf with empty hands. Wanted to ask why his wound had healed overnight. Wanted to ask what he was, because the answer was sitting right there at the edge of my mind, a shape I could almost see, and all I had to do was turn my head and look at it straight.

I didn't ask. I wasn't ready. Because if the answer was what I thought it was, then the man lying on the floor between me and the door, the man who'd fed my fire and cleaned my wounds and run through a frozen forest to save my life, was the same kind of creature that had just tried to pin me in the snow.

And I'd asked him to sleep beside my bed.

"Thank you." The words were all I could manage. "For coming after me. Even after what I did."

He was quiet for a long time. Then. "Go to sleep, Talia."

I closed my eyes. The last thing I heard was his breathing. Steady and even and close.

I didn't understand him. Didn't understand what he was or why he was protecting me or what he was hiding behind those intoxicating eyes.

But lying in the furs with my wounds bandaged and his breathing filling the silence, I realized what should have terrified me.

I felt safe.

And that was the most dangerous thing of all.

Chapter Thirteen

We stopped fighting. I wasn't sure when it happened, there was no truce, no conversation, just the slow erosion of hostility into something neither of us had a name for.

He started teaching me things without either of us deciding he would. It began with the snares. I'd watched him mend them enough times that one morning I picked up a broken one from the table and turned it over in my hands.

"You're holding it wrong." He didn't look up from the hearth.

"Then show me," I challenged.

He crossed to the table and sat down across from me, took the snare from my hands and held it up. "The loop needs to sit here," he explained, threading the gut string through the wooden frame with fingers that made the work look effortless. "Too high and the rabbit runs under it. Too low and it triggers before anything steps through."

"How do you know where to set it?" I watched his hands, trying to memorize the movements.

"You look for the runs." He leaned forward, elbows on his knees. "Tracks in the snow. Droppings. Places where the bark's been chewed low on the trunks. Rabbits are creatures of habit — they use the same paths over and over. Find the path and the snare does the rest."

"Who taught you?" I asked, taking the frame back and trying to copy what he'd done. The gut string slipped through my fingers and I swore under my breath.

"Taught myself." He shrugged. "After my father left. First winter I nearly starved because every trap I built fell apart." He reached across and adjusted my grip without thinking about it, his fingers over mine, repositioning them on the string. "Took me months to figure out the tension. Lost a lot of rabbits."

"My grandmother tried to teach me once." I worked the string through the loop the way he'd shown me. "I was too young. My fingers wouldn't do what she told them to."

"They're doing fine now." When I looked up he was watching my hands with an expression I couldn't read.

"You always do that." I kept my eyes on the string.

"Do what?"

"Watch." I tied the knot — clumsy, but it held. "You've always watched. Even before all this."

His fingers stilled on the table.

"I remember you." I tossed it out like it meant nothing, my eyes on the snare in my hands like it was the most interesting thing in the room. "At the market. When I was small. You were standing behind your father near the baker's stall and you wouldn't stop staring at me."

He didn't answer. The quiet between us pulled tight, charged, the air before a storm.

"I was eating a honey cake," I continued, still working the snare, still not looking at him. "And Grandmother was holding my hand. And this boy was just — watching me. Like I was the only thing in the whole market worth looking at."

I heard him exhale. Long and slow.

"Grandmother noticed." I kept my tone even. "She pulled me behind her skirt and said something to your father. I couldn't hear what. I was too small. But the way she spoke told me she was frightened underneath." I glanced up. "Your father grabbed your arm and pulled you away. You looked back at me over your shoulder while he dragged you through the crowd."

He was very still. His eyes were on the table, on the snare frame between us, on anything that wasn't my face.

"You remember." It wasn't a question.

"The honey cake," he confirmed after a long pause. "The red ribbon in your hair." He picked up a piece of gut string and wound it around his finger, unwound it, wound it again. "I remember your grandmother's face when she saw me looking."

"Why were you staring?" I asked.

"I was a boy." He kept winding the string. "Boys stare."

That was not an answer. His hands were shaking on the gut string. His shoulders had gone rigid. I understood then that whatever the real answer was, it lived in the same locked room as everything else he would not tell me, the healing wound, the not-quite-human sound he made when he told the gray wolf to leave.

"Here." I held up the finished snare. "Did I do it right?"

He looked at it. Looked at me. Gratitude, maybe, that I'd let him off the hook. Or surprise that I'd chosen to.

"The knot needs tightening." He reached across to adjust it, and we went back to the lesson like the conversation hadn't happened.

But it had. And I could see it sitting in him for the rest of the day, thc memory, the market, the boy who wouldn't stop staring at the girl with the honey cake and the red ribbon. He carried it the way he carried everything, silently, with his back straight and his face turned away, like if he didn't look at it directly it couldn't hurt him.

I wondered how long he'd been watching me. How many years. How many times he'd stood in the trees while I lived my small, ordinary life in the village and never knew he was there.

The thought should have frightened me.

It didn't.

And that frightened me more than anything.

The dream started the way running starts, with the ground already moving under my feet.

I was in the forest. Barefoot, bare-skinned, wearing nothing but the red cloak, the wool rough against my body and the cold sliding past me like water around a stone. I should have been freezing. I wasn't. The dream wouldn't let me feel anything except the running and the thing behind me and the strange, reckless joy of being chased by something that didn't want to catch me. Only to keep me moving.

The black wolf.

I could hear it behind me, the heavy rhythm of its paws on frozen ground, the sound of its breathing, the soft chuffing noise it made when I changed direction. Playing. That's what this was. A game with rules I knew in my bones even though my waking mind had never learned them. I ran and it followed and neither of us was afraid.

The trees opened into a clearing and I burst through the gap between two ancient oaks and stopped, my chest heaving, my hair tangled with pine needles, the cloak settling around me like a second skin. I turned.

The wolf stood at the edge of the tree line. Enormous and black and beautiful — fur so dark it ate the moonlight, eyes like liquid gold, its body still and watchful. Steam curled from its mouth with each slow exhale.

It took a step into the clearing. Then another. Moving toward me the way the tide moves toward shore, patient, inevitable, certain of where it was going because it had been going there forever.

I backed up until the bark of the oak pressed against my bare shoulders. The wolf kept coming. Closed the distance until I could feel the heat pouring off its body, could see the individual hairs in its black fur catching the starlight, could smell pine and earth and a musk underneath that was wild and male and made my stomach clench.

It stopped in front of me. Its head was level with my chin, the golden eyes looking up at me with an expression that had no business being on an animal's face. Patience. Devotion. A hunger so vast and so carefully leashed that looking at it felt like standing at the edge of a cliff.

The fear drained out of me like water through open fingers. What replaced it was warmth — heavy, nameless, that started in my chest and spread downward, loosening my muscles, softening my spine against the bark, gathering in the low, dark places of my body where wanting lived.

The wolf lowered its head.

And then it wasn't the wolf anymore.

Dietrich knelt in front of me in the snow, naked, his hands sliding under the cloak and gripping my hips, his fingers pressing into the flesh hard enough to anchor me to the tree. His mouth was on my stomach before I could draw breath, warm and open, moving downward in a line that left heat blazing in its wake, each kiss lower than the last, deliberate and unhurried, like a man who knew exactly where he was going and intended to take his time getting there.

"Please," I heard myself say. The word came out wrecked. I didn't know what I was begging for. Just knew I'd die if he stopped.

His mouth found me.

The pleasure was blinding — a white-hot surge that buckled my knees and tore a cry from my throat and would have dropped me if his hands hadn't been holding me up, pinning my hips to the bark while his mouth worked and my fingers twisted into his hair and my head fell back against the oak and the stars blurred above me into streaks of silver light.

I looked down.

The black wolf looked back up at me. Golden eyes. Dark fur. Its mouth still on me, still moving, and the pleasure didn't stop, it intensified, sharpened, climbed toward something I couldn't outrun.

I should have screamed. Should have shoved it away, should have felt the horror of what was happening crash over me like cold water.

I couldn't. The pleasure had swallowed the horror whole and left nothing behind except the climbing, the tightening, the wave building at the base of my spine that was going to break me apart.

It broke.

I screamed and the clearing went white and I felt myself falling and there was cold. Nothing but cold.

I was standing in snow. The shift I'd worn to bed was soaked through and plastered to my skin and the wind was cutting through it like it wasn't there. My feet were bare and already numb and I was shaking so hard my teeth rattled.

The dream was still in my body. I could feel it, the phantom heat, the lingering pulse between my thighs, the evidence of my release cooling against my inner thighs in the freezing air. The shame hit me like a wave of nausea. The wolf. The man. The way they'd been the same thing. The way I'd wanted it.

I shoved the thought down so hard it left a bruise in my mind.

The night wandering. The same curse that had followed me my whole life, walking in my sleep, ending up in places I had no memory of choosing. The river when I was a girl. The forest when Sophia disappeared. And now here, wherever here was.

The cottage door stood open behind me, maybe thirty feet away, firelight spilling into the darkness. The bar lay on the ground beside the threshold. I'd moved it in my sleep, moved that heavy wooden bar with the power I couldn't control, even unconscious, even lost in a dream about a wolf with golden eyes.

I took a step toward the cottage. Toward warmth. Toward safety.

My foot broke through something.

The crack split the silence — a hard, brittle snap beneath my weight, nothing like snow. Lines raced outward from my foot in every direction, black veins spreading across a white surface.

Ice. I was standing on ice.

I looked down and my heart seized. A frozen lake stretched around me in every direction, white and flat and featureless except for the cracks spreading from where I stood. The water beneath the ice was black. Bottomless. I could see it through the fractures, dark and patient, waiting for the surface to give way.

I didn't dare breathe. Didn't dare shift my weight. Stood absolutely still with the cold burning the soles of my feet and the cracks widening with soft, terrible sounds like whispered warnings.

The ice was already failing. I could hear it — a low groan building beneath me, the sound of a hold giving way.

Then it stopped.

The surface dropped out from under me and the black water swallowed me whole.

The cold was beyond anything I had language for. It wasn't a sensation — it was an erasure. It wiped out thought, wiped out feeling, wiped out everything except a single screaming nerve that knew I was dying. My lungs locked. My muscles froze. The water closed over my head and the world became black and silent and absolute.

I tried to kick. Tried to claw my way upward. My body wouldn't respond — the cold had severed the connection between what I wanted and what my limbs could do. I was sinking. Deeper. The darkness thickening around me and the pressure building in my chest and the black spots at the edges of my vision spreading like ink dropped into water.

This was how I died. In a frozen lake in the middle of nowhere because I'd sleepwalked out of a dream about a wolf's mouth between my legs.

Then something crashed through the surface above me.

Arms wrapped around my chest. Strong, sure, impossibly warm against the cold that had frozen me solid. They pulled me upward through the dark water with a strength that shouldn't have been possible, one arm locked around my ribs, legs kicking beneath us, driving us toward the surface with a force that felt less like a man swimming and more like a current reversing itself.

We broke through. I gasped and choked and coughed water that tasted like mud and rot and old copper underneath. The air burned my lungs worse than the water had.

"I have you." Dietrich pulled me tighter against him, his mouth near my ear. "Hold on. I have you."

He dragged me toward the edge of the broken ice, kicking hard, his breath coming in sharp grunts with each stroke. Hauled himself out first, his hands finding purchase on the solid edge, his shoulders bunching with effort, then reached back and pulled me up after him with hands that shook from cold or fear or both.

He didn't pause. Didn't catch his breath. He gathered me up in his arms and ran, barefoot on frozen ground, soaking wet, carrying my weight like it was nothing, his legs driving through the snow in long strides that ate the distance to the cottage.

I couldn't stop trembling. Couldn't feel my hands or feet

or face. Couldn't do anything except hang in his arms and let the shaking run its course.

He kicked the cottage door wide and carried me to the bed and set me down on the furs. His hands went to my shift immediately, pulling the soaked fabric over my head with quick, efficient movements that left no room for modesty or hesitation.

"You're hypothermic." He was already stripping off his own drenched shirt. "Body heat. Fastest way."

The shift came off. Then his trousers, his boots, everything, stripped with the practiced speed of a man who understood that seconds mattered and embarrassment didn't. He was bare in the firelight, pale skin and lean muscle and the scars I'd traced with my eyes for weeks, and then he was in the bed beside me and his arms were pulling me against him and the furs were coming up over both of us. Heat poured off his skin like he was burning from the inside, radiating from every point where our bodies touched, his chest against my back, his thighs pressed behind mine, his arms wrapped tight around my ribs. This wasn't normal body warmth. This was something else entirely, something that defied every piece of medical knowledge I possessed, a furnace behind his skin that shouldn't exist in any human body.

I didn't care. I pressed myself into it — pressed every frozen inch of my skin against every burning inch of his, trying to steal every scrap of heat I could, trying to stop the shaking that wouldn't stop. My teeth chattered so hard I thought they'd crack.

"You're safe," he murmured against my hair, his breath warm on my scalp. "You're alive. You're safe."

I was crying. The sobs came from somewhere deep and raw, shaking through my body in waves that had nothing to do with the cold and everything to do with the dream and the ice and the feeling of the water closing over my head and the certainty, absolute, bone-deep certainty, that I was going to die alone in the dark.

He held me through it. One hand cradled the back of my head, the other rubbed slow circles on my back, and he said nothing because there was nothing to say. Just held me and let me cry and kept the heat pouring off his impossible body into mine.

Minutes passed. Maybe longer. The trembling slowed. The sobs lost their edges and turned to shuddering breaths and then to silence. His heat had found the frozen places inside me and was thawing them one by one, my fingers first, then my feet, then the deep core of cold that had settled behind my ribs and made every breath feel like inhaling broken glass.

I should have pulled away. I was warm enough now, warm enough to survive, warm enough that continued contact was no longer medical necessity but something else entirely. I could feel him, all of him, pressed against my back, and despite the cold, despite the terror, despite everything, my body was aware of his in ways that had nothing to do with heat exchange.

I didn't pull away.

"I can't sleep," I whispered into the dark.

"You don't have to," he replied, his arms tightening slightly. "Just rest. Just breathe."

"I keep seeing a horrible sight." I pressed my face against his shoulder. "Every time I close my eyes."

His hand stilled on my back. "The lake?"

"You." The word came out small and frightened. "I see you dying."

His body went quiet beneath me. Every muscle suddenly still, his body held.

"Tell me." His arms tightened around me.

So I told him. In halting, broken pieces, the way visions come out when you try to translate them from the language of blood and bone into words that other people can understand. I told him about seeing him on frozen ground with his chest torn open, blood steaming in the cold air. About the gray wolf circling him, yellow eyes gleaming with triumph. About feeling his ribs crack and his blood pour and his lungs fill, feeling it like it was happening to me, like the pain was mine, like we were connected in a way I couldn't see or name or understand.

He listened without speaking. His arms stayed around me and his heartbeat stayed steady beneath my ear and he let me talk until the talking was done.

When I finished, the silence lasted a long time.

"It's happened before." I closed my eyes. "The visions. I've seen things that came true."

"What do you mean?" He asked, carefully.

"William." I swallowed against the tightness in my throat. "The morning he died."

He already knew about William's death. He'd said *I know* when I'd told him about the six men, about the pieces in the clearing. He'd known the sound of William's laugh and the way he hunted and things he shouldn't have known unless he'd been watching from the trees for years.

But he didn't know this part.

"I woke up that morning with a vision sitting on my chest like a stone." I pressed my face against his collarbone. "I'd seen something in the forest. A creature with teeth. And I knew, knew in my bones, that if William walked into those woods he wouldn't come back."

His hand found my hair. Threaded through the wet strands slowly, gently, the way you soothe an animal that's been hurt.

"I begged him," I whispered. "I got on my knees in front of the door and begged him not to go. I told him about the dream. Told him I had a nightmare and saw him in it." The tears came again, sixteen years of them, stored up and compounding interest. "And he kissed my forehead and told me I worried too much and walked out anyway."

Dietrich's hand stilled in my hair. He'd gone still.

"I couldn't make him believe me." The words tasted like the thing I'd been choking on for sixteen years. "I couldn't make anyone believe me. They looked at me like I was hysterical. Like my fear was a woman's weakness and nothing more." I pressed my face harder into the hollow of his shoulder. "And that night they brought his body back in pieces and all I could think was that I'd known. I'd warned him and he didn't listen and now he was dead because I wasn't enough to make him stay."

"You were enough," Dietrich said, and his tone had an edge I hadn't heard before, fierce and sharp and aimed at something that wasn't me. "You warned him. You begged him. You got on your knees. He chose not to listen. That's his failure and the failure of every man who laughed at you and told you your fear was nothing." His arms tightened around me. "The guilt isn't yours to carry. It was never yours."

"I should have done more," I whispered.

"You can't force people to believe you," he replied, his knuckles grazing my cheekbone, wiping the tears that had pooled there. "You can't make them listen when they've already decided you're not worth hearing. All you can do is warn them and hope. And you did. You did everything a person can do."

We lay in silence for a long time. His words didn't erase the guilt… it was too old, too deep, woven into the foundation of who I'd become. But the way he said it, the anger on my behalf, the certainty that I wasn't to blame, shifted the weight. Like someone had put their hands under the stone I'd been carrying alone and was helping me hold it.

I tilted my head back to look at his face. He was already looking down at me.

"Thank you," I whispered. "For saying that. Even if I can't believe it yet."

"You will." His breath stirred my hair. "Someday."

His touch lingered on my face, the backs of his fingers against my cheekbone, careful and tentative, as if I were something he'd found in the forest and was afraid of breaking.

Then he leaned down and pressed his mouth to my forehead. Soft. Tender. A kiss that was nothing like the one I'd used to destroy him, no hunger in it, no calculation, just the quiet pressure of lips against skin and the warmth in my hair.

I closed my eyes. A knot loosened inside me — one I'd been carrying so long I'd stopped feeling the rope.

His mouth moved to my temple. Then my cheekbone, right where his fingers had been. Then the corner of my eye, his lips coming away wet with my tears.

Each touch was feather-light. Given, not taken. Offered, not demanded. The opposite of everything that had happened between us — the pinning, the mortar, the seduction, the lies.

I turned my face toward his. Our mouths were an inch apart. Less. I could feel his breath on my lips, the coarse edge of his beard almost touching my chin, and see every fleck of gold in his amber eyes and the small scar at the corner of his mouth I'd never noticed before.

We stared at each other. The fire crackled. The wind pressed against the boarded windows. Somewhere in the forest the gray wolf was waiting and the world outside this bed was full of teeth.

But inside it there was only this. His eyes and mine. His breath and mine. The inch between us that neither of us was willing to close because closing it meant choosing it and choosing it meant meaning it.

I closed the distance.

I kissed him.

Chapter Fourteen

He made a sound against my mouth, low and broken, somewhere between surprise and relief, like a man who'd braced for a blow and gotten mercy instead. His hand came up to my face and his fingers were shaking so badly he couldn't hold them steady against my cheek. He tried to cup my face and his thumb missed, grazed my ear, found my cheekbone on the second try. The clumsiness of it undid me more than any smooth touch could have.

He kissed me back and it was nothing like the wall. The wall had been hunger unleashed, a man breaking apart. This was careful and uncertain, his mouth moving against mine, his beard soft and rough at the same time against my face, like he was learning the shape of it, like kissing was a thing he'd imagined a thousand times but the reality of it was bigger than the imagining and he didn't know where to put all of it.

I shifted in his arms, turning so I was facing him fully. We were already bare, had been since the lake, since he'd stripped us both for warmth and pulled me against him under the furs. Our bodies pressed together now with a different intent, chest to chest, hip to hip, skin against skin, and the heat from his body was still impossible, still more than any human should produce, and I pressed into it and felt every inch of him. The scars. The muscle. The hard evidence of what this was doing to him pressed against my hip.

He flinched. Tried to pull his hips back, his whole body going rigid with shame, like his body's reaction was a confession he needed to take back, an apology he couldn't get out fast enough.

"Don't," I whispered, and pressed closer.

His whole body shuddered. His forehead dropped against mine and his breathing came apart, ragged, uneven, a man drowning in a current he had no practice surviving.

"Talia." My name in his mouth, rough and desperate. "I haven't. I've never ..."

He couldn't finish. The words jammed in his throat and his face twisted with humiliation, a grown man confessing the one thing he'd clearly rather die than admit. His eyes dropped away from mine and his hands went still on my body and I felt him start to pull back, start to retreat behind the walls he'd lived inside his whole life.

The realization landed in my chest like a stone dropped into still water. The ripples spread outward and touched everything, how he'd smelled my wrist on the floor like instinct had overridden every conscious thought, hovered his hands over my body at night without ever making contact, broken so completely when I'd kissed him by the mortar. The clumsiness of his hands just now. Trying to hide his arousal. The trembling that wasn't just emotion but the raw, overwhelming terror of a man facing a hunger his body understood and his mind never had.

He'd never been touched. By anyone. In nearly forty years of his life.

"Look at me." I tried to make it gentle.

He wouldn't. His teeth were clenched and his eyes were fixed on a point somewhere past my shoulder and the muscles in his neck stood out like cords.

I put my hand on his face, felt the beard, the warmth, the tension in his jaw, and turned it toward me. Gently.

His eyes found mine. Bright. Shame and want and fear all tangled together, fighting each other to the surface, a man standing at the edge of something he was convinced would prove every terrible thing he'd ever believed about himself.

"It doesn't matter," I told him. My thumb traced the scar on his cheekbone. "It doesn't change anything."

"You don't understand," he managed. "I won't know how to. I'll be ..."

"You'll be fine." I traced his collarbone. "I'll show you."

His expression cracked. The shame was still there but underneath it, pushing up through the rubble, was a hope so raw and fragile it made my throat ache to look at.

I kissed him again. Slower this time. Gentler. Let my mouth teach his what to do, how to move, how to match my rhythm, when to press and when to ease back. He learned fast. His mouth softened against mine, found the pace I was setting, began to answer instead of just receive. His hand came back to my face and this time his fingers knew where to go, cradling my face with a steadiness they hadn't had before.

"Good," I murmured against his lips. "That's good."

His hand slid from my face down to my neck, my collarbone, and then lower, and here the clumsiness vanished. His palm found my breast and cupped it with a sureness that made me arch, his thumb finding my nipple with no fumbling, no hesitation, rolling it the way he'd pulled at it with his mouth by the mortar. He remembered. The one piece of my body he'd already mapped, the one thing he'd learned in those frantic seconds against the wall before the stone came down on his skull. His fingers knew this territory and the confidence of that touch against the uncertainty of everything else sent a jolt through me.

I'd taught him this. With a lie and a weapon in my hand. And his body had kept the lesson.

He bent his head. His mouth found my nipple and closed

around it and any thought of guiding him evaporated. He didn't need guidance here. His tongue circled and pulled with the same desperate focus he'd shown against the wall, warm and wet and greedy, and the vibration of his groan rolled through my breast and into my ribs and settled low in my belly like a coal catching fire.

My fingers twisted into his hair. I arched into his mouth and the sound that came out of me was raw and graceless and I didn't care. Sixteen years. It had been sixteen years since anyone had touched me and my nerve endings were screaming awake after years of silence and every pull of his mouth magnified a hundredfold.

But his free hand was lost. It moved from my hip to my ribs to my waist and back again, restless and uncertain, touching everything and knowing nothing.

I took it.

"Here," I whispered, guiding it down my stomach.

His mouth left my breast. He lifted his head and looked at me. His eyes were so wide and dark there was almost no amber left.

I guided his fingers between my legs and he made a choked sound, surprise, wonder, the shock of finding me wet and ready.

"For you," I managed. "This is real."

I showed him what I needed. Placed my fingers over his and taught him the pressure, the rhythm, the place that made my hips roll and my fists clench. He was shaking so hard I could feel it through both our bodies but his fingers followed my lead with desperate concentration, adjusting when I adjusted, pressing when I pressed.

Then his mouth dropped back to my breast. He couldn't help it — pulled my nipple between his lips and sucked while his fingers worked between my thighs, and the combination was a fist closing around something white-hot at the base of my spine.

I stopped being able to think. His mouth, tongue circling, teeth grazing, and his fingers between my legs, following the rhythm I'd taught him. He was doing both at once and he didn't know what it was building toward, didn't understand the way my body had gone tight and trembling, didn't recognize the way my thighs were tensing or my hips were rolling against his hand in a rhythm I couldn't control.

"Don't stop," I gasped. "Whatever you do, don't ..."

He didn't stop. His mouth pulled at my nipple and his fingers circled and pressed and the wave built and built, climbing higher with every stroke, every pull, every graze of teeth, until there was nothing left except the tightening and the heat and finally I broke.

The orgasm hit so hard my whole body seized. My back bowed off the bed and a cry tore out of me, sharp and high and completely beyond my control, and my thighs clamped around his hand and my fingers ripped at the furs and I shook while the waves crashed through me one after another, relentless, blinding.

His mouth ripped away. His hand froze. He scrambled upright, his eyes wide with panic, his face draining of color.

"What happened?" Fear sharpened his face. His hands hovered over me without touching, terrified of making whatever he'd done worse. "Talia — did I hurt you? Are you ..."

I was still shaking. Still gasping. The aftershocks were rolling through me and I couldn't form words, couldn't do anything except lie there with my chest heaving and my eyes wet and a smile breaking across my face that I couldn't have stopped if my life depended on it.

"Talia." He was over me now, his face stricken, his hands cupping my face. "Talk to me. Please. Did I ..."

"You didn't hurt me," I managed, shaking, and the laughter came, helpless, breathless, bubbling up through the aftershocks. "Dietrich. You didn't hurt me. That was, that's what's supposed to happen."

He stared at me. Blinking. Processing.

"That?" he repeated. "The shaking? The sound you made?"

"That," I confirmed, still trembling, still coming back to myself. "That's what it feels like. When it's good."

He looked down at his hand, the fingers still glistening, and then back at my face, and the expression that moved across his features was something I'd carry for the rest of my life. The fear dissolved first, replaced by confusion, then realization, then a wonder so pure and vast it made him look ten years younger. Like a boy who'd just been told the thing he'd been afraid of was actually a gift.

"I did that." Soft. Like he needed to hear it out loud.

"Your mouth." I reached up to touch his face. "And your hand. Together."

The wonder hardened in his face, want flooding in behind it, so intense it thickened the air between us.

"Can we ..." He swallowed. "I want to ..."

He couldn't say it. His face was burning and he was harder than I'd ever felt him, pressed against my thigh, and the question was written across every inch of him even though his mouth couldn't form the words.

I answered by pushing him onto his back.

His eyes went wide. He lay beneath me breathing hard, his hands hovering at my hips like he wasn't sure he was allowed to hold on.

"You can touch me," I told him, settling my weight across his hips. "Wherever you want."

His hands found my waist. Gripped. I took him in my hand and he gasped, his hips bucking, and a sound tore from his throat that was animal and human at the same time.

I guided him. Positioned him. And then slowly, so slowly, I sank down.

The stretch was intense. Sixteen years of nothing and then this, the fullness, the pressure, the overwhelming intimacy of having another person inside my body. My hands braced on his chest and my eyes closed and I heard myself make a sound that was surprise and relief and grief, because I'd forgotten what this felt like and the remembering was almost too much to bear.

Beneath me he'd stopped breathing entirely. His hands

gripped my hips with a force that would leave bruises and his eyes were wide and glassy and his mouth was open and I could see every muscle in his body locked tight with the effort of not moving, not thrusting, not doing the thing every instinct in him was screaming at him to do.

"Breathe," I told him.

He gasped. A ragged, shuddering intake that sounded like a man surfacing from deep water.

I rocked my hips. Just once. Just a small, slow movement to show him how this worked.

The sound he made. I'd never heard anything like it. A groan that started in his chest and tore its way up through his throat and broke apart in the air between us. His fingers dug into my hips and his head pressed back into the pillow and I watched tears leak from the corners of his closed eyes and slide into his hair.

He was crying. The man who'd slept in caves and survived alone for decades and driven wolves off with nothing but teeth and fury was crying because a woman was making love to him for the first time in his life.

I leaned down and kissed the tears from his temples. Kissed his closed eyelids. Kissed the scar on his cheekbone and the corner of his mouth.

"Stay with me," I whispered against his lips. "Open your eyes."

He opened them. Amber and wet and completely undone.

I moved again. Slow. A rhythm for him to learn, the way

I'd shown him everything else, patient, deliberate, giving him time to feel each sensation before the next one arrived. His hands on my hips followed the movement, gripping and releasing, learning the pace.

"You can move," I told him. "Move with me."

His hips lifted. The first thrust was clumsy, too hard, wrong angle, and I adjusted, shifted my weight, guided him with the pressure of my hands on his chest. The second was better. The third made us both gasp.

"There," I breathed. "Like that. Just like that."

He found the rhythm and held it, tentative at first, then steadier, his body learning what his mind couldn't teach it. His eyes watched my face with fierce concentration, cataloguing every sound, every roll of my hips, every shudder I made.

His rhythm faltered. His rhythm broke and his grip on me tightened and I could feel him losing the thread, the pleasure pulling him under faster than he could fight it.

"I can't ..." He choked on the rest, his face burning. "It's too. I'm going to ..."

"Let go." I rolled my hips. "It's all right. Let go."

He shattered.

His whole body arched beneath me, every muscle locking at once, and the sound that came out of him was nothing I had language for, raw and wrecked and primal, ripped from somewhere so deep it left the rest of him empty. His hands clamped on my hips and held me still while his body pulsed inside me, wave after wave, his face twisted with a pleasure so intense it looked like pain.

I held myself above him and watched him come apart and felt the wall I'd built the day William died crack wide open. Because the look on his face wasn't the look of a man getting what he wanted. It was the look of a man receiving everything he'd believed he would never, ever have.

He went limp beneath me. His chest heaved and his face was wet and for a long moment neither of us moved.

Then his eyes opened. Amber and dazed and immediately, devastatingly ashamed.

"I'm sorry." He sounded utterly wrecked. "You just, before, but I couldn't last long enough to ..."

"Stop." I leaned down and pressed my mouth against his. Soft. Unhurried. "That was perfect."

"But you didn't, we didn't, together ..."

I kissed him quiet. Held his face in my hands and kissed him until the shame loosened its grip and he settled.

"We have time," I murmured against his lips. "This doesn't have to be everything at once."

He looked at me with surprise.

"Stay," he whispered. "Please stay."

"I'm here." And for now, that was enough.

I eased off him and settled against his side, my head on his chest. His arms wrapped around me and held on like a man who'd spent his whole life drowning and had just been taught what air was. His heartbeat slammed against my ear, too fast, too hard.

We lay like that while the fire burned low. His hands moved over my back in slow, aimless patterns, touching me because he could, because I'd said he was allowed, because someone had finally meant it.

After a long time, he stirred. He was hard again against my thigh, impossibly soon, inhumanly soon, and his face was flushed and hopeful and terrified in equal measure.

"Already?" I couldn't hide the surprise.

He looked away. Ashamed again.

I turned his face back to me. "That wasn't a complaint."

This time I guided him onto his side and pulled him into me from behind, his chest against my back, his arms wrapped around me, his face buried in my hair. The angle was deeper and I heard him choke when he pushed inside, felt his teeth graze the back of my neck, felt the groan vibrate through his chest into my spine.

"Slow," I murmured, reaching back to grip his hip and set the pace. "Like this. Feel it."

He moved behind me — slow and deep and shaking with the effort of following my lead instead of chasing the need. His arms wrapped around my ribs, holding me against him, his mouth pressed open against the nape of my neck, breathing me in with every stroke.

This time was different. The desperation had burned off and what was left was an instinct that was rawer and more fragile, two bodies learning each other in the dark. He figured out that a certain depth made me moan and he sought it again and again. I reached between my legs and touched myself while he moved inside me and he made a broken sound against my hair when he felt my fingers working.

"I want to feel you," he whispered against my neck. "I want to feel it when you ..."

"You will," I whispered. "Keep moving. Don't stop."

The pleasure built like a tide, slower this time, deeper, fed by the warmth of his body behind mine and the steady rhythm he'd found and the sound of his breathing in my ear. When the orgasm came it rolled through me in long, slow waves and I clenched around him and heard him gasp.

"Go." I pressed back against him. "With me."

He came with his face buried in my hair and his arms locked around me and a sound that might have been my name or might have been something older than language. His whole body shook against mine and I held his arms where they wrapped around my ribs and let the aftershocks roll through both of us until they faded into stillness.

We lay tangled together while the logs popped in the fire and the light through the boards turned from black to gray. His arms didn't loosen. His face stayed pressed into my hair.

"Talia." A long time passed before he spoke.

"Hmm."

"Thank you." He said it so quietly I felt it more than heard it. "For showing me. For being patient. For not making me feel like less."

My eyes burned. I laced my fingers through his where they rested against my stomach.

"You're not less." I squeezed his fingers where they laced through mine. "You've never been less."

He pressed his mouth against the back of my neck and didn't say anything else. He didn't need to. His arms said it. His heartbeat said it. The way he held me said it louder than words ever could.

I closed my eyes and listened to him breathe and felt his body warm and solid against mine and for the first time since William died, the bed didn't feel empty.

After a while I shifted, rolling onto my back. He followed the movement without letting go, settling his head against my chest, his arm draped across my ribs. I ran my fingers into his hair.

"There's one more thing." I stared at the ceiling.

"About the dream," I continued. "Before I woke up on the ice."

He went still against me. His breathing didn't change but his body did, a subtle tightening, a gathering, the way an animal goes quiet when a shadow moves wrong.

"I was running through the forest." I stared at the ceiling because I couldn't look at him while I told him this. "A black wolf was chasing me. Like the one from the night I escaped the village, enormous, dark fur, golden eyes. But it wasn't hunting me. It was playing. Like we knew each other."

His hand had gone still on my ribs.

"And then it changed." My face was burning. "It became you. And then it changed back. And I ..."

I stopped.

"And you what?" he asked. He kept everything out of it on purpose.

"I didn't want it to stop," I whispered. "Either of them. The wolf or the man. And when I woke up I was on the ice and I ..."

The silence said it for me.

He was rigid against me now, every muscle locked. His heart hammered so hard I could feel it against my breast.

"A black wolf," he repeated. The control in him was almost painful to hear, too tight, too even, like a wire stretched to its limit.

"Yes." I swallowed. "What does it mean? Is something wrong with me?"

"Nothing is wrong with you." He pulled me closer, his arms tightening with a fierceness that contradicted every measured word. "The dream doesn't mean anything."

He was lying. I could hear it in the tension threaded through every word. Could feel it in the rigidity of his body, the way his heart refused to slow down. He knew what the dream meant. The silence told me that much. So did the way he wouldn't look at me.

I lay against his chest and listened to his heart race. I knew he was hiding something. But I didn't push. I wasn't ready for the answer.

Chapter Fifteen

I woke to his mouth on my shoulder. His lips traced the line of my collarbone softly while his arm tightened around my waist and pulled me closer against the warmth of his chest. I made a sound that was not quite a word, and I felt him smile against my skin.

"Morning," he murmured against my shoulder.

"Morning," I replied, and the word felt strange in my mouth, ordinary, domestic, what people say when they've been waking up beside each other for years instead of days. I turned in his arms and his mouth found mine and we kissed slowly, lazily.

We dressed in the easy silence of two people who'd seen each other bare and weren't pretending otherwise. He pulled on his trousers and shirt and crossed to the hearth to build the fire. I pulled grandmother's dress over my head and sat at the table with the grimoire open in my lap, watching him crack eggs into the pan.

The domesticity of it should have felt wrong. A week ago I'd been his prisoner. Two days ago I'd cracked his skull open with a mortar. And now he was cooking me breakfast while I read at the table and neither of us found it strange.

He set a plate in front of me, eggs, bread he'd baked on the hearthstone, a cup of water. Then he leaned down and kissed the side of my neck, his mouth warm against my pulse, lingering there a beat longer than he needed to.

The pleasure that rolled through me was sudden and sharp, a bright flare in the center of my chest, and the power detonated before I could catch it.

The door blew off its hinges.

The oak slab sailed through the doorway and landed in the snow ten feet from the cottage, one hinge still dangling. Cold air flooded the room. Eggs slid off the spatula and hit the floor.

We both stared at the doorway.

He straightened slowly. Looked at the door in the snow. Looked at me, my hands still raised, power crackling and fading around my fingers.

"I'll get wood to fix that," he announced, his mouth twitching.

The laugh burst out of me before I could stop it, helpless, ridiculous, my body not knowing what else to do with it. He was fighting it too, the scar on his cheekbone twitching, his mouth pressed tight against the grin trying to escape.

"I'm sorry," I managed.

"Don't apologize," he countered, pulling on his coat. "Just don't do that when I'm near the fireplace."

He kissed my forehead, quick and warm, and stepped through the empty doorway into the snow. I watched him disappear into the trees, his footsteps crunching away until the forest swallowed the sound.

The cottage was cold with the doorway gaping open. I pulled a fur around my shoulders, scraped the eggs off the floor, and went back to the grimoire.

The grimoire had new pages waiting for me.

I turned past the entries I'd already read and found fresh text where blurred ink had been, sharp and legible, the magic in the book responding to whatever had grown stronger in me since the clearing.

On the Nature of the Gift

The old blood manifests differently in each of us. The gift takes many forms, each unique to the woman who carries it.

Some have the Sight — visions of what has not yet come to pass. They dream true and see the threads of fate before they are woven.

Some have the Sensing — they feel what cannot be seen. Presences, intentions, the pull of supernatural things calling from beyond the tree line. They are drawn to what others cannot perceive and it is drawn to them.

Some have the Healing Touch — wounds close beneath their hands, bones knit, illness flees their presence.

Some have Elemental Mastery — they call fire from nothing, summon water from air, command earth and wind to their will.

And some have Forceweaving.

My finger traced beneath the word.

Forceweaving is the gift of raw power. Those who possess it can project force from their body, pushing, shoving, repelling with tremendous strength. A Forceweaver cannot lift a cup delicately but can send a man flying across a room. Cannot move a chair carefully, but can shatter a door with a thought.

I glanced at the empty doorway. A door with a thought. That was exactly what I'd just done.

The power responds to emotion. Fear creates barriers and shields. Anger creates blasts that destroy. And in rare moments, other strong emotions, joy, pleasure, grief, can trigger it as well, the force erupting in all directions without control.

To harness Forceweaving, one must learn to separate emotion from execution. The power lives beneath your skin like a second heartbeat. Feel it humming there, recognize it as distinct from what you feel. Then direct it with intention rather than letting it explode in response to every strong emotion.

Picture the force as threads. Golden threads emanating from your body, from your chest, your hands, every part of you. Gather the threads in your mind. Twist them together. Aim them at your target. Push with your will, not your feelings.

Master this, and you become a weapon. Fail, and you become a danger to everyone around you.

I closed the book and reached inward. There — a humming beneath my skin. Warm and alive and waiting for direction.

I looked at the water jug on the counter. Gathered the threads. Aimed. Pushed. The jug exploded. Shards of clay and water sprayed across the room.

Too much.

I tried with a wooden cup. Gathered. Aimed. Pushed — gently. The cup shot off the counter and cracked against the far wall.

Still too much.

A spoon. Gathered the threads. Held them. Pushed with the barest whisper of intent. The spoon slid across the table and dropped off the edge.

Better. Still clumsy. Still imprecise. But the difference between the jug and the spoon was the difference between screaming and whispering, and I was learning where the volume lived.

I spent the next hour practicing. Moved everything that wasn't breakable — spoons, a wooden bowl, a folded cloth, a boot Dietrich had left by the hearth. Some I could nudge.

Some I sent flying. Once I tried to move two things at once and the Forceweaving split and scattered and I couldn't move either.

I was reaching for the boot again when a voice came from the doorway.

"Forgive me."

I spun. The Forceweaving flared around my hands, crackling and unstable, half the threads already unravelling.

An old man stood in the open doorway, careful not to step inside. He held up both hands — palms out.

"I didn't mean to startle you," he offered, dipping his head. "I was passing through these woods and heard a loud sound. Wanted to make sure no one was hurt."

I stared at him, my heart slamming against my ribs. He couldn't have come at a worse time, no door, no Dietrich, my Forceweaving spent from an hour of practice.

He was past fifty, maybe older, with silver threading through dark hair that hung past his collar. Tall and broad through the chest and shoulders in a way that suggested he'd been powerful in his youth. His clothes were worn but had been good quality once. His face was weathered, lined around the eyes and mouth.

And he was staying outside. Just standing there in the snow like he understood the rules of threshold and invitation, even though there was no door to enforce them.

"I'm fine," I assured him, holding the words steady by sheer will. "There was an accident. I'm not hurt."

"That's good." He smiled slightly, keeping his hands visible. "Though that's quite a sound for an accident."

I said nothing. Dietrich was somewhere in the forest looking for wood. The doorway gaped between us with nothing to stop this man walking through.

He seemed to sense my wariness because he took a small step back.

"I don't mean to intrude," he added, his tone apologetic. "Just an old traveler who's been walking these woods too long. Saw smoke from your chimney and thought I might ask for some water."

"You can have water," I told him. "Stay there. I'll bring it to you."

"Of course." He settled himself on the step outside the doorway. "I wouldn't dream of entering uninvited."

I filled a cup with unsteady hands. Closed the grimoire on the table. When I brought the water to the doorway, I kept several feet between us.

"Thank you kindly." He took the cup with hands that shook. Drank deeply. "Bless you, child."

I watched him. Something was bothering me about his face. Something familiar in the set of his eyes that tugged at a memory I couldn't reach.

"You used to live in these woods?" I asked carefully.

"A long time ago," he replied, handing the cup back. "Before things went wrong. Just passing through now."

"Alone?"

"Always alone these days." A heaviness settled behind

his gaze. "Haven't had company in more years than I care to count."

"Are you hungry?" The question came out before I could stop it. "I have bread. Some dried meat."

His face lit with gratitude. "I couldn't impose ..."

"It's not an imposition," I cut in. "Stay there."

I brought him bread and meat. He ate with the careful movements of someone who'd gone too long without food.

"You're very kind," he remarked between mouthfuls. "Especially a woman alone ..." He paused. "You are alone, aren't you?"

"He'll be back soon," I blurted, the lie obvious even to my own ears.

"Ah." Curiosity flickered across his face. "Well then. I should probably be on my way before he returns. Some men don't take kindly to strangers near their women."

The way he said *their women* made my skin prickle.

"What's your name?" I pressed.

He paused mid-bite and looked at me for a long moment. "Does it matter?"

"I just gave you food and water. I think I deserve to know who I helped."

He smiled, but it didn't reach his eyes. A coldness crept into his expression which made the hair on the back of my neck stand up. "Fair enough. You can call me Erik."

Everything stopped. My breath. My heart. The floor tilted beneath my feet and the room went bright at the edges and I was suddenly back at the market, seven years old, grandmother's hand crushing mine while she pulled me behind her skirt. A man with amber eyes had been watching Sophia from behind the baker's stall. His son beside him — a boy with the same strange eyes.

Erik. Dietrich's father. The man who'd taken Sophia.

I stumbled back from the doorway. The Forceweaving flared around my hands, hot and bright and wild, crackling in directions I couldn't control.

His smile widened, showing too many teeth. The pretense of a harmless old man dropped away like a shed skin.

"Ah." He straightened, his eyes brightening with recognition. "So you do know who I am."

"Get away from here," I warned, shaking, trying to hold the power steady.

"Why would I do that?" He stood slowly, unfolding from the step with a predator's grace that had nothing to do with his apparent age. His shoulders went back. His spine straightened. He moved like an animal wearing human skin. "I came all this way to find you. Been watching for weeks, waiting for the right moment."

"Dietrich will ..." I started.

"Dietrich is deep in the forest." He stepped over the threshold. No door to stop him. "Looking for timber, I'd wager. Heard that door blow clean off its hinges this morning." His mouth curled. "Generous of you, leaving the way open for me."

I threw the Forceweaving at him. The blast went wide

— caught the doorframe instead of his chest, splintering what was left of the wood.

He didn't flinch. Just tilted his head and breathed in through his nose, slow and deep, like a man savoring what he'd been starving for.

"There it is." His eyes shifted from brown to amber. "The power." Another step toward me. "I felt it from miles away the night it woke in you. Fear and anger cracked you open and the old blood came pouring out." His nostrils flared. "I've been smelling it ever since. Every night, the scent getting stronger."

"Now I'm here to take what I lost," he said, and the hunger in him was vast and specific and had nothing to do with me as a person. "What your aunt gave me for two years before she..."

He didn't finish. Perhaps he couldn't, but his expression shifted. His eyes narrowed, and the muscle at his temple twitched once. "Sophia had the Sensing," he explained. "She could feel me in the forest at night. Feel what I was. What I could do." He paused. "I wanted her. Her gift. Her power. The way it would feel pouring into me when I claimed her."

"So you took her," I spat.

"I gave her a choice." His lips twisted around the word like it tasted sour. "Come with me, or I'd kill the old woman and the girl. Your grandmother. You." He studied my face. "Sophia had the Sensing. She could feel the truth of a threat the way you can feel the weather changing, in her bones, in her blood. She felt mine. She knew I meant every word."

My legs buckled. I braced myself against the table.

"She walked into the forest that same night," Erik continued. "Came to the tree line and stood there and waited for me because she'd felt the shape of what I'd do to her family if she didn't."

The room was spinning. Sophia. My aunt. The girl who'd braided my hair and called me little Red. She'd known what was waiting in the forest. She'd felt the truth of his threat with the Sensing, felt the violence coiled inside him, felt the absolute certainty that he would kill a child and an old woman without hesitation. And she'd gone. Walked into the dark and offered herself to a monster because the alternative was burying her family.

"Every time I mated her, I grew stronger," he continued. "Her power fed mine. The more I took, the more I needed." He stepped closer. "And then I broke her. An accident. She fought and I — it doesn't matter. She died. And the power stopped. And the world went dark."

Something shifted in him. Got heavier. "Twenty-two years," he ground out. "Feral. Running through these woods like a sick animal. Forgetting what I was. Forgetting everything except the hunger and the absence of what she'd given me." His eyes locked with mine. He breathed in deep through his nose, pulling the air through his nostrils like tasting wine.

"Sophia was a candle, girl. You … You're a bonfire. The

Forceweaving — raw power, not passive Sensing. I could taste it on the wind and it burned away more than two decades of madness in a single breath." The amber burned brighter. "If claiming Sophia made me this strong, claiming you would make me ..."

He didn't finish. He didn't need to.

Unstoppable.

"You don't want me," I realized, and the understanding was somehow worse than the alternative. "You want what's inside me. The power. You'd drain me the same way you drained her."

"I loved Sophia," Erik snarled, and the self-deception in it was breathtaking. "I loved what she gave me. What she made me feel. If that's not love then the word has no meaning."

"That's not love," I spat. "That's feeding."

"Call it whatever you like." He crossed the threshold. "I've been starving for almost two decades. And you smell like the first meal I've had since she died."

I gathered the Forceweaving and threw it with everything I had. This time it connected — caught him in the chest and sent him staggering backward, his boots skidding across the stone. But it didn't send him flying. The power was scattered, uncontrolled, half of it dissipating before it reached him.

He straightened. Rolled his neck. Smiled.

"Good," he acknowledged. "But not good enough."

I threw another blast. It went wide and shattered the

shelf behind him, grandmother's jars exploding, herbs and glass spraying across the room, the smell of sage and yarrow flooding the air.

Grandmother's jars. Years of careful labels in her slanting script, destroyed in a second.

Erik lunged. He crossed the distance faster than any human body should move and his hand closed around my throat and drove me back against the table. The grimoire slid off the edge and hit the floor. His face was inches from mine and his eyes were fully amber now, glowing, the pupils elongated and vertical.

"Your husband smelled like you," he hissed, his grip tightening. "Sixteen years ago. He walked into my forest with your scent soaked into his skin and his clothes and I could smell it from a mile away."

William. The word formed in my mind but wouldn't leave my mouth. His hand was too tight on my throat.

"I tore him apart," Erik continued, his nostrils flaring. "Every man with him. Followed the scent of you on his skin and killed everything that carried it. The way he screamed. The way he called out your name at the end like you could save him."

Rage burned through the terror. I gathered every thread I could find, twisted them together, and detonated them at point-blank range.

The blast threw him off me and across the room. He hit the far wall hard enough to crack the stone and slid to the floor. I doubled over coughing, my throat burning where his fingers had been.

He was already getting up. Coming at me again, faster, his body low and coiled and wrong, moving in a way that had nothing human in it. He grabbed my arm and spun me toward the open doorway and shoved.

I flew through the threshold and hit the snow hard, the impact driving the air from my lungs. The grimoire was still inside. The cloak was still inside. I had nothing except the shift on my back and the Forceweaving sputtering beneath my skin.

I rolled onto my back.

Erik stood in the doorway. The light behind him framed his silhouette and the amber in his eyes was all that was visible, two points of hot gold burning in the shadow of his face.

"Watch," he ordered.

Chapter Sixteen

He stepped into the snow and his body came apart.

It happened in the daylight, in full view, close enough that I could hear every sound. The cracking came first, wet and organic, bones snapping and reforming, joints dislocating and reshaping. His back arched and a scream tore from his throat that became a howl halfway through. His shirt split as his shoulders widened. His spine curved and extended. His hands hit the ground and the fingers shortened, thickened, nails darkening into claws. His face elongated, jaw pushing forward, teeth lengthening, skin rippling and tearing as gray fur pushed through from underneath.

I couldn't look away. My body was locked, every muscle frozen, my eyes forced open by a horror so complete it overrode every survival instinct I had.

The man fell apart. The wolf stood up.

Gray fur. Massive body. Scars across its face and flanks. The long pale line across its muzzle where the fur refused to grow.

The wolf from the clearing. The one that had pinned me in the snow. The one that had tried to …

Its yellow eyes found me lying in the snow and its lips pulled back from teeth stained dark with old blood.

I ran.

I was on my feet and running before my mind caught up, barefoot through snow that burned and cut and swallowed my ankles, in a shift that caught on every branch and tore and I didn't care because the sound behind me was claws on frozen ground, heavy and fast and getting closer with every stride.

The trees swallowed me. I ran the way I'd run the night I escaped the village, blind, desperate, powered by nothing except the animal certainty that stopping meant dying. Or worse than dying.

The wolf was faster. I could hear it closing the distance, the rhythm of its paws, the low rumble building in its chest. The same sounds I'd heard in the clearing. The same sounds that meant it had stopped hunting to kill and started hunting to possess.

I threw Forceweaving behind me without looking. Heard it connect with a tree instead, the trunk cracking, branches crashing down. The wolf didn't slow.

I threw again. Empty. The well was dry. I'd spent everything on Erik in the cottage and the practice before that and there was nothing left.

My foot caught a root. I went down hard, face first into frozen mud, my lip splitting, my mouth filling with blood and dirt.

I tried to get up. My arms wouldn't hold.

The wolf's shadow fell over me.

I rolled onto my back and saw it standing above me, massive and gray and panting, steam curling from its mouth. Its body lowered over mine and I felt the heat of it through the shift, felt its weight pressing down, felt its muzzle push against my neck and inhale, long and deep, tasting my scent. Its body shifted. Adjusted. Its hindquarters moved and I felt the intent of it with a clarity that turned my blood to ice.

I screamed.

The black wolf hit the gray wolf like a boulder thrown from a cliff.

The weight vanished from my body as the two of them collided and rolled, a tangle of fur and teeth and blood that crashed through the underbrush and into the base of an oak. The impact shook snow from the branches and they were on their feet instantly, circling, snarling, two enormous wolves facing each other in a clearing that smelled like blood and pine and terror.

The gray wolf was bigger. Broader through the shoulders and chest, built with the dense, scarred musculature of something that had been fighting for decades. It lunged first and caught the black wolf by the throat and drove it sideways into a tree. The black wolf yelped and twisted free, leaving fur and blood behind on the bark.

They circled. The gray wolf lunged again and its jaws found the black wolf's shoulder and clamped down. I heard bone crunch. The black wolf howled and its claws raked down the gray wolf's flank, opening four long gashes that poured blood onto the snow. The gray wolf held. Bit deeper. The black wolf slammed its body sideways, driving them both into a fallen trunk.

The gray wolf lost its grip. The black wolf drove upward, its jaws closing on the gray wolf's belly. It bit down and tore and the gray wolf screamed, a sound so human it raised every hair on my body, and dark blood spilled across the snow.

The gray wolf staggered. Its back legs buckled. It snapped at the black wolf's face, caught its ear, tore through the cartilage. The black wolf didn't let go. It held the belly wound and shook its head, tearing the gash wider, and the gray wolf's snarls turned to whines turned to something desperate and terrified.

The gray wolf broke free. Lurched toward the deeper forest trailing blood. The black wolf pursued, three strides, four, then its injured shoulder gave out and it crashed to the snow.

The gray wolf fled. Its howl faded through the trees until the forest swallowed it.

I lay in the snow where I'd fallen, my shift torn, my lip bleeding, my body shaking so hard my teeth rattled. The black wolf lay in the clearing ten feet away, its sides heaving, blood matting its dark fur and staining the snow beneath it. Its shoulder was twisted wrong. Its ear was torn nearly in half. The gashes down its flank were deep enough to show white bone beneath the muscle.

Then the black wolf began to change.

The sound came first. That wet, organic cracking I'd heard minutes ago when Erik's body had broken apart. Bones snapping. Joints grinding. Fur receding into skin.

The muzzle shortened, flattened, became a jaw and a mouth and a nose. The paws elongated into hands — scarred, familiar hands that I knew the feel of on my skin. The spine compressed. The ears rounded. The black fur thinned and disappeared.

Dietrich lay naked in the snow.

His left shoulder was dislocated, the joint bulging wrong beneath the skin. His side was torn open in four parallel gashes that ran from his ribs to his hip. His ear bled where the cartilage had been torn through. His skin was gray with shock and blood loss and he was shaking, full-body tremors that made his teeth chatter.

He lay on his side with his eyes closed and his arms curled against his chest and he looked nothing like the man who'd kissed my neck over breakfast and everything like a wounded animal left to die in the snow.

I stared at him.

Dietrich was the black wolf. The black wolf was Dietrich.

The man who'd carried me out of the forest. The wolf that had sent Klaus's dogs screaming. The man who'd hovered his hands over my sleeping body. The wolf I'd dreamed about — the one that had chased me through moonlit clearings, the one that had become him while pleasure tore through me.

The same. They were the same.

He was a werewolf. Like his father. The same blood, the same magic, the same creature built to hunt women like me.

They hunt us by scent, by instinct, by a hatred they cannot choose to put down.

I'd let one inside me. Kissed one and touched one and guided one into my body. Lain in the dark and listened to one breathe and felt safe.

The fury arrived like a wave. He'd lied. Every single day. Every touch, every silence, every careful deflection, lies built on lies built on the foundational lie that he was human.

But he was bleeding in the snow. And the blood was real and spreading and his skin was turning the color of old ash and his breathing was getting shallow and if I stood here being angry while he bled out I'd be the woman who let a man die because she was too furious to help.

I was a healer. Whatever else was true, that was still true.

"Can you walk?" I demanded, kneeling beside him.

His eyes opened — amber, glazed, unfocused. "Talia ..." he croaked, scraped raw by the transformation.

"Don't," I snapped. "Don't say my name like that. Can you walk?"

He tried to push himself up with his good arm. Collapsed. Tried again. Got his knees beneath him. Standing was worse — he swayed and nearly went down and I caught him, bracing my shoulder under his good arm, staggering under his weight. His skin was so hot against mine it felt feverish, that impossible furnace heat pouring off him even now, even half dead.

"Move," I ordered. "One foot in front of the other. Don't think about it. Just move."

We moved. Slowly. Agonizingly. He leaned on me with his good arm across my shoulders and I held his wrist and braced his weight against my hip and we stumbled through the snow. Every few steps he'd stagger and I'd have to plant my feet and hold him upright and the rage made it easier because I was too angry to let him fall.

"You're a werewolf." I hauled him over a fallen branch through gritted teeth.

He said nothing. His breathing was labored and wet.

"Your father is a werewolf. You are a werewolf. The black wolf that saved me in the forest was you. The wolf that's been howling outside the cottage every night was you." I adjusted my grip on his wrist and pulled him forward. "You've been lying to me since the moment I opened my eyes in that bed."

"I was ..." He coughed. Blood flecked his lips. " — protecting you."

"From what?" I snarled, dragging him around a boulder. "From the truth? From knowing what I was sleeping beside?"

He flinched. Even half conscious, even bleeding out, the words found their mark.

"I couldn't tell you," he managed. "If you knew what I was, you'd have ..."

"Run?" I finished for him. "I tried to run. You barred the door. I tried again and you dragged me back. So don't pretend my choices mattered to you."

He went quiet. Just the sound of his breathing and our feet crunching through the snow and the occasional wet sound from his wounds that told me he was bleeding faster than he should.

The cottage appeared through the trees. The doorway gaped open, the door still lying in the snow where my Forceweaving had blown it that morning. Through the gap I could see the wreckage, shattered shelves, broken table, rubble where the wall had crumbled.

A lifetime ago we'd been laughing about that door.

I dragged him through the threshold. He collapsed on the floor and I quickly got out of the way before his weight would have taken us both down. He hit the stone and groaned and curled around his injured shoulder and the blood from his side started pooling on the packed earth.

I stood over him breathing hard, my shift soaked with his blood, my bare feet numb, my hands shaking with cold and exhaustion. "You lied to me." I broke on the last word.

He looked up at me from the floor. His eyes were glazed with pain. The same eyes I'd looked into last night while he was inside me.

"I know," he whispered. And closed his eyes.

I stood there for ten seconds. Fifteen. Let the fury burn.

Then I went to the shelf, what was left of it, and started looking for anything that had survived. Grandmother's salve in a jar that had rolled under the remains of the table, unbroken. Clean cloth from the chest in the corner. Water from the water pail.

I knelt beside him and started cleaning the wounds on his side. My hands were steady because I was a healer and healing was what I did, even when I wanted to hit the patient more than save him.

"This is going to hurt," I warned, pressing cloth against the deepest gash.

He hissed through his teeth. His hand found my knee — reached for it blindly, instinctively, seeking contact the way a drowning man reaches for anything solid.

I let him hold on and cleaned each gash with care, packed the deepest one with salve, and wrapped his torso in bandages torn from the cleanest cloth I could find. His shoulder needed setting — the joint was out and swelling fast. I braced my foot against his ribs and gripped his arm and pulled, and the pop when it went back in made us both gasp.

He lay on the floor while I worked, his eyes half-closed, his hand still on my knee. The tremors were easing as his body started doing whatever impossible thing werewolf bodies did, knitting, healing, repairing damage that should take weeks in hours.

"Talia," he rasped when I'd finished wrapping the last bandage.

"I'm not ready to talk to you," I replied, wiping his blood from my hands onto my ruined shift. "And I'm especially not ready to hear you explain why lying to me for weeks was actually some noble act of protection."

He went quiet.

"You're going to heal," I continued, standing and looking down at him. "Because apparently that's what your kind does. And when you're healed, you and I are going to have a conversation. A real one. With the truth this time. All of it."

"All of it," he repeated.

"Every lie. Every omission. Every time you let me believe something that wasn't true." I held his gaze. "Starting with the night you carried me out of the forest. Starting with why a werewolf, a creature bred to hunt bloodkeepers, saved one instead of killing her."

His eyes held mine. Amber and bright and full of something I didn't want to examine because examining it might soften the rage, and I needed the rage. The rage was the only clean thing I had left.

"Rest," I ordered. "I'll keep watch."

I crossed to the corner where the grimoire lay half-buried in rubble. Pulled it free, brushed the dust from the cover, and sat down against the wall with the book in my lap.

He lay on the floor between me and the ruined doorway, bleeding and healing and watching me with wolf's eyes in a man's face.

I opened the grimoire and started reading.

I had questions. The book had answers.

And Dietrich could lie there and bleed while I found them.

Chapter Seventeen

The third morning, I looked at the hole in the wall and the door lying in the snow and the cold pouring through both, and I made a decision that had nothing to do with forgiveness and everything to do with the fact that winter was trying to kill us and the cottage was losing.

"Get up," I ordered from across the room.

He lifted his head from the furs. His eyes were wary, uncertain — the look of a man who'd spent two days of silence waiting for the axe to fall.

"The wall needs patching," I continued, pulling on my cloak and grandmother's boots. "The door needs hanging. I can't do either alone."

He stood, slowly, carefully, favoring his left side where the deepest gash was still closing, and pulled on his shirt and trousers and boots without a word.

We worked through the morning. He cut timber from a fallen oak near the clearing while I hauled the pieces back and held them in place while he fitted them into the gap. We packed moss and mud between the logs. My hands went numb from the cold and his were steady despite the injuries and neither of us spoke except to coordinate.

"Higher on the left," I directed, bracing a log against my shoulder.

He adjusted without comment.

The door took longer. He hammered iron scraps into new hinges on a flat rock near the hearth, the clang of metal filling the cottage. I held the door in place while he fitted them, my arms aching, his hands working above mine, close enough that I could feel the heat of his skin.

When the door swung closed and latched for the first time, we both stood there looking at it.

"It works," I confirmed.

"It works," he agreed.

I turned to go inside and he spoke.

"There's something I need to show you."

I stopped. Didn't turn around.

"You don't have to talk to me," he added. Two days of silence had roughened everything about him. "You don't have to forgive me or listen to me or look at me. But you need to see this."

I turned. He was standing in the snow with soot on his hands and blood seeping through his bandages where the work had pulled at the healing gashes, and his face held something I hadn't seen on it before. Grief. Old and heavy and carried so long it had worn grooves into him.

"Follow me," he requested quietly.

He walked around the back of the cottage. Past the woodpile. Past the spot where he drew water. I followed because curiosity was stronger than anger, and because the look on his face told me this wasn't a trick or a defense or an attempt to win me back.

A birch tree stood alone against the tree line, its white bark peeling in thin sheets, its bare branches scratching against the gray sky.

At its base, a mound. Low and weathered and covered in snow, so old it had almost disappeared back into the earth.

Dietrich stopped a few feet away. He didn't say anything. Just stood there with his hands at his sides and let me look.

I knelt in the snow and brushed the white away until I could see the frozen earth beneath.

I looked at the trunk. There — carved deep into the bark, the letters thick and uneven, cut by a young man's hand:

SOPHIA

The sound that came out of me wasn't a word. It was something older than language, a raw, animal noise from the deepest part of my chest. My aunt was under this dirt. Had been under it for a long time.

"I found her when I first came here," Dietrich offered from behind me, and the words fell apart as he said them.

"On the floor near the hearth. The fire had gone out. She was still wearing the red dress your grandmother had made her."

I pressed my hand flat against the frozen earth and felt nothing, no warmth, no pulse, no ghost. Just cold ground and a dead girl underneath it.

"I was nineteen," he went on, each word pulled from him like a splinter from deep in the flesh. "I buried her and carved her name because I didn't know what else to do. I didn't know any prayers. Didn't know any words that would be enough. So I just — put her in the ground and said I was sorry and stayed."

I pressed my forehead against the cold bark and sobbed. For Sophia. For the girl who'd braided my hair and called me little Red. The girl who'd walked into the forest at nineteen to save her family and died behind boarded windows in her own mother's home.

Dietrich stood behind me. He didn't touch me. Didn't try to comfort me. Just stood there while I wept, and I could hear his breathing, uneven and hitching in a way that told me he was crying too.

When the sobs ran dry, I stayed kneeling. The cold had soaked through my dress and numbed my knees and I didn't care.

"You visit her," I stated. I could see it — the path worn in the snow between the cottage and the tree, packed down by years of feet. His feet.

"As often as I can. She deserved someone remembering her," he replied quietly. "Even if it was just me."

The anger didn't leave. But it shifted. Made room for the recognition that the man standing behind me had buried a girl he'd never known, carved her name into a tree, and visited her grave because he believed she deserved to be remembered.

Monsters didn't do that. Whatever else he was, wolf, liar, predator bred to hunt my kind, he'd done that.

I wiped my face. Stood. My knees buckled and I caught myself against the trunk.

"I'm sorry," I whispered to the frozen earth. "I'm sorry I didn't come sooner. I'm sorry you walked into the forest for us and I spent so many years not understanding what you'd done."

The birch tree creaked in the wind.

"I'm going to kill him," I told her. "For you. For grandmother. For William. I'll find a way."

Snow fell — light, fine flakes that landed on the mound and melted.

I turned and walked back toward the cottage. Dietrich followed at a distance. Neither of us spoke until we were inside and the new door was shut and the fire was crackling and the wreckage of our shared life was all around us on the floor.

I sat on the bed. He stood by the hearth. Sophia's grave had done something that two days of silence and a morning of labor couldn't. It hadn't fixed us. It had just made the breaking more complicated.

"Your father was feral for twenty-two years after Sophia," I began. "And the night my Forceweaving woke, it snapped him back."

"Yes," he confirmed.

"You brought me to Sophia's prison," I continued, each word laid down like a stone. "The one place in this forest that reeks of blood-keeper. And your father found me here."

"I didn't know he'd woken," Dietrich insisted. He cracked on the last word. "I thought he was still feral ..."

"Feral," I spat. "Your feral father killed my husband and six armed men. Tore them to pieces in a clearing. That's not feral, Dietrich. That's a killer."

"Feral doesn't mean stupid," Dietrich clarified, his eyes going distant. "It means the man is gone and the wolf is running the body. And wolves are brilliant hunters, they ambush, they flank, they coordinate kills without a single conscious thought. My father killed your husband on instinct. Smelled blood-keeper scent on a human male, registered it as a territorial threat, and eliminated it. Seven men, six minutes. The wolf didn't plan it. Didn't think about it. It just happened the way a hawk happens to a rabbit." He swallowed. "The feral wolf is pure reflex. What woke up when your power called to him, that's the man coming back. And the man is worse than the wolf ever was, because the man can plan."

"I know what you thought," I cut in. "I'm telling you

what happened. He walked through that doorway and told me he'd been watching for weeks. He laid a trail to lure you away. He was thinking, Dietrich. Planning. The same man who caged my aunt was coming for me."

He flinched. The full-body kind.

"Were you there?" I demanded, and the question had been sitting inside me since the bow conversation, since he'd known William's laugh, since he'd said *I know* with a weight that told me he wasn't guessing. "When William died. Were you in the forest?"

His hands stilled on his knees.

"I heard it," he admitted. "I was half a mile away. By the time I reached the clearing it was over. Your husband and his men were ..." He stopped. His Adam's apple bobbed. "My father was already gone. There was nothing left to save."

"You could have warned them," I pressed, tears burning my face. "You watched the village for years. You knew William hunted in that forest. You could have ..."

"And told him what?" Dietrich's voice cracked. "A stranger walks out of the woods and tells your husband not to hunt here because a feral werewolf is running these trails?" He looked at me and the grief in his face was old and deep and worn smooth from carrying. "He'd have laughed at me the way he laughed at you when you begged him to stay home."

He was right. William had laughed. William had kissed

my forehead and promised he'd come back and walked out the door anyway.

"I couldn't save him, Talia." He stripped himself bare with it. "I've carried that for sixteen years. I couldn't save *him* and I couldn't save *you* from the grief and I've hated myself for both every single day."

Neither of us spoke. We'd each blamed ourselves for the same death for sixteen years, and neither of us was wrong.

"Your father told me what taking a blood-keeper does to a werewolf," I went on, because stopping now would mean feeling it and I couldn't afford to feel it yet.

His face went gray.

"And you knew," I pressed, my nails digging into my own arms. "You knew what your father became after Sophia. You could smell her power on him."

"I more than knew," he corrected, low and strained. "It's not something that has to be taught. It's instinct. The wolf knows what claiming is the way it knows how to hunt. The way it knows how to track a scent or fight for territory." He stared at the fire, his hands gripping his own knees. "The ritual. The mating. Under the moon. The bite that opens the bond. The way the power flows through blood and body. I've known it since my wolf arrived at fifteen. It lives in my bones like a second language I never asked to learn."

The admission landed in my stomach like a stone.

"So you knew exactly what you could do to me," I said it the way you state weather. Fact. Nothing underneath. "Every time you were near me. Every time you smelled my blood. You knew the steps. You knew how to take my power and make it yours."

"Yes," he confirmed, and the word was unflinching. "I know exactly how it works. I know the moon phase. I know where the bite goes. I know what the wolf does during the claiming, the shift, the teeth, the way the bond locks into place." His gaze found mine. "I know all of it the way a wolf knows how to kill. It's written into what I am."

He turned back to the fire, his throat working around what came next.

"But there's something my father never understood," he went on, and the next part came out like a confession. "He took Sophia's power by force and it drained her. Piece by piece. Every time he claimed her, she had less. He got stronger and she got weaker until there was nothing left." He looked at me, the firelight catching the scar across his cheekbone. "I don't think it has to work that way. I think, the wolf in me believes, that if the giving is willing, the power doesn't drain. It flows. Both ways. Amplifies instead of consuming."

"You think," I repeated flatly, folding my arms across my chest. "You believe."

"I can't prove it," he admitted, pressing the heels of his hands against his eyes. "No werewolf has ever tried. No blood-keeper has ever survived long enough for anyone to find out. It's instinct, not knowledge. A feeling in the wolf's blood that consent changes the equation." He dropped his hands and held my gaze. "I could be wrong."

"And if you're wrong, I end up like Sophia," I stated.

He dipped his chin once. "Yes. Which is why I will never ask."

"And you expect me to believe you'd never ..."

"I would die first," he snarled, and the ferocity of it shook dust from the ceiling. His whole body had gone rigid, not with shame this time but with something fiercer, revulsion aimed inward. "I watched what my father did to Sophia. I was seventeen years old. I heard it through the walls. I heard her screaming and I heard him ..." He stopped. His throat worked. "I would tear the wolf out of my own chest with my bare hands before I did that to you. To anyone."

"Pretty words," I shot back. "Your father probably told Sophia something similar."

"My father is a monster," Dietrich ground out, and the sound that came with it wasn't entirely human, a vibration beneath the words, the wolf pressing close to the surface. He caught himself. Breathed. Pulled it back. "My father is a monster and I am his son and I carry the same instinct in my blood. I won't pretend otherwise. The wolf wants the claiming. Every time I'm near you, every time I smell your power, it's there, the pull, the ritual, the knowledge of exactly how to do it."

He stepped closer. I refused to budge.

"But wanting and doing are not the same thing," he continued. "I have wanted to claim you since the night I carried you out of the forest. The wolf has screamed for it every single night. And every single night I've walked into the snow and changed and run until the wanting was small enough to lock away."

"And the night we were together?" I demanded, tears burning my face. "Was the wolf screaming then?"

"Louder than it ever has," he admitted, and a tear tracked down his cheek. "You were beneath me and the moon was up and your blood was singing and every instinct I had was telling me to shift and bite and take." He broke on the next part. "And I didn't. I held it back. I stayed human. I stayed the man you were choosing to be with. Because that's who I wanted to be."

"How do I know?" I pressed, relentless. "How do I know what I saw on your face that night, the shaking, the tears, wasn't you fighting the claiming instinct instead of being overwhelmed by what I was giving you?"

"Both," he whispered. "Both were happening. The tears were real because a woman was touching me for the first time in my life and I didn't know a body could feel that much. And I was fighting the hardest battle of my life at the same time, keeping the wolf caged while you showed me what it meant to be human."

He swallowed hard.

"Both things are true," he repeated. "And I'm not going to pretend one cancels the other because it doesn't. I was the man crying in your arms and I was the wolf fighting to claim you and they were happening in the same body at the same moment and that's the truth of what I am. Man and wolf. Love and hunger. Both. Always."

He rubbed his face with both hands. When they dropped, his eyes were red. "You turned me into this, Talia. You didn't mean to, but you did. Before you came here I was nothing. A dead man walking circles in an empty cottage. Then you showed up with your blood and your fire and your stubborn, impossible heart and the wolf woke up and I woke up with it and now I can't put either of us back to sleep."

I stared at him.

"You watched me fight my father," he added, steadying himself. "You watched him throw me into trees. Tear my shoulder apart. Nearly kill me. If I'd claimed you, if your Forceweaving had poured into me the way Sophia's Sensing poured into him, do you think that fight would have gone the way it did?"

The memory was vivid. The gray wolf's superior strength. Dietrich outmatched from the first lunge, fighting on stubbornness and desperation.

"If I had your power, I would have torn him apart in seconds," he went on quietly. "Instead I nearly died in the snow. That's not the body of a man who's stolen his lover's magic."

He was right. I hated that he was right. Hated it because being right about this didn't erase the lie and didn't change the fact that every time he'd touched me the question had been there, was this love or was this hunger?

Both. The answer was both. And I didn't know how to live with that.

"We are not what we were," I declared.

He didn't move.

"Whatever happened between us, the night I let you inside my body, that was between me and a man I thought I knew." I held the words in place through sheer will. "I don't know you. I don't know where the man ends and the wolf begins. And until I do, you don't get to touch me. You don't get to hold me."

He bowed his head.

"The wolf," I continued, and the anger sank into something worse. "You just told me it screams for the claiming every time you're near me. That it was screaming while we ..." I stopped and after a pause spoke again. "Can it take over? Can the instinct override the man?"

"I've held it back every time," he replied, his eyes on the floor.

"That's not what I asked," I pressed. "Can it win?"

He was quiet for a long time. His hands gripped his own thighs until the knuckles went white.

"If I stopped fighting," he confessed, each word pulled from somewhere deep. "If I let go. If the wolf was strong enough and I was weak enough, yes. It could win." He looked up at me and his face held nothing back. "That's why I left every night. That's why I slept outside. It wasn't just to patrol. It was because the wolf doesn't understand consent. It just wants. And I've been holding it back since the night I carried you out of the forest."

Every night he'd left the cottage. Every morning he'd arrived at first light with shadows under his eyes. The night he'd hovered over my sleeping body and made that low, strained sound, a growl caught between need and restraint.

He'd been fighting the instinct to claim me. Every single night. Standing on the edge of something monstrous and choosing to walk away.

"If the wolf ever wins," I told him, and the Forceweaving hummed beneath my skin, warm and ready and mine. "If you ever lose that fight, even for a second, I will kill you. I will put every thread of power I have into your chest and end you. For Sophia. For me."

He looked into my eyes. The amber burned in the fire-light and behind it I could see the wolf, watching me, wanting me, straining against chains held by a man who loved me too much to let it free.

"I know," he replied quietly. "I'd want you to."

"Good." I crossed back to the bed and pulled the furs around my shoulders. "Sleep by the fire. Stay on your side of the room. Tomorrow you rebuild the shelf."

He wiped his face with the back of his hand and settled by the hearth.

I opened the grimoire in my lap and stared at the pages. The rage burned low and steady in my chest. Banked coals that refused to go out.

But underneath the coals, buried so deep I could barely

feel it, something else was smoldering. The image of a name carved into birch bark by a nineteen-year-old boy who'd buried a stranger and visited her every day for more than two decades. The way he'd sounded when he told me he'd tear the wolf from his own chest before he hurt me. The admission, raw and unvarnished and terrifying, that both the love and the hunger were real and he couldn't separate them and he'd been fighting every second and he was still fighting even now, sitting ten feet away from me with his head bowed and his shoulders shaking.

Man and wolf. Love and hunger. Both. Always.

I didn't know how to live with that.

But I didn't know how to leave it either.

Tomorrow there would be more questions. About the dream with the black wolf. About what it meant that his wolf had found me in my sleep. About Erik, and how to end him before he came back for the power he craved.

But tonight I sat with the grimoire and listened to him breathe across the room, and I let the new door hold against the winter wind, and I thought about Sophia under the birch tree and the boy who'd carved her name and the wolf who loved me and the man who was afraid of what that love could become.

Chapter Eighteen

The bark exploded off the pine in a shower of white splinters that caught the pre-dawn light like sparks.

I gathered the threads again. Aimed at the next tree. Pushed.

The blast went wide and shattered a branch ten feet above where I'd been aiming. I swore under my breath, wiped the blood from my nose with the back of my hand, and gathered the threads again.

I'd been out here for an hour. Maybe longer. The snow around me was littered with debris, broken branches, scattered bark, a boulder I'd cracked clean in half with a blast that had drained me so completely I'd had to sit in the snow for ten minutes before my hands stopped shaking. Beyond the clearing, through a gap in the pines, the frozen lake glinted flat and gray in the early light, the same lake I'd nearly drowned in, its surface unmarked, patient, pretending it hadn't tried to kill me. I kept my back to it and trained facing the cottage. My shift was soaked with sweat despite the cold. My fingers were raw. The humming beneath my skin had gone from a roar to a whisper, the well running low.

I didn't stop. Stopping meant thinking, and thinking meant remembering, and remembering meant the sound of bones cracking on a forest floor and gold eyes in a wolf's skull and the taste of a man's tears on my lips while he —

I threw another blast. It connected this time — hit the trunk dead center and sent a crack running up the wood that split the tree nearly to the crown. Better. Still too much force, not enough precision, but better.

The back of my neck prickled.

I didn't turn around. I didn't need to. My body had learned to register him before my mind did, the shift in the air, the warmth that shouldn't carry this far, the scent of pine and smoke and the animal musk underneath that my stupid, treacherous body still leaned toward like a plant toward light.

I hated it. Hated that my skin knew him. Hated that the same nerve endings he'd woken with his shaking hands still fired when he stood within twenty feet of me. Hated that my body didn't care about lies and wolves and broken trust, it just remembered his mouth on my collarbone and wanted more.

"You're wasting power," Dietrich observed from the doorway behind me.

"Go away," I snapped, gathering the threads again.

"You're hitting the tree but you're using ten times the force you need. You'll drain yourself in minutes in a real fight."

"I don't recall asking for your opinion." I threw the blast. It went wild — caught a low-hanging branch and sent it spinning into the clearing where it buried itself in the snow like a javelin.

"You can't prepare for my father by hitting trees," he pressed.

I spun around. He was leaning against the doorframe with his arms folded, the bandages on his ribs visible through the gap in his shirt. His face was careful. Neutral. Giving nothing away except the truth of what he'd just told me.

"And what do you suggest?" I demanded.

"A moving target," he replied. "One that fights back."

"You're injured."

"I'm healing." He pushed off the doorframe and stepped into the clearing. "And I'm still faster than anything you've fought before. If you can learn to hit me, you can hit him."

I wanted to refuse. Wanted to tell him I'd rather train alone than spend another minute in his proximity, feeling his heat creep across the distance between us and hating myself for noticing.

"Fine," I agreed instead, because he was right and because Erik was out there somewhere getting stronger and I didn't have the luxury of letting pride outweigh survival.

He crossed to the far side of the clearing and settled into a stance I hadn't seen before, weight forward, knees bent, hands loose at his sides. Even injured, even holding back, the way he moved was wrong. Too fluid. Too quiet. The body of a man wrapped around the reflexes of something faster and more dangerous.

"Come at me," he invited.

I gathered the threads. Aimed. Threw.

He wasn't there. He'd moved the instant before the blast left my hands, a sidestep so fast my eyes couldn't track it, smooth and silent, and the Forceweaving hit nothing but empty air and buried itself in the snow behind where he'd been standing.

"You're telegraphing," he called from three feet to the left of where I'd aimed. "Your shoulders tense before you release. Your fingers curl. I can see it coming before you've committed."

I threw again. He dodged again. I threw a third time and he circled behind me and I spun and threw wild and the blast caught the edge of the woodpile and sent logs rolling across the clearing.

"Stop aiming at where I am," he instructed, moving back to his starting position without a hint of exertion. "Aim at where I'm going to be."

"How am I supposed to know where you're going to be?" I snarled, gathering the threads again with hands that were starting to tremble from the drain.

"Watch my feet," he answered. "The body commits to a direction before the mind decides to move. The weight shifts. The lead foot turns. Read that and throw where the turn is taking me."

I watched his feet. He moved. I saw the weight shift, left, his right foot pivoting, and I threw where the turn was carrying him.

The blast caught his shoulder and spun him sideways. He caught himself against a tree, his hand slapping bark, and looked at me with something that might have been surprise.

"Good," he acknowledged, rubbing his shoulder.

We trained for hours. He moved and I threw and I missed and I missed and I missed and then I didn't. The pattern was agonizingly slow — nine misses for every hit, my Forceweaving scattering wide or arriving too late or hitting with so much force that I drained myself in a single blast. But the hits were coming more frequently. By midmorning I was landing one in five. By noon, one in three.

He was teaching me without teaching me. Every dodge showed me what I'd done wrong. Every hit showed me what I'd done right. He never praised beyond a clipped "good" or "better" and never criticized beyond the practical, "too wide," "too slow," "you're broadcasting again." The distance between us stayed useful. Two people with a job to do and no room for anything else.

Until he corrected my stance.

I was planting too wide, he explained, which threw off my aim. He stepped closer and his hand hovered near my hip, not touching, just indicating where my weight should shift. But the heat of his palm radiated through the fabric of my dress and sank into the skin beneath and my concentration shattered like a jug hit with too much Forceweaving.

The blast went sideways. Took out a section of the woodpile I'd already damaged.

We both stared at the scattered logs.

"Sorry," I muttered, stepping away from him. Putting distance between my body and the memory of his hands.

"Wider stance," he repeated, moving back to his side of the clearing like nothing had happened. "Try again."

We didn't acknowledge it. Filed it away in the growing catalog of things we weren't discussing, alongside the way I'd caught him watching my mouth while I drank from the waterskin, and how I'd turned away too fast when he'd pulled his shirt off to check his bandages, and that thickening in the air every time we got within arm's reach and neither of us knew how to thin it out again.

I collapsed onto the stump near the cottage door and pressed my hands against my thighs to stop the shaking. My nose was bleeding again — a steady trickle that dripped onto my shift and wouldn't stop. The Forceweaving had gone quiet beneath my skin, the well drained to its dregs.

Dietrich disappeared inside and came back with water and a cloth. He held them out without getting too close, letting me take them from his hands with a gap between our fingers.

"Drink," he directed. "The power replenishes faster when you're hydrated."

I drank. Pressed the cloth against my nose and tilted my head back and stared at the gray sky and tried not to think about how natural it had felt, training with him. How his body and mine had fallen into a rhythm, attack, dodge, adjust, attack, that felt less like combat practice and more like a conversation.

"How do you kill a werewolf?" I asked, still looking at the sky. "Not injure. Kill."

He was quiet for a moment. Then he sat on the ground near me, close enough to be heard, far enough to respect the boundary.

"Silver," he began. "It burns on contact. Like pressing a hot coal against your skin. A silver blade will slow us down, weaken the healing. But it won't kill unless you get it into the heart or sever the spine." He paused. "And getting close enough to a werewolf to use a blade means getting close enough to die."

"What about fire?" I pressed.

"Can work," he conceded, picking up a twig and turning it between his fingers. "If you can trap the wolf in it long enough. The healing is fast but not infinite, sustained burning will overwhelm it eventually. But fire is wild. Hard to aim. Hard to control in a fight where the wolf is moving."

"And Forceweaving?" I lowered my head and looked at him. "What can my power do to a werewolf?"

His eyes met mine and held. "Everything," he answered quietly. "A focused blast to the skull will crack it open. Enough sustained pressure on the chest will collapse the lungs. A precise, concentrated strike to the heart ..." He mimed it with his hand, a single pointed thrust toward his own sternum. "The heart stops. The wolf dies."

"But I'd have to be precise," I replied.

"Very precise," he confirmed. "A wild blast will knock a werewolf back but it won't kill one. My father took your Forceweaving at close range in the cottage and walked it off. The power has to be focused, a spear, not a wave. Everything you have, concentrated into a point no bigger than your fist, aimed exactly where it needs to go."

"I can't do that yet," I admitted, wiping the blood from my nose.

"That's why we're training," he reminded me.

I consulted the grimoire over the last of the bread. Turned to the Forceweaving combat pages and read while I chewed, tracing the instructions with a blood-crusted fingertip.

"The book describes something called threading," I announced, studying the diagram, golden threads twisted together into a tight spiral, the point narrowed to a needle. "Gathering the force into a single concentrated line instead of throwing it wide. Like the difference between throwing a bucket of water and forcing it through a nozzle."

"Makes sense," he acknowledged from where he sat. "Can you do it?"

"I don't know." I studied the diagram. The technique required holding the threads together under enormous pressure, keeping them from scattering while simultaneously aiming and releasing. Every instinct would tell me to let go, to throw wide, to explode instead of pierce. "The book says it's the hardest technique. Most blood-keepers never master it."

"You're not most blood-keepers," he observed.

I looked up sharply. His face was neutral but his eyes held something that wasn't neutral at all, a fierce, quiet certainty that looked like faith.

I looked away before it could do any more damage than it already had.

"Again," I declared, standing and brushing crumbs from my shift. "Slower this time. I want to try the threading."

We trained through the afternoon. The threading was impossible at first, the threads scattered every time I tried to compress them, the pressure too great, my focus too fragmented. The blasts came out wide and weak, dissipating before they reached him.

"Tighter," Dietrich called, dodging a blast that hardly ruffled his hair. "You're letting them spread."

"I'm trying," I ground out through clenched teeth.

"Don't try," he countered, circling to my left. "The book

said separate emotion from execution. You're angry and the anger is blowing the threads apart. Pull the rage out of the weaving and use your will instead."

"Easy for you to say," I snapped, gathering the threads again. "You're not the one whose ..."

I stopped. He was right. The anger was a fuel but it was also a fire, too hot, too wild, burning through the threads before I could shape them. I needed cold. I needed precision. I needed the part of me that was a healer, methodical, exact, clinical, instead of the part of me that wanted to burn the world down.

I gathered the threads. Pulled the anger out of them the way I'd pull poison from a wound, carefully, deliberately, leaving behind only the clean golden force. Twisted them together. Tighter. Tighter. Felt them resist, felt them vibrate with the pressure, felt the narrowing point form between my palms.

I aimed at the tree behind him. Released.

The blast punched a hole through the trunk. Clean. Round. The size of my fist. The tree groaned and tilted and fell with a crash that shook snow from every branch in the clearing.

We both stared at the fallen tree. At the hole through its center, the edges smooth, a wound that looked surgical instead of explosive.

"There it is," Dietrich breathed, and his whole face opened up.

I looked at my hands. They were shaking. My nose was

pouring blood and my vision was graying at the edges and I'd used almost everything I had left. But I'd done it. The threading. A spear instead of a wave.

I swayed. My knees buckled.

He was there before I hit the ground, catching my arm, bracing my weight, holding me upright with one hand while the other pressed the cloth against my bleeding nose. I leaned into him without meaning to. My body tilted toward his warmth the way a plant tilts toward the one crack of light in a dark room. My shoulders were against his chest, my face inches from the hollow of his throat where his pulse beat steady and warm beneath the beard.

I could smell him. Pine and smoke and the musk underneath that still made something in my belly tighten despite every argument I'd had with myself about it. My body didn't care about arguments. My body remembered his hands and his mouth and the sound he'd made when I'd sunk down onto him and it wanted, it wanted—

I pulled away. Stepped back so fast I nearly fell again.

"I'm fine," I insisted, too quickly.

"You're about to collapse," he corrected, but he let me go. His hand dropped to his side and curled into a fist and I knew, knew from the way his teeth clenched and his nostrils flared, that my scent had done the same thing to him that his had done to me. That the space between wanting and having was destroying us both from opposite sides.

"I'm fine," I repeated, and walked past him into the cottage.

I sat on the bed and buried my face in the pillow and waited for my heart to stop hammering. My body was a traitor. Sixteen years of celibacy and it had woken up and now it wouldn't go back to sleep. Every time he was near me, every time his heat reached my skin, every time I caught the animal smell of him beneath the pine, it responded. Tightened. Remembered. Wanted.

I wanted to hate him for it. Wanted to blame the wolf, the instinct, some magic in his blood that called to mine. But the truth was simpler and uglier than that. The truth was that I'd touched him and he'd trembled and I'd felt powerful and tender and alive in a way I hadn't felt since William, and my body didn't care that the man it wanted turned into a wolf when the moon rose. My body just wanted to feel that way again.

I pulled the pillow over my head and refused.

He rebuilt the shelf that evening while I read by the fire.

I hadn't asked him to start tonight. He just did it — measuring wood with his hands, cutting joints with the knife, fitting the pieces together with quiet, practiced movements. His hands knew wood the way my hands knew herbs. The work came from his body, not his mind, and I found myself watching despite my best efforts not to.

The way his forearms flexed when he drove the pegs in. The width of his hands, the scars across the knuckles. The concentration in his face — brow furrowed, lower lip caught between his teeth, eyes tracking the wood the way they'd tracked my body in the clearing.

I looked away. Turned a page I hadn't read.

"The grimoire mentions the Fae," I announced, because talking about ancient mythology was safer than watching his hands and remembering where they'd been.

"Hmm?" He didn't look up from the shelf.

"The source of everything. Blood-keepers, Sanguinarians, werewolves, all of it traces back to the Fae. Ancient beings who were here before humans. Their presence seeped into the earth and woke the blood of the women who lived closest to the old places. That's what blood-keepers are, Fae power, diluted, carried in mortal blood." I traced the cramped handwriting with my finger. "The Sanguinarians were the Fae's mistake, they tried to pour their power directly into humans and the bodies died but wouldn't stay dead. Came back wrong. Beautiful and cold and needing blood to survive. And the Sanguinarians made werewolves to hunt us down."

"My father told me the story when I was young," he replied, fitting a shelf bracket into place. "Called the Fae the ones who started the fire and walked away from the blaze."

"The grimoire says a blood-keeper who reaches her full power can kill a Sanguinarian," I continued, reading. "Can kill a werewolf." I looked up at him. "Can, in theory, wound a Fae."

He stopped working. Turned to look at me.

"That's why they hunt us," I went on. "Your kind. The Sanguinarians. All of them. It's not just hunger or instinct. It's fear. Every generation, one of us is born stronger than the last. And we terrify the things that were designed to control us."

His eyes caught the light. "Good." He spoke so quietly it pulled me in. "Be terrifying."

I looked at him a beat too long. Felt the pull — the magnetic draw of his body across the room, the tug in my chest, the hum beneath my skin that intensified when his eyes were on me. My body leaning toward his the way it always did, traitorous and relentless.

I looked down at the book. Turned another page.

He went back to the shelf.

We worked in our separate corners while the fire burned and the wind pushed against the boards and the night settled around us. He finished the shelf and loaded grandmother's surviving jars onto it, the ones that had escaped the fight intact, lining them up the way they'd been before, labels facing out.

I watched him place the sage jar, the one I'd opened that first day, the one that had dropped me to my knees with memory, on the bottom shelf, exactly where grandmother had always kept it.

He remembered where it went. He'd been living in this cottage for a long time and he remembered where an old woman had kept her sage.

The anger loosened. Just a fraction. Just enough to let something else breathe underneath it, something I still wouldn't name but could no longer pretend I didn't feel.

"Thank you," I offered. "For the shelf."

He nodded without turning around. "Tomorrow we train again. Earlier. Before your power drains from practice."

"All right."

"And I want to show you something about the wolf," he added, his back still to me. "How it moves. The patterns. The tells you can read before it attacks. My father and I fight differently but the instincts are the same. If you learn to read me, you'll be able to read him."

"All right," I repeated.

He crossed to the fire and lay down on his furs. I stayed on the bed with the grimoire open in my lap, everything swirling through my mind, the Forceweaving entry, the combat techniques, the Fae passage, the memory of his hands on the shelf brackets and the sage jar in its proper place and the way he'd caught me when I fell and the way I'd leaned into his chest before I could stop myself.

Erik was out there. Healing. Coming back. And when he came, he'd be stronger and smarter and he wouldn't make the same mistake twice.

I had to be ready. Had to be precise enough to thread the Forceweaving into a spear that could punch through a wolf's skull. Had to be strong enough to do it more than once. Had to be fast enough to hit a target that moved like smoke.

And I had to do all of it while standing next to a man whose proximity turned my concentration to rubble and whose hands I could still feel on my skin every time I closed my eyes.

I closed the grimoire. Blew out the candle. Pulled the furs to my chin.

"Dietrich." His name fell into the dark.

"Hmm." The sound came from across the room, low and rumbling, and my body responded to it the way a string responds to a tuning fork, vibrating at a frequency I couldn't control.

"When Erik comes back," I began, staring at the ceiling. "If we fight him together and we win, what happens after?"

He was quiet for a long time.

"I don't know," he admitted. "I've never thought past keeping you alive."

"Start thinking," I told him.

More quiet. Then — "What do you want to happen?"

I didn't answer. Because the answer was complicated and contradictory and involved wanting things I wasn't ready to want from a man I wasn't ready to forgive, and the wanting was tangled up with the anger and the grief and the memory of Sophia under the birch tree and the question I couldn't stop asking myself, was this love or was this instinct? Was I choosing him or was my blood choosing his blood? Was there even a difference?

"I don't know either," I finally replied. "But I want to be alive to figure it out."

"Then we train," he concluded.

"We train," I agreed.

The new door held. Somewhere in the forest, a wolf howled, and I didn't know if it was wild or something else, and the not-knowing sat in my chest like a second heartbeat, familiar and frightening and impossible to ignore.

I closed my eyes. Him across the room. Steady and even and close.

I didn't sleep for a long time.

And from the way his breathing never quite settled, neither did he.

Chapter Nineteen

The days bled together after that. We trained and we fought and we ate and we didn't talk about the things we weren't talking about, and the silence between us filled with bruises and bark dust and the particular exhaustion of two people working toward something they couldn't name.

I lost count around the second week. Mornings started before dawn, me in the clearing throwing Forceweaving at trees until my nose bled, him circling at half speed while I tried to thread the power tight enough to hit a moving target. Afternoons I spent with the grimoire. Evenings he built things, a second shelf, a rack for drying herbs, repairs so quiet and steady they felt like apology and penance rolled into one. Nights we slept on opposite sides of the cottage and pretended the distance was a choice.

His ribs were still mending. Werewolf wounds from

another werewolf didn't close the way a human cut would. He moved better each day but I caught the flinch when he twisted wrong, the shallow breath when he reached too high. The wolf in him was stitching the damage together from the inside, but it was slow work. Whatever magic his kind carried, it had limits when the teeth that made the wound carried the same curse.

Then the rain came.

The first rain since I'd arrived in the forest, warm enough to melt the top layer of snow and turn the clearing into a patchwork of white ice and dark, churned earth where weeks of Forceweaving blasts had stripped the ground bare.

I didn't notice until I was already moving.

Dietrich came at me from the left, half speed, still favoring the healing ribs, but fast enough that I had to pivot hard to track him. I gathered the threads, aimed where his feet were taking him, and released.

The blast connected. Caught his shoulder and spun him sideways. I was already gathering for a second strike, my weight shifting, my back foot turning on the muddy ground.

My boot hit ice beneath the mud. Both feet went out from under me and I went down hard, face first, arms too slow to catch myself. The mud was cold and thick and it swallowed me, hands, chest, face, hair. I slid three feet before I stopped, the Forceweaving scattering into nothing as my concentration shattered.

I lay there for a moment. Face down in freezing mud. The taste of earth and ice in my mouth.

"Talia ..." His boots appeared in my peripheral vision, crunching through the muck.

"Don't," I warned, spitting mud. "Don't you dare laugh."

He didn't laugh. He reached down and pulled me to my feet and his face was perfectly, carefully neutral, though a muscle in his cheek was doing something suspicious.

I looked down at myself. Grandmother's mended dress was ruined — soaked through with black mud from collar to hem, the fabric heavy and cold against my skin. My hands were caked. My hair was matted with it, dark clumps hanging in my face. I could feel it in my ears, between my fingers, inside my boots.

"Training's done for today," I muttered, scraping mud off my chin.

He nodded. The muscle in his cheek twitched again.

"I saw that," I snapped, and stalked back toward the cottage, leaving a trail of muddy footprints in the snow.

By the time I got through the door I was shivering so hard my teeth rattled. The mud was drying in patches against my skin, pulling tight and cracking, and the parts that were still wet were turning my body to ice from the outside in. I stood on the stone floor and dripped and looked at the ruined dress and wanted to scream.

I heard him come in behind me. Heard him cross to the hearth without a word, add wood to the fire, fill the kettle and set it over the flames. Then fill it again. And again.

He was heating water. Without being asked. Without

making it a negotiation or a peace offering or anything other than what it was, a practical response to a woman covered in freezing mud.

The wooden tub sat in the corner near the hearth. I'd seen it there since my first day in the cottage but had never used it. He dragged it out, positioned it close enough to the fire that the heat would reach the water, and started filling it from the kettle. Trip after trip, kettle to tub, the water steaming in the cold air.

"There's a cloth screen in the back room," he offered, not looking at me. "I'll set it up."

He found it behind the medicine shelf, a folding screen of stretched linen over a wooden frame, spotted with age but intact. He set it between the tub and the rest of the room, creating a barrier that gave me privacy from the chest down while still letting the fire's heat reach the water.

Then he turned his back and busied himself at the far end of the cottage, sorting through the salvaged herb jars on the new shelf, making more noise than the task required so I'd know where he was.

I peeled off the ruined dress. The shift beneath was nearly as bad, mud had soaked through to the linen, staining it brown and black. I pulled it over my head and dropped it on the floor and stepped into the tub.

The water was perfect. Hot enough to sting, deep enough to cover me to the waist. I sank down and felt the warmth hit my frozen skin and for a moment nothing existed except the heat and the relief and the loosening of muscles I'd been clenching against the cold.

I scrubbed. Arms, chest, stomach, legs — the cloth and the hot water turning the mud to brown rivulets that ran into the tub and turned the water the color of weak tea. My face, my neck, behind my ears. The mud came off in layers, revealing pink skin underneath that stung where I'd scraped it raw.

But my back was a different matter. The mud had soaked through my dress and my shift and dried against my skin in a solid sheet from my shoulders to my lower back. I twisted, reaching behind me with the cloth, and got as far as my shoulder blades before my arms refused to bend any further.

I tried from the other direction. Reached up from my waist. Got the small of my back but not the center, where the worst of it had caked into the grooves of my spine and hardened like plaster.

I sat in the water and tried again. And again. The cloth scraped uselessly against my side while the mud on my back dried tighter and pulled at my skin.

"I need help with my back." I pulled my braid over one shoulder.

The sorting sounds stopped.

"I can't reach it," I continued, staring at the screen and not at the space beyond it where he was standing. "The mud's dried. I need someone to ..."

"All right." He took a breath. A man being handed something fragile and knowing it.

I heard his footsteps cross the room. Heard him pick up a fresh cloth and dip it in the hot water from the kettle. Then he came around the screen and knelt behind the tub.

I pulled my hair over one shoulder, baring my back. The water covered me from the waist down. From behind, all he could see was my back, mud-caked and tensed and waiting.

The cloth touched between my shoulder blades and I flinched. Not from cold or pain but from the intimacy of it, the weight of his hand through the fabric, the careful pressure as he began to work the dried mud loose.

He washed my back the way he did everything, methodically, thoroughly, with a focus that left no room for anything but the task. The cloth moved in slow circles, softening the mud, lifting it away in dark smears that ran down my spine and into the water. He started at my shoulders and worked down, his knuckles pressing into the tight muscles along my spine, and I had to close my eyes against the sensation because the combination of warm water and strong hands was doing things to me that had nothing to do with getting clean.

"There's mud in your hair," he observed quietly.

"I know."

He set the cloth aside. I heard him pour water from the kettle into a smaller basin, testing the temperature with his fingers. Then his hands were in my hair, working through the tangles, loosening the mud, his fingers against my scalp careful and slow.

I tipped my head back without meaning to. My eyes closed. His fingers moved through my hair in long, gentle strokes, separating the strands, combing the mud free, cupping water in his palms and pouring it over my head to rinse. The water ran warm down my temples and over my closed eyelids and I felt every callus on his fingers, every ridge of scar tissue, the impossible heat of his skin against my scalp.

His hands slowed. His fingers stopped combing and just, rested. Against the back of my head, threaded through my wet hair, holding me with a tenderness that made my breath catch.

I turned my face toward him.

He was right there. Kneeling beside the tub, his hands in my hair, his face inches from mine. Water dripped from his fingers onto my bare shoulder. His amber eyes were dark and close and full of something he was trying very hard not to let me see.

I kissed him.

I didn't decide to. My body closed the distance before my mind could intervene, my mouth finding his, wet and warm, tasting of nothing except heat and proximity and the ache of weeks of denial. He made a sound against my lips, soft, surprised, almost wounded, and his hand tightened in my hair and he kissed me back.

It was slow. Slow and devastatingly tender, nothing like

the desperate collision against the wall or the tearful, trembling first time. This was a kiss between two people who knew exactly what they were doing and exactly why they shouldn't be doing it and couldn't bring themselves to stop. His mouth moved against mine and his hand cradled my head and the steam from the bath rose between us and I could feel his heartbeat in his fingertips where they pressed against my scalp.

He pulled away — just enough to break the contact. His forehead resting against my temple, his breathing ragged and uneven.

"I'll be outside," he managed.

He stood. His hands left my hair and I felt the absence of them like cold water. He didn't look at me, kept his eyes on the floor, on the wall, on anything that wasn't my bare shoulders above the waterline, and walked to the door and opened it and stepped through it and closed it behind him.

I sat in the cooling water and pressed my fingers to my mouth and tasted him on my lips and didn't pretend I didn't want more.

The water went cold before I got out.

I was sitting by the fire in my damp shift, combing my wet hair with my fingers, when he came back.

He didn't come in empty-handed. He carried a bundle folded over his arm. White fabric, soft, carefully held like it mattered.

"I found this," he began, holding it out without quite meeting my eyes. "In the back room. Your grandmother's medicine cupboard, behind the jars. Wrapped in cloth and hidden." He paused. "I think she put it there on purpose."

I took it from him. Unfolded it.

A dress. White linen, finer than anything else in the cottage. Not rough homespun but a weave that was softer, woven tight and smooth. The collar was embroidered with small flowers in thread that had once been bright and had faded to soft colors. Blue cornflowers, red poppies, green leaves stitched with tiny, precise stitches I recognized immediately.

"Grandmother made this," I breathed, my fingers tracing the embroidery. "The stitching — it's the same hand that labeled the herb jars. The same tiny flowers she put on everything."

He nodded. "I thought so too."

I held the dress up against myself. The bodice was fitted, the waist narrow, the skirt falling in a simple line to the floor. It had been made for a woman my size, my grandmother's size when she was young, or Sophia's size, or mine.

"I'll turn around," he offered.

He faced the wall. I pulled the damp shift over my head and dropped it, then lifted the white dress and let it fall over my body. The linen settled against my clean skin, cool and soft and smelling faintly of cedar from the chest where it had been stored for two decades. The bodice fit close, the embroidered collar sitting just below my throat. The sleeves were long, the cuffs stitched with the same tiny flowers. The skirt whispered against my legs when I moved.

It fit. As if it had been waiting for me.

I reached for the red cloak where it lay folded on the bed. Drew it around my shoulders and fastened it at my throat. The red wool against the white linen. The cloak I'd stitched by candlelight over the dress my grandmother had sewn. A piece of a woman's life, separated by decades and a forest and a death, brought back together on her granddaughter's body.

"You can turn around," I told him.

He turned.

He stopped.

His mouth opened and nothing came out. His eyes moved from the red cloak to the white dress to the embroidered collar to my face, clean and flushed from the bath, framed by damp dark hair that was already starting to curl as it dried, and whatever he'd been about to say died somewhere between his brain and his tongue.

I'd never seen a man look at a woman the way he was looking at me. Not with desire, though that was there. Not with admiration, though that was there too. It was recognition. Like he was seeing a person he'd imagined so many times that the reality of her had become impossible to believe.

"What?" I demanded, self-conscious under his stare.

He swallowed. Tried to speak. Swallowed again.

"You look like..." He stopped. His words had gone

strange. Thick and rough, catching on a knot in his throat. "At the market. When you were a girl. You had a red ribbon in your hair and honey on your fingers and I couldn't..." He broke off. Pressed the heel of his hand against his eyes. "I'm sorry. I just… I wasn't expecting..."

"Wasn't expecting what?" I asked softly.

He dropped his hand. His eyes were bright and the amber in them caught the firelight and turned it to gold.

"You," he answered. "Standing in this cottage. Wearing her dress and your cloak. Looking like everything I ever ..."

He didn't finish. He didn't need to. The sentence completed itself in the way he looked at me, a man seeing the girl from the market grown into the woman in front of him, standing in a cottage he'd kept for twenty-two years, wearing the red that meant blood-keeper and the white that meant something new.

I didn't know what to say. The moment was too large for words, too full of history and grief and longing and the strange, impossible fact that everything in this cottage had been waiting for me to arrive. The dress in the chest. The sage on the shelf. The cloak around my shoulders. The man by the fire.

"Thank you," I managed. "For finding it. For keeping it safe."

He nodded. Looked at the fire. Looked back at me. Looked at the fire again, like he couldn't hold his eyes on me for too long without a part of him giving way.

"I'll start supper," he offered.

He crossed to the hearth and started working with his back to me, and his hands were shaking on the pot and his shoulders were rigid and I stood by the bed in my grandmother's dress and my grandmother's cloak and felt a crack open inside me that all the anger in the world couldn't seal shut again.

I looked down at the embroidered flowers at my wrists. Traced a cornflower with my fingertip. Grandmother's hands had stitched these tiny petals decades ago, sitting by a fire just like this one, in a cottage that was now mine by inheritance and survival and the stubborn refusal to die.

The white dress and the red cloak. The healer and the blood-keeper. The woman who'd been hunted and the woman who was learning to hunt back.

I sat down at the table and opened the grimoire and started reading the combat pages again, and if my eyes kept drifting to the man at the hearth, to the breadth of his shoulders and the steadiness of his hands and the way the firelight played across the scars I'd traced with my mouth, well.

That was between me and the dress and the red cloak and the ghost of a woman who'd stitched flowers into linen because she believed her granddaughter would someday need something beautiful to wear in the middle of a war.

Chapter Twenty

The claw marks appeared on the cottage wall overnight.

I found them when I stepped outside at dawn, four deep gouges raked through the stone right beside the window boards, the rock dust still pale on the snow beneath. Erik had stood here in the dark. Close enough to hear us breathing. Close enough to touch the wall where I slept on the other side.

Dietrich was already in the clearing, staring at the marks. His face had gone blank in the way that meant everything underneath was moving too fast to show.

"He's healed," I concluded.

"Enough to mark territory," Dietrich confirmed. "Enough to announce he's coming back."

"How long?" I pressed.

"Days." He touched one of the gouges. "Maybe less."

"Then stop going easy on me," I demanded. "Full speed. Today."

He didn't argue.

The first time he came at me full speed I didn't see him move. One moment he was at the edge of the clearing, the next his hand was on my throat, not squeezing, just there, demonstrating how fast a werewolf could close distance when it stopped pretending to be human.

"Dead," he stated, removing his hand.

"Again," I ordered.

He came again. I threw the threading — tight, focused, aimed where his feet were taking him. It missed by a foot. He was inside my guard before the blast dissipated, his palm flat against my sternum.

"Dead," he repeated.

"Again."

We went for hours. He stopped being gentle. Stopped telegraphing. Moved the way his father would move, fast, brutal, unpredictable, and I threw everything I had and missed and missed and missed.

By midmorning my nose was streaming blood and my hands were shaking and I'd landed exactly two hits out of maybe forty attempts.

"Not enough," I gasped, bent over with my hands on my knees.

"You're getting faster," he observed, barely winded.

"Not fast enough," I shot back. "Again."

I broke open that afternoon. The anger I'd been using as

fuel, the rage at his lies, at Erik, at everything, I'd been pouring it into every blast. But anger was wild. Anger scattered the threads.

I needed a steadier source.

Dietrich came at me from the left. Fast. I gathered the threads and instead of reaching for the anger I reached for what lived underneath it. The thing I'd been refusing to name since the bath. Since the shelf. Since the birch tree. The pull that made my body hum when he was near and my hands steady when he was watching.

I released the threading.

The blast caught him square in the chest. Tight. Focused. Precise enough to stop his momentum and send him back three full steps.

He looked at me. Breathing hard for the first time all day.

"What did you just do?" he asked, pressing a hand to his sternum.

"Found a better fuel," I replied, and didn't explain further.

We trained until I collapsed. I threaded a blast that cracked a boulder clean in half. The two halves steamed in the cold air and Dietrich stared at them with a look caught between pride and fear.

I swayed on my feet. He caught my arm. I leaned into him — my shoulder against his chest, my face near the hollow of his throat. His scent filled my lungs and my body tilted toward his warmth the way it always did.

I didn't pull away. Not immediately.

His arm came up. Slowly. And wrapped around my shoulders.

We stood in the clearing with the cracked boulder steaming behind us and neither of us spoke. His heartbeat was too fast beneath my ear. Too hard for a man who'd just been moving at full werewolf speed.

I pulled away eventually. But not quickly. And not far.

The second set of claw marks appeared the next morning. On the door itself.

Deep grooves raked through the new oak he'd hung days ago. Erik had come while we slept, close enough to touch the door we'd built together.

"He's not just circling," I realized, tracing the gouges. "He's announcing."

"Testing how close he can get," Dietrich corrected, his expression grim. "How much he can take before I respond."

"Next time it won't be marks," I stated.

"Next time it won't be marks," he agreed.

We trained until dark. I landed one in three at full speed. The threading held tighter with each attempt. But it wasn't enough and we both knew it.

That night, by the fire, I sat on the bed with the grimoire closed in my lap and watched him feed the flames.

"Claim me," I suggested.

His hands stilled on the log he was placing.

"The claiming," I continued. "The bite. The bond. Do it."

He turned, and the expression on his face wasn't what I expected. Not hope. Not desire.

Fear.

"I can't do that to you," he replied, and the stillness in him told me he'd been thinking about this for a long time.

"You told me what it means," I challenged, standing from the bed. "The bond. The protection. Other wolves sensing it. You told me you wanted ..."

"I know what I want," he interrupted, the steadiness fraying. "I've wanted it since the night I carried you out of the forest. The wolf has been screaming for it every day since." He pressed his hands against his face. Breathed. "But wanting and doing are different things."

"I'm asking you," I insisted, stepping closer. "I'm choosing ..."

"You're choosing because Erik is coming," he cut in, dropping his hands. His eyes found mine — fierce and bright and full of pain. "You're choosing because you're frightened and you think the bond will give us an advantage." He broke. "The claiming isn't a strategy, Talia. It's permanent. It's my teeth in your skin and my heartbeat in your chest for the rest of your life. And if I do it because you're scared instead of because you're sure ..."

"You think I'm not sure?" I stepped into his space.

"I think you're brave and you'd do anything to survive," he countered, and his composure finally broke. "And I love you too much to let you do this for the wrong reasons."

Everything stopped.

He'd said it in pieces before. In the confession about the wolf and the man. In the way he'd wept during sex and carved Sophia's name and placed the sage jar where Grandmother kept it. A hundred ways without ever saying it plainly.

I love you too much.

He didn't say the wolf wants you. Didn't say the instinct pulls.

I love you. So much that I'll refuse the thing I've wanted my entire life because I'm afraid it isn't what you truly want.

"I'll die protecting you," he went on, stripped down to nothing. "If Erik comes tomorrow, I'll fight him. Without the bond, without the claiming, without anything except teeth and claws and the need to keep you alive." He swallowed hard. "And if he kills me, then at least I'll die knowing I never took something from you that you might regret giving."

I stared at him.

This man. This impossible, infuriating man who would walk into a fight he couldn't win, who would die on the forest floor with his chest torn open, rather than claim me without being absolutely certain I wanted it.

His father had caged a woman and claimed her by force because he couldn't bear the thought of not having her.

His son was willing to die rather than put his teeth on a woman who was standing in front of him begging for it.

The anger, the last ember of it, the final coal I'd been keeping banked since the day I'd watched his bones reform, went out.

What replaced it was heat of a different kind entirely.

I reached for the laces of the white dress.

His eyes tracked my fingers. "Talia, what are you ..."

"Be quiet," I told him, and pulled the first lace free.

The second. The third. The bodice loosened. I pushed it down over my shoulders, past my hips, and let it fall. The white linen pooled at my feet.

I pulled the shift over my head.

His whole body jerked. A shudder that ran from his shoulders to his boots.

"You're not doing this because of Erik," I stated, stepping toward him. "And neither am I."

"Talia ..." He could hardly get it out. His eyes kept dropping from my face to my body and dragging themselves back up and the effort was visibly killing him. "I just told you I wouldn't ..."

"You told me you loved me," I corrected, closing the distance. "You told me you'd die before you'd let anyone hurt me. You told me you'd walk into a fight you can't win and bleed out in the snow rather than claim me without my consent." I put my hands on his chest. Felt his heart slamming beneath my palms. "So here it is. My full, free, honest consent. Given by a woman who is not frightened and not desperate and not thinking about Erik at all."

"Then what are you thinking about?" he managed.

"About the sage jar," I replied. "About Sophia's name carved into birch bark. About the way you wept the first time I touched you and the way you held the wolf back every single night and the way you just looked me in the eye and told me you'd rather die than take something I might regret."

I rose onto my toes and put my mouth beside his ear.

"I love you," I whispered. "I love you and I want you to claim me. Because I choose you. Both of you. Man and wolf. Tonight and every night after."

His control broke.

His hands found my waist and his mouth found mine and the kiss was nothing soft, thirty years of wanting released in a single moment, his body pressing me backward toward the bed, his hands gripping me like I'd dissolve if he loosened his hold.

I pulled at his shirt. He tore it over his head. I ran my hands down his chest, feeling the ridges, the scars, the intense heat of him.

"Take what you want," he breathed against my mouth, coming apart on every word. "Whatever you want. However you want it. I'm yours."

I pushed him onto the bed.

He landed on his back, chest heaving, eyes blazing up at me. I climbed over him and straddled his hips and the sound he made, low and broken, sent heat flooding through me.

I stripped his trousers off him and then it was just us, skin against skin, the fire crackling, his body beneath mine.

His hands found my breasts with that single-minded devotion, his mouth finding my nipple, tongue circling, the groan vibrating through my ribs. I let him because the pleasure was sharp and real. But tonight I wanted more.

I pressed my palm flat against his chest and pushed him down. He went, his back hitting the furs, his eyes wide.

I kissed his mouth. Then his throat. Then lower — down the center of his chest, following the dark line of hair from his navel downward.

His breathing changed. Got ragged.

"Talia ..." He propped himself up on his elbows. "What are you ..."

"Lie back," I told him.

He didn't. He watched me move lower and I could see the moment he understood because his whole body went rigid and his elbows gave out and he dropped flat against the furs.

"You don't ..." he started, choking on it, his hands fisting the furs. "I've never — no one has ever ..."

"I know," I murmured against his hip bone. "That's why."

I took him in my mouth.

The sound he made wasn't human. A raw, guttural cry that tore from his chest and bounced off the stone walls. His hips bucked, involuntary, uncontrollable, and I pressed my hands against his thighs and held him down and worked him slowly. Learning the shape of him. The weight, the heat, the way his body responded to pressure and the flat of my tongue.

He lasted less than a minute.

His hand found my hair, not gripping, just holding on, and his body fractured, hands fisting my hair.

"Talia, I'm going to, you need to ..."

I didn't pull away.

He came with a shout that split him in half. His body arched off the bed and his hand tightened in my hair and I kept my mouth on him through every wave until his body went limp and his hand fell away and his chest heaved.

I lifted my head. He was staring at the ceiling with his mouth open and his eyes glassy, a man who'd just had his mind wiped clean.

"What ..." He swallowed. "What did you ..."

"Took what I wanted," I replied, wiping my mouth with the back of my hand.

He covered his face with both hands and made a sound that was half laugh and half sob.

Then he went still and dropped his hands, his eyes found mine and they weren't glassy anymore. They were burning. The amber had swallowed everything and the pupils had gone narrow and dark and the look on his face was nothing I'd seen before.

This was the wolf.

He moved before I could react.

His hands closed around my waist and I was on my back before I understood what had happened, lifted, turned, put down on the furs with a strength that made my weight feel like nothing. My head hit the pillow and he was already pushing my thighs apart with his shoulders, already settling between my legs, already lowering his mouth with a single-mindedness that left no room for asking.

His mouth found me and the sound that came out of him was a growl, low and sustained and vibrating against the most sensitive part of my body. This wasn't the careful, searching tongue from the first time. This was instinct. The wolf knew what it wanted and it wanted to devour me.

His tongue was broad and flat and relentless, stroking with a pressure that made my back arch off the furs. He gripped my thighs and spread them wider and buried his face between them and ate me like a man who'd been starving for decades and had finally found sustenance.

I couldn't think. Couldn't see. The pleasure was savage — nothing gentle, nothing tentative, just his mouth and his tongue and the growl that never stopped vibrating through me. He found the rhythm that made me cry out and locked onto it with predatory focus, driving it home again and again.

My hands found his hair. Twisted. Pulled. He groaned

against me and the vibration sent a spike of pleasure so sharp I screamed and my hips lifted off the bed and he followed, his hands sliding under me, lifting me to his mouth, holding me suspended between his palms and his tongue while my legs shook.

I came so hard I lost time. One moment I was arching off the bed with his name tearing out of me and the next I was flat on my back with the aftershocks rolling through me and his mouth still on me, gentler now, lapping, tasting, that low growl still rumbling.

He wasn't finished.

He rose up from between my thighs and his body covered mine and his face was above me, flushed and wrecked and his beard glistening wet with me, the coarse hair dark and slick from chin to throat. He didn't wipe it away. Didn't seem to know or care. His mouth found mine and I could taste myself on him, sharp and salt, and feel the wet scratch of his beard against my face. The rawness of it, the animal intimacy of kissing a man still wearing the evidence of what he'd just done, made something deep in my belly clench hard.

His hips pressed against mine and he was hard again, impossibly hard, and his eyes were still burning with that amber-swallowed look that was all wolf.

"I need ..." he started.

"Take it," I told him.

The last restraint snapped loose.

He thrust into me in one stroke, no guidance, no hesitation, instinct finding the angle that nature had designed, and the sound we both made filled the cottage. He didn't wait for me to set the pace. The wolf had taken the reins and it drove his hips with a rhythm that was primal and deep and exactly what my body was screaming for.

His wet beard dragged against my throat as his mouth worked along my neck, not kissing, just tasting, his teeth scraping and his tongue following. I could feel the slickness of his beard leaving traces of me on my own skin and the filthy intimacy of it made my hips lift to meet every thrust.

"Harder," I gasped, and the word came out before I could catch it.

He obeyed. His hips slammed into mine and I felt every inch of him, deep, deeper, finding places that hadn't been touched in sixteen years, hadn't been touched ever, because William had been gentle and careful and this was neither of those things and my body was singing with it.

This wasn't the trembling virgin who'd cried the first time. This was the animal underneath, and it was magnificent.

He pulled out and I made a sound of protest. Desperate, needy, furious at the loss. But his hands were already turning me and I was on my stomach before I understood what had happened. Flipped like I weighed nothing. Like my body was a thing he could arrange however he wanted.

"Yes," I breathed into the furs. "Yes."

He entered me from behind and the depth of it made us both cry out. His hand found my hair, twisted into it, pulled, arching my back until the stretch ran from my scalp down my spine, and his other arm wrapped under my hips and lifted them and the angle was devastating. Every thrust hitting a spot that sent sparks cascading through my vision.

His beard scraped against the back of my neck, rough and still damp, and his breath came hot and ragged, punctuated by sounds that weren't words, growls and snarls and the occasional broken syllable of my name. I could feel his body changing against mine, not fully shifting, but the edges of it, the heat intensifying, the muscles hardening, the teeth against my skin growing sharper.

His hand twisted harder in my hair and I moaned and pressed back against him. The pleasure was building again, waves stacking faster than I could process. The pull on my scalp and the depth of him and the wet scrape of his beard against my nape and the growl rumbling from his chest into my spine, all of it feeding into the same tightening coil.

I liked it. Liked it so much it frightened me, the fist in my hair, the weight of his body driving mine into the furs, the rawness of being taken by something that was more than a man. I wanted more of it. Wanted him to pull harder and thrust deeper and lose himself completely.

"Don't hold back," I told him, muffled by the furs. "I can take it."

He snarled against the back of my neck and his hips found another gear, harder, faster, his grip on my hair tightening until the pain bloomed bright at my scalp and fed straight into the pleasure building at the base of my spine.

"Talia ..." My name mangled by teeth that weren't quite human. "The bite. I can't hold ..."

"Do it," I gasped. "Now."

His hand released my hair and found my right shoulder instead, not because I'd told him to, but because the wolf knew where it wanted to mark. His fingers dug into the flesh, holding me still. His mouth opened against the muscle where neck met shoulder, I felt the heat of his breath, the wet scratch of his beard, the points of teeth that were too sharp, too long, pressing dents into my skin.

He thrust deep, once, twice, and on the third his teeth sank in.

The pain was sharp and bright and real. It cut through the pleasure and then fused with it, the two braiding together into something that had no name. His teeth were in my flesh, deeper than human teeth could go, and I felt the bond snap into place, not gradually, not gently, but like a door kicked open from both sides at once.

And I could feel him.

Everything. All at once.

His pleasure, a wave so vast it nearly drowned us both. His love, older than I'd understood, deeper than I'd believed, a river flowing since boyhood without once changing course. His terror that the teeth were too deep. His triumph that they were exactly deep enough. The wolf howling inside him with a joy so fierce it brought tears to my eyes.

And a sensation I hadn't expected. Being inside me, felt

from his side. The tight, wet heat of my body around his. The pull of it. The way it felt to him. Overwhelming, sacred, like being allowed inside a temple he'd spent his whole life circling from the outside.

The orgasm detonated through us both.

His poured into me and mine poured into him and the combined force arched my spine and tore a sound from my throat I'd never made, raw and animal and completely beyond control. His body locked behind mine, teeth still buried in my shoulder, his fist finding my hair again and gripping hard and I came with his teeth in my flesh and his hand in my hair and his body buried inside mine and I was pinned and claimed and completely, devastatingly his.

Everything amplified, his pleasure feeding mine feeding his in a loop with no beginning and no end. I could feel him pulsing inside me and feel what that pulsing felt like from his side, the release so intense it bordered on agony, the relief of a man who'd been clenching every muscle for years finally letting go.

I was crying. He was crying. I could feel his tears before I felt them hot against the back of my neck, sliding from his eyes and mixing with the blood from the bite and the dampness of his beard.

When it passed, when the waves retreated and the bond settled from a roar to a hum, his teeth released my shoulder. His tongue found the wound immediately, lapping with slow, careful strokes that made me shudder. The contrast between the savagery of the bite and the tenderness of his tongue cracked open a place in my chest I didn't know how to close again.

His hand loosened in my hair. His fingers combed through the strands. Gentle now, untangling the knots his fist had made, smoothing the hair from my face. The wolf was receding. The man returning. I could feel it through the bond. The wildness pulling back like a tide, leaving behind a man who was awed and shaking and desperately grateful.

He was still inside me. Still trembling. His beard was a mess — wet with me, streaked with blood from the bite, pressed against the nape of my neck where he'd buried his face. His body came in shuddering waves that I felt in my own chest as much as through his body.

"Talia," he breathed. Wrecked and raw and shaking against me. "I can feel you."

"I know." I pressed my face into the furs. "I can feel you too."

His heartbeat, wild and gradually slowing. His love, vast and warm, so close I could touch it. His fear that he'd been too rough. That the wolf had crossed a line.

I reached back and found his hand and laced my fingers through his and squeezed.

"You didn't hurt me," I told him before he could ask. "I liked it. All of it."

Relief flooded the bond so hard it made my eyes sting. The knot of shame unwound. The terror dissolved. A fierce bright joy rushed in to fill the space. He'd been so afraid.

Even in the grip of the wolf, some part of him had been terrified that he was becoming his father.

He wasn't. The difference was as clear as two different heartbeats. Erik's hunger had been consumption, a mouth that only knew how to swallow. Dietrich's was devotion, a hunger that wanted to give as much as it took, that trembled with the privilege of being allowed to want.

"The hair," he managed, his fingers still combing through it. "I didn't mean to — the wolf just ..."

"I liked it," I repeated firmly. "The hair. The wolf. Being flipped and held down. All of it."

Shock poured through the bond — genuine astonishment that the roughness was what I'd liked best. Old shame rearranged itself inside him.

He eased out of me, carefully, slowly, and the loss echoed from both sides of the bond. The emptiness. The cold air replacing his heat. He made a small sound that matched mine.

He gathered me against him. Turned me so we were face to face, lying on our sides in the furs. His beard was a disaster — dark with moisture, streaked with blood. His eyes were amber fading back to their usual shade, the wolf settling deeper behind them.

I cupped his face in my hands. Felt the wet coarseness of his beard against my palms. The last of his fear dissolved between one breath and the next, and what remained was just us, two people in the furs with a bond humming between them and a bite throbbing on my shoulder and the taste of each other on their mouths.

"I love you," I told him.

"I know. I can feel it. I love you too," he replied.

We lay there while our bodies settled. I could sense his awareness of me, my exhaustion, my satisfaction, the pleasant ache between my thighs, the sting of the bite, the deep contentment that had settled into my bones like warmth after years of cold.

He pulled the furs over us and pressed his mouth against the bite one more time, gentle, reverent.

"The mating," I murmured after a long time. My fingers traced a scar on his chest, following it absently, learning the texture. "That's different. That's the wolf fully."

"Yes," he confirmed. His fingers found the bite on my shoulder and traced around it. "The claiming is the bond. The mating is everything else. The full shift. The power transfer. The knot." His breath caught. "It has to be the full moon. I'd be in the form between, not full wolf, not fully human. And your Forceweaving would flow into me."

"Strong enough to beat your father?"

"Maybe," he admitted. "With your power and mine together, maybe."

"But you won't ask for it," I concluded.

"The mating will be your choice," he confirmed. "The same way the claiming was."

I kissed him quiet. Pressed my mouth against his until

he stopped talking and the bond settled between us like a living thing finding its resting place.

"When is the next full moon?" I asked against his lips.

I felt the answer before he gave it, fear and hope and hunger intertwined.

"Three days," he whispered.

I laced my fingers through his. Felt the bite throbbing on my shoulder in the same rhythm.

"Three days," I repeated. "Train me until then. And when the moon rises ..."

I didn't finish. I didn't have to because he felt the rest, the intention, the decision, the fierce wanting that had nothing to do with strategy and everything to do with him.

His arms tightened around me. I felt him fighting the hope. And then I felt the moment he stopped fighting and let it bloom, cautious and fragile and bright.

"Together," he finished.

"Together," I agreed.

The new door held. Erik's claw marks scarred the wood. And between us, the bond hummed, warm and alive, carrying his heartbeat to me and mine to him.

Three days until the full moon.

Three days to become strong enough to kill a monster.

And in the space between now and then, I lay in the arms of a man who was also a wolf, with his teeth marks on my shoulder and his love in my blood, and I felt, for the first time since I'd been driven into this forest, not just safe.

Ready.

Chapter Twenty-One

Three days passed in a fever of preparation.

We trained from dawn until my hands shook. At night, the bond widened between us, and his wolf pressed closer to the surface with every hour. By the third morning, I could feel the full moon in his blood like a second pulse beneath my own.

"Tonight." He stood at the window, his back to me, his fingers gripping the sill.

I'd been watching him all morning. The way he couldn't sit still, couldn't focus, couldn't keep his hands from clenching and unclenching at his sides. I could feel a restless current churning beneath his skin, energy that pulsed and receded and pulsed again, tidal, as if the wolf inside him was breathing and pressing against the walls of his body.

The full moon. I'd felt it building in him for days, each night the wolf closer to the surface, the amber in his eyes brighter, the heat pouring off his skin hotter. Each night his hands gripping me harder than he meant to, the growl creeping into every sound he made when I arched beneath him, the chains on the wolf stretching thinner.

"I need you to understand what tonight means," he continued, still facing the window. "What it will actually be. Not the mechanics. I've told you those. The reality."

"Then tell me the reality," I replied from the bed, pulling grandmother's dress over my head.

He turned. His eyes were already changing — the amber flickering, the wolf pressing close behind them in a way I hadn't seen during daylight before.

"It won't be me," he warned. "Not the way you know me. The shifted form is ..." He searched for the words. "Bigger. Stronger. More wolf than man. The mind is still mine but the instincts are louder. The body is ..."

"I saw your father shift," I reminded him. "In the cottage. I know what ..."

"This is different," he cut in, and something in his tone made me stop. "My father shifted into a full wolf. The mating form is between. Half and half. Standing upright but wrong. Clawed. Fanged. Covered in fur." He forced the next part out. "You've never seen anything like it. And when you do, every instinct you have, every blood-keeper instinct, every survival instinct, is going to scream at you to run."

I felt the fear underneath his words, not fear of the mating but fear of my face when I saw what he became. Fear that the woman who'd said *I love you, man and wolf both* would look at the thing standing in front of her and take it back.

"I won't run," I assured him.

"You might," he countered quietly. "And if you do, if you change your mind at any point, I need to know. Scream it at me through the bond and I'll stop. I'll find a way to stop."

"And if I don't want you to stop?"

His nostrils flared, and I felt his spike of hunger so sharp it made my breath catch.

"Then you need to understand how it works," he went on, the wolf pressing closer to the surface with every word. "The wolf doesn't make love, Talia. It mates. There's a difference. The instinct is, predator and prey. The chase. The catch. The claiming of territory." His eyes held mine. "It will want to chase you. It will want you to run. That's how it works, the blood gets up, the scent gets stronger, and the wolf needs to hunt what it's about to take."

My mouth had gone dry. My heart was beating in places it shouldn't have been, low in my belly, between my thighs, in the palms of my hands.

"You're telling me to run from you," I stated.

"I'm telling you it will feel like running from a predator," he clarified. "Because that's what the wolf is. What I'll be. And the fear will be real, your body won't know the difference between danger and ..." He stopped. His hands were shaking. "I need you to know what you're walking into."

"I know what I'm walking into," I told him. "I've dreamed about it."

His eyes snapped to mine. Recognition hit him so hard he went still. The shock of it rippled between us. The dream. The black wolf in the moonlit clearing. The chase through the forest. The cloak and the bare skin and the pleasure that had shattered me awake on the ice.

He'd felt that dream every night since the claiming. Had felt me dreaming it again and again, the wolf and the woman and the forest and the wanting. He knew I wasn't afraid of it. He knew I craved it.

That was what terrified him.

"When the moon rises," he managed, his hands white-knuckled on the table edge, "I'll go outside. I'll shift. And I'll wait." He swallowed. "If you want this, when you want this, come into the forest. I'll smell you before I see you. The wolf will find you."

"And then?" I pressed.

"And then it begins," he replied. "However it begins. Whatever happens between the predator and the prey in the dark."

The room was very warm. The fire danced in the hearth. His hunger and mine were feeding each other in a loop that was getting harder to break. "I'll be there," I promised.

He closed his eyes. Nodded once. Then he crossed to the door and went outside to train me for the last time before the moon changed everything.

. . .

The hours passed like water through a cracked bowl.

We didn't speak about what was coming. Every time we tried, the bond flooded with so much want that words became impossible. I ran through one last training session in the clearing, the Forceweaving sharp and steady, three hits in five at full speed. His grin when the third blast caught him square made the bond sing.

By late afternoon the restlessness in him had become visible. His skin flushed, his movements too fast, his eyes flickering between amber and gold with increasing frequency. He kept scenting the air when he thought I wasn't looking. Kept turning toward me like a compass needle.

I bathed while there was still daylight. Heated water in the tub and scrubbed my skin clean and washed my hair and let it dry by the fire in dark waves that curled against my shoulders. I didn't braid it. I didn't pin it back. I left it loose the way the dream had shown me. Wild and free and smelling of nothing but clean skin and the faintest trace of grandmother's soap.

When dusk came, he stood.

I felt the shift beginning. Not physical yet but internal, the wolf rising up inside him like a tide, pressing against the surface, demanding release. His eyes had gone full amber. He was deep and slow and controlled in the way of a man holding a door shut with everything he had.

"I'm going." He was already changing. Deeper in the

chest, the edges of him roughening into a register below human speech.

"I know," I replied.

He crossed to the door. Stopped with his hand on the latch. Didn't turn around.

"Talia."

"Hmm."

"The cloak." A pause. "Wear the cloak."

Then he opened the door and stepped into the dusk and I heard him walking toward the tree line and then I heard the cracking, distant, muffled by the trees, but unmistakable. Bones breaking and reforming. The wet sound of a body being unmade and remade in a new shape.

A howl rose from the forest. Long and deep and resonant with invitation. Not grief or hunger or warning. A wolf calling to its mate across the dark.

I stood by the fire and let the sound move through me and felt a trembling inside my chest. His wolf reaching for me, pulling at a place deep behind my ribs.

I undressed.

Pulled the white dress over my head and folded it carefully on the bed. Pulled the shift off after it. Stood naked in the firelight and felt the warmth play across my skin and the cold press at the edges and the bite on my shoulder throb with the rhythm of his heartbeat.

I picked up the red cloak.

Drew it around my shoulders and fastened it at my throat. The wool was rough against my bare skin, my nipples, my stomach, the backs of my thighs. Red wool over naked flesh. The same image from the dream. The same woman walking into the same forest to find the same wolf.

I pushed the door open and stepped into the dark.

The cold tore through me. The snow burned the soles of my bare feet and the wind cut through every gap in the cloak and found the bare skin underneath. The moon was rising above the tree line, full and huge and silver-white, casting shadows so sharp they looked carved into the snow.

I walked toward the forest.

My breath clouded in the freezing air. My feet left prints in the fresh snow, bare toes, arched soles, a trail that anything with a nose could follow. I sensed the moment he caught my scent, a spike of awareness, sharp and electric, the wolf's attention locking onto me like a predator sighting prey.

The tree line swallowed me. The moonlight filtered through the bare branches and turned everything silver and black and the shadows were deep enough to hide anything. The forest was utterly silent — not the peaceful silence of sleeping woods but the held-breath silence of something watching.

I kept walking. Deeper. My feet crunching on snow that no one else had walked on. The cloak catching on branches and pulling free and catching again. The cold burning my bare legs and my bare feet and the exposed skin at my throat where the cloak parted with each step.

A branch cracked somewhere to my left.

I stopped. My heart hammered against my ribs so hard I could feel it in my teeth. His presence, close, closer than I'd realized, but muffled now, filtered through the animal in him that made the familiar contours of his mind harder to read.

Another crack. Behind me this time. A low sound. Not a growl, not quite, but deeper. A rumble that I felt in the ground beneath my feet before I heard it with my ears. The sound of a massive, hungry body drawing breath.

I turned slowly.

The werewolf stood between two oaks twenty feet away.

My legs nearly gave out.

This wasn't the black wolf I'd seen fighting Erik. That had been an animal, terrifying but recognizable, a creature that moved on four legs and had a shape my mind could process. This was different entirely. A form my mind recoiled from, a wrongness that triggered every survival instinct I possessed and set them all screaming at once.

It stood upright. Seven feet tall at least, maybe more, its shoulders so broad they blocked the moonlight between the trees. Its body was covered in black fur, dense and coarse, rippling over muscles that bunched and shifted beneath the pelt with every breath. Its arms hung at its sides, long and thick, ending in hands that were wrong, too large, the fingers tipped with claws that curved like skinning knives and gleamed wet in the moonlight.

Its legs were bent wrong. Jointed like a wolf's hind legs, digitigrade, the knees reversed, the massive feet ending in clawed toes that gripped the frozen ground. It stood the way a man stands but nothing about it was human. It was a wolf forced into a man's posture, or a man twisted into a wolf's shape, and the result belonged in neither world and was terrifying in both.

I'd seen this shape before. In the clearing, the night I ran. The gray wolf had stood like this. The same impossible height, the same backward legs, the same clawed hands that weren't hands at all.

Its head was a wolf's head on a man's neck. Elongated muzzle, ears pricked forward, lips pulled back from teeth that were longer than my fingers and gleaming with saliva. The fur around its muzzle was dark and sleek and its nostrils flared wide, scenting the air with slow, deliberate breaths that steamed in the cold.

And its eyes. Golden. Burning. Fixed on me with an intensity that went beyond hunger, beyond desire, beyond anything I had a name for. The bond confirmed what I already knew. Dietrich was in there, behind those eyes, thinking and feeling and aware. But the wolf was driving now. The wolf was in control. And the wolf was looking at me the way Erik had looked at me in that clearing. Except this wasn't horror. This was older and darker and infinitely more dangerous.

I was trembling. Not from the cold.

Every blood-keeper instinct I possessed was shrieking at me to run. My legs wanted to run. My hands wanted to throw Forceweaving. My body was flooded with adrenaline so potent I could taste the copper of it on my tongue. This was the thing my bloodline had been fleeing from for centuries. This was the predator that had been built to hunt us down and drag us back and take what it wanted.

And it was standing between me and the only way out of the forest.

In my mind I reached for him. Found the Dietrich beneath the wolf, a steady presence burning like a candle flame inside a furnace. He was there. He was aware. And he was holding the wolf back with everything he had, giving me time to choose.

Run or stay. I'm here either way. I love you either way.

The thought came — not words exactly, more like a feeling shaped into meaning. His love, vast and unwavering, wrapped around the wolf's hunger like hands around a throat.

The werewolf didn't move. Just stood there, breathing, watching, its massive chest rising and falling. Waiting. Patient in the way only a predator can be patient, the patience of a being that knows its prey can't outrun it and is content to let the chase begin on the prey's terms.

I looked at it. At the claws and the teeth and the impossible body and the golden eyes that held the man I loved inside a monster's skull.

My hands were shaking. My knees were shaking. Every nerve I had was on fire with fear so primal it predated language.

And beneath the fear, beneath the adrenaline and the

survival instinct and the blood-keeper's ancestral terror, my body was responding in ways that had nothing to do with danger and everything to do with the dream I'd been having since the first night in the cottage. The heat gathering low in my belly. The pulse between my thighs. The cloak suddenly too rough against my nipples.

The words came from a place I didn't know I had. From the cloak and the forest and the wolf and the woman standing barefoot in the snow.

"What big eyes you have," I whispered.

The werewolf went still. Its ears twitched forward. Through the bond, a flicker of recognition from the man buried inside the beast.

All the better to see you with.

I took a step toward it. My bare feet crunched in the snow and the cold bit my soles and I didn't care. I was looking at the claws, the curved black hooks that could open me from throat to navel with a single swipe.

"What big claws you have."

All the better to hold you with.

Another step. Close enough now to feel the heat pouring off its body, close enough to see the saliva gleaming on those teeth, each one longer than my finger, each one built to tear and grip and never let go.

"What big teeth you have."

All the better to eat you with.

Its muzzle lowered toward my face. I felt the hot exhale against my mouth, the wet heat of it, and then its tongue dragged across my lower lip in a single broad stroke that buckled my knees and pulled a sound from my chest I'd never heard myself make.

"What big tongue you have," I breathed.

All the better to taste you with.

I unfastened the clasp at my throat and the cloak fell.

Red wool pooled around my bare feet on the white snow. I stood naked in the moonlight, pale skin and dark hair and the bite mark on my right shoulder that throbbed with his heartbeat. The cold cut into me like glass but I barely felt it because the werewolf's eyes had dropped from my face to my body and the sound it made, a low, shuddering rumble that vibrated through the ground and up through my bare feet and into my bones, set every hair on my body upright and sent a flood of wet heat between my thighs that I couldn't have stopped if I'd wanted to.

It scented the air. Its nostrils flared wide and I knew, knew with absolute certainty, that it could smell my arousal. Could taste it on the wind the way Erik had tasted my Forceweaving. Could track the exact chemical signature of a woman's want across miles of frozen forest.

The werewolf took a step forward. The ground shook beneath its weight. Its claws left deep furrows in the frozen earth.

I ran.

I didn't decide to. My body made the choice — the blood-keeper instinct and the prey instinct and the woman's instinct all firing at once, sending me spinning on my heel and sprinting into the dark forest as fast as my bare feet could carry me. Branches whipped my face and roots grabbed at my ankles and the snow burned my soles and the moonlight turned the trees to silver bars of a cage that was closing around me.

Behind me, the sound of pursuit. Not footsteps. Heavier, faster, the drumming of massive clawed feet on frozen ground that ate the distance between us with every stride. The crashing of branches as a body too large for the gaps between trees forced its way through. The sound of it. Deep and rhythmic and hungry, getting closer with every heartbeat.

The dream. This was the dream. Except the dream had been warm and painless and tinged with the haze of sleep and this was real. The cold searing my bare skin, the branches drawing blood across my arms and face, the terror so sharp I could taste it, and underneath the terror the arousal burning so hot it was making me dizzy.

I could feel him. Not just behind me but around me, his awareness encompassing mine, the wolf's senses mapping the forest in ways I couldn't fathom. He knew where I was going before I did. Knew every turn I'd take before I took it. Was letting me run because the chase was part of it. The blood rising, the scent intensifying, the prey's fear and the predator's hunger building together toward an end neither of us could stop.

I burst into a clearing and the moonlight hit me full and

bright and I was naked and silver-skinned and gasping and the werewolf broke through the tree line behind me.

It was faster than I'd imagined. It crossed the clearing in three strides and its arm caught me around the waist and lifted me off the ground like I weighed nothing, nothing at all, a doll, a leaf, and pulled me back against its chest.

The fur was coarse and hot against my bare skin. The arm around my waist was thick as a tree limb, corded with muscle, the claws curving carefully away from my flesh. Its other hand came up and gathered my hair, all of it, one fistful, and pulled my head back against its shoulder, baring my throat to the moonlight.

It pressed its muzzle against my neck and inhaled.

The sound it made, a rumble so deep it bypassed my ears and went straight into my chest cavity, made my legs give out entirely. I sagged against it and felt the hard length of it against my lower back, hot even through the fur, and my body clenched around nothing and the whimper that came out of me was the most honest sound I'd ever made.

Dietrich. Still there. Still aware. His love wrapping around the wolf's hunger, not fighting it anymore but braiding with it, the two of them looking out through the same golden eyes at the woman trembling against their chest.

I'm here. I'm here. I love you. I'm here.

"I know," I whispered into the cold air.

The werewolf lowered me to the ground. Face down on the cloak — the red wool spread across the snow where I'd dropped it, and he'd carried me back to it, had circled back to the place where I'd stood and laid me down on the only soft surface in the frozen forest.

Even now. Even with the wolf driving. He'd brought me back to the cloak so I wouldn't be bare against the snow.

The tears came and I let them because they weren't fear. They were the realization that the man inside the monster was still choosing me, still protecting me, still thinking about my comfort while his body was something out of a nightmare and his instincts were screaming at him to take.

His weight settled over my back. Fur against bare skin — rough and hot, impossibly hot, the heat of him pouring through the pelt like a furnace. I could feel the musculature of his chest against my shoulder blades, the power in it, the coiled, barely restrained violence of a body built for one purpose.

His muzzle pushed between my thighs from behind.

I gasped and my hands fisted in the red wool. His tongue, broader and rougher than the human version, textured in ways that made my nerve endings detonate, lapped against me in a long, slow stroke that dragged a moan from somewhere I didn't know existed. He tasted me the way he'd tasted me in human form, with that same focused, devoted attention, except the wolf's tongue was longer and his mouth was wider and the sounds he made against my flesh were animal.

He lapped at me until my thighs were shaking and my face was pressed into the cloak and I was making sounds I didn't recognize as my own voice. I could feel what my taste did to him, the wolf intoxicated by it. The predator had caught its prey and was savoring it before the final act.

Then his weight shifted. His body rose over mine, the fur dragging against my spine, and I felt him, the wolf's version of him, harder and larger than the human, hot against the backs of my thighs.

Ready?

"Yes," I breathed into the cloak.

He pressed forward.

The stretch was — I cried out. Pressed my face into the wool and gripped the cloak with both fists and tried to hold still through the overwhelming fullness of it. Larger than the human form. Thicker. My body strained to accommodate and the burn was sharp but the bond was there, pouring his awareness into me, his care, his restraint, the wolf fighting its own instinct to thrust because the man inside it was monitoring my pain and refusing to move until it eased.

I breathed. The burn faded. The fullness remained — immense and stretching and so deep I could feel him in places I didn't know I had.

"Move," I managed.

He moved.

The first thrust drove the air from my lungs. The second made me scream into the cloak. The third found the angle that turned the screaming into something else entirely, pleasure so sharp it whited out my vision, crashing through me in a wave that the bond amplified and sent back to him, and

I felt his answering surge of pleasure pour through the connection and feed my own in a loop that built exponentially with every stroke.

His clawed hands gripped my hips, careful even now, the razor edges turned away from my skin, holding me with devastating strength that lifted my hips higher and changed the angle and the new depth drew a sound from both of us that the forest had never heard before.

I could feel everything from his side, the tight, slick heat of my body around him, the intoxicating flood of my scent, the pleasure building at the base of his spine in waves that matched mine. And threaded through all of it, Dietrich. His mind clear and present behind the wolf's golden eyes, feeling everything I felt, loving me through every thrust, his awareness wrapped around mine like a hand cradling a flame.

His pace was relentless. The wolf's rhythm — nothing like the man's careful strokes, nothing learned or deliberate. This was instinct pure and absolute, the ancient engine driving the act with a force that shook the ground beneath us and sent snow cascading from the branches overhead.

His fist closed in my hair and pulled. My back arched and a cry tore from my throat and the pleasure of it, the stretch in my scalp, the vulnerability, the surrender, fed straight into the coil building at the base of my spine.

I was close. So close. The bond was amplifying everything — every sensation doubled, every wave of pleasure cresting higher because I could feel his building alongside mine, the two of us climbing the same peak from different sides.

Then I felt something else. The base of him swelling where our bodies joined. Growing thicker with each thrust. Catching at my entrance, pressing, stretching.

The knot.

The stretch intensified, wider, fuller, my body straining at its limit. My hands tore at the cloak and the burn was back but the pleasure was there too, tangled with it, the two inseparable, and I could sense his desperation, the wolf needing to lock, needing to seal, needing to complete the bond in the oldest way it knew.

"Let it," I gasped. "I want it. Let it."

He thrust deep and the knot pushed inside.

My body locked around it. The fullness was beyond anything — a pressure so complete it left no room for thought or breath or fear. Only sensation. Only the stretch and the heat and the pulse of him inside me and the bond between us blazing so bright I could almost see it, a golden thread connecting his heart to mine.

The power came.

I felt it leave me, not painfully, not like draining, but like exhaling. Like releasing a breath I'd been holding my whole life. My Forceweaving poured into him, warm and golden and alive, flowing from my blood into his through the place where our bodies were locked together. I could feel it filling him, lighting him up from the inside, making him more than he'd been, stronger, faster, the wolf's already formidable power amplified by the living magic in my veins.

He howled. The sound split the night — not pain, not triumph, but something between the two. The sound of a creature being remade by something it hadn't known it was missing.

The orgasm hit us both at the same time. It was annihilation. His pleasure and mine colliding and fusing and detonating in a blast that wiped out everything, thought, sight, sound, self. I screamed and he howled and the trees shook and the snow fell from every branch in the clearing and for a moment, one blazing, endless moment, I couldn't tell where I ended and he began. We were the same thing. The same creature. The same heart beating in two bodies that were locked together on a red cloak in the moonlight while power poured between them like light through a broken window.

The knot pulsed inside me. Each pulse sent another wave crashing through us both, aftershock after aftershock, the bond carrying them back and forth until they faded into tremors and the tremors faded into stillness.

He collapsed around me. His massive body curled protectively over mine, the fur hot against my sweat-soaked skin, his arms pulling me against his chest. The knot held us together — locked, inseparable, exactly as he'd warned.

His mind, clearer now, the wolf settling, the man surfacing. Wonder and love and a fierce protective tenderness that felt like being wrapped in something warm and indestructible.

Are you all right?

I pressed back against the wall of fur and muscle behind me. Felt his heartbeat through his chest, rapid, powerful, vibrating through my spine.

"More than all right," I whispered.

The knot. Does it hurt?

"It's ..." I shifted slightly and felt the fullness and the pulse and the strange, deep pleasure of being stretched around something that wasn't letting go. "It's a lot. But it doesn't hurt."

His muzzle pressed against the bite on my shoulder. His tongue, rough, warm, impossibly gentle, traced the claiming mark.

I can feel your power in me. The Forceweaving. It's. I don't have words for what it feels like.

"Strong?" I murmured.

Alive. Wonder colored the thought. *Like a fire that's been burning since before I was born. I can feel it in my bones. In my blood. You're in my blood, Talia.*

The tears came softly. Not from pain or fear. From the enormity of what we'd done, two creatures from opposite ends of a chain that was built to keep them apart, choosing each other, locking together, pouring power and love through a bond that shouldn't have existed between predator and prey.

We lay on the red cloak in the moonlit clearing while the

knot held and the power hummed and the forest stood witness. His body curled around mine — massive and furred and wrong by every measure of the world we'd been born into, and more right than anything I'd ever felt.

His thoughts drifted to me in fragments, not words but images, sensations, the wolf's version of language. The warmth of my body against his fur. The scent of my hair. The taste of me still on his tongue. The steady, living pulse of my Forceweaving flowing through his veins like a second heartbeat.

And beneath all of it — a single, clear thought that needed no translation:

Mine. Yours. Ours. Forever.

I laced my fingers through the thick fur at his forearm and held on.

"Yours," I whispered. "Ours. Forever."

The moon moved across the sky above us. The knot softened gradually, releasing its hold in slow increments, the fullness easing, my body adjusting to each small change. When it finally released, the loss was sudden and sharp and he whined behind me, a high, uncertain sound that was nothing like the monstrous creature he'd been an hour ago.

He shifted. The cracking was quieter this time, gentler somehow, the bones reshaping with less violence than I'd witnessed before. The fur receded. The massive body compressed. And then it was Dietrich behind me, naked and human and trembling, his arms still around me, his face pressed against the bite on my shoulder.

"Talia," he managed, wrecked and shaking against me. "I can feel everything. Your power. Your heart. Every breath you take. It's ..."

He couldn't finish. He just held me tighter and pressed his face into my hair and shook.

I turned in his arms and looked at him in the moonlight. His face was pale and damp with sweat and his eyes were amber fading back to their usual shade and his expression was the face of a man who'd just been handed the keys to a kingdom he'd believed was imaginary.

"Strong enough to beat your father?" I asked.

He was quiet for a moment. I felt him reaching inward, testing the new power, feeling the Forceweaving running through his blood alongside the wolf's own magic. The two forces braided together — mine and his, blood-keeper and werewolf, the hunted and the hunter, woven into something that was neither and both.

"Yes," he confirmed, and I perceived the truth of it, not arrogance but certainty. A certainty that comes from knowing exactly what you are and exactly what you can do and being ready to prove it. "With your power and mine together, yes. I can beat him."

I kissed him. Tasted moonlight and sweat and the salt of tears on his lips.

"Then let him come," I declared.

We walked back to the cottage naked in the moonlight, his arm around my shoulders, my body aching in places I hadn't known existed and thrumming with a satisfaction so deep it felt geological. The red cloak was bundled under his other arm, stained with snow and sweat and the evidence of what we'd done, the red that every woman in my line had worn, carrying one more story in its color.

He stopped walking. Pulled me against him in the snow and held me with his face buried in my hair.

"I spent twenty-two years walking these woods telling myself it was duty," he murmured against my temple. "Patrol. Protection. But the wolf never stopped circling back to this cottage. Every night, ending up at the same door. I thought something was wrong with me." His arms tightened. "Turns out it was just looking for you."

The cottage was warm. The fire still burning. The door still holding against the wind with Erik's claw marks scarred into the wood.

He carried me to the bed and cleaned me with warm water and gentle hands and wrapped me in furs and held me against his chest while the bond hummed between us, complete now, fully formed, carrying every heartbeat and every breath and every flicker of thought from one to the other.

I could feel his new strength settling into his bones. My Forceweaving woven into his wolf's power, the two magics fused and multiplied. He was more than he'd been. More than his father. More than any werewolf who'd ever hunted a blood-keeper instead of loving one.

And I was more than I'd been too. The mating hadn't diminished my power, it had deepened it, given it roots that went down through the bond and into his body and drew strength from the connection. I could feel the Forceweaving humming stronger than ever beneath my skin, fed by the bond, amplified by the love.

Erik had drained Sophia because he'd taken her power by force. A leech feeding on stolen blood.

I'd given mine freely. And the giving had made us both stronger.

That was the difference. That was the answer the grimoire had never written down because no blood-keeper had ever survived long enough to discover it. Forced claiming drained. Willing mating amplified. The power didn't diminish when it was given with love, it multiplied.

I pressed my face against Dietrich's chest and listened to his heartbeat, steady and strong and carrying the echo of my own, and felt, for the first time, like we might actually survive what was coming.

Erik had Sophia's stolen Sensing.

We had something he'd never had. Something he'd never understand.

A bond built on choice instead of chains.

And when the gray wolf came for the power he craved so much, he would find out exactly how much that difference was worth.

Chapter Twenty-Two

Weeks passed. The claw marks on the door went untouched, no new gouges, no fresh scratches, no territorial markings in the snow. The forest had gone quiet in a way that should have felt like relief but sat in my chest like a held breath.

"Maybe he knows," I ventured one morning, watching Dietrich clean his knife by the fire. "About the claiming. The mating. Maybe he can smell the bond and decided it's not worth the fight."

Dietrich shook his head without looking up. "He knows. He can smell it from miles away, my scent on you, yours in me, the bond between us." The blade stopped moving and he looked at me. "He's known since the night I bit you."

"Then why hasn't he come?" I pressed.

"Because he's cunning." I felt something cold moving beneath his calm, the wolf's unease, a predator's instinct recognizing another predator's patience. "My father doesn't charge into fights he hasn't already won. Twenty-two years feral didn't burn the strategist out of him. It sharpened it." He tested the blade against his thumb. "He's planning something. I just can't see what. The fight nearly killed him too. He's healing from what I did to him. Watching. Learning our patterns. He won't move until he's certain."

He set the knife down. Crossed to where I sat and leaned down and kissed me, slow, thorough.

"I need to check the eastern traps," he murmured against my mouth. "And the perimeter. I don't want him circling close without me knowing."

"Be careful," I told him.

He pulled on his coat and crossed to the door. I felt his alertness sharpen the moment he stepped outside, the wolf rising, the senses expanding. He looked back at me once. The amber in his eyes catching the morning light.

Then he disappeared into the trees.

I watched the space where he'd been. His presence dimmed as he moved further, never gone, just distant, the difference between standing next to a fire and feeling its warmth from the next room.

I turned back to the cottage. Swept the floor. Built up the fire. Checked the food stores and made a mental note about the dried meat. My body still carried the deep, pleasant ache from the night before. The bond throbbed gently in my chest. Dietrich's heartbeat beneath my own.

I hadn't touched the grimoire in weeks. It was still under

the bed where I'd left it before the claiming because after that night I stopped thinking about books and pages and creature entries and honestly I stopped thinking about most things that weren't Dietrich and the bond and the way my body felt like it belonged to me for the first time in my life. But he was out checking the traps and the perimeter and the cottage was quiet and warm and I felt good. Not bracing. Not waiting for something terrible. Just good.

I pulled it out and sat at the table and opened it and turned past everything I already knew. Grandmother's entries, her mother's, the creatures, the werewolves. I got to Sophia's section and expected the blur because that was what always happened, every single time, the ink swimming away from my eyes like the book was pulling it back.

The words were clear. All of them. I could read every line on the page and my hands started shaking so hard I had to flatten them on the table to hold the pages still.

The ice broke on the creek this morning. I heard it through the walls, a sound like glass falling. I closed my eyes and let myself pretend I was standing on the bank with Mama and Red, watching the water come back to life the way it does every spring. Mama would have her sleeves rolled to the elbow. Red would be barefoot already because she never could wait for the ground to warm.

I held the sound as long as I could. Pressed it against my chest and breathed it in. He cannot take what I keep inside my own head. The creek. Mama's hands. The smell of her garden after rain. Red pulling ribbons from my hair and stuffing them into her mouth because everything red belonged to her, even then.

These are mine. He can take my blood and my years and the strength in my bones but he cannot reach the places where I keep the people I love.

I shoved my knuckles against my teeth because my whole face was doing things I couldn't control and I kept going.

I have been thinking about destiny. Mama told me once that our blood chose us before we were born. That we didn't become blood-keepers — we arrived as them, already marked, already carrying the thread that tied us back through the generations to the first woman who bled and the world bent around her.

I used to believe that meant we had no choice. That the blood decided and we simply followed.

I don't believe that anymore.

Destiny is not a road. It is a river. It carries you, yes. But you can still choose which bank you swim toward. You can still choose what you hold onto and what you let the current take. I chose to write the note. I chose to walk out that door. I chose wrong. But I chose. And that matters.

Freedom is not the absence of cages. I know that now better than anyone. Freedom is knowing you would choose differently if you could. Freedom is the choosing itself.

The next entry looked different. The letters were pressed harder into the page and the handwriting was tighter like she'd been pushing the quill down too hard or writing without enough light to see.

We are not the last. I can feel them — not clearly, not the way I feel the village, but like a hum at the edge of hearing. Other women. Other bloodlines. Scattered and hiding and surviving the way we have always survived. Some of them carry gifts I cannot name. Some of them have forgotten what they are. But they are out there. Beyond the forests and the mountains and the borders of every map Mama ever showed me. Others like us. Living. Enduring.

Mama spoke of the Sanguinarians once, late at night when she thought I was sleeping. Old ones. Older than the wolves. They are the ones who made the first werewolves, and they did not stop wanting what they made. She said they would come again. Not soon, they move in centuries the way we move in years, but they would come. And when they did, it would not be for the wolves. It would be for us. For the blood.

If someone reads this and the old ones have not come yet, they will. Prepare. Find the others. You are stronger together than you will ever be alone.

I kept turning pages. Sophia had written for two years in this cottage and she'd filled more pages than I expected. Birds she heard through the boards. The way the light through the cracks changed when the seasons turned. Grandmother's recipe for burn poultice because she was terrified the knowledge would die with her. Wildflowers she couldn't see but could smell through the gaps in the wood.

A dream about the village market where she had to lie still after waking because she couldn't tell which was real. I flipped through every page. Read some, skimmed others, but I checked every one.

Two years of my aunt in her leftward tilting handwriting and not a single mention of Erik in any of it. He got nothing from her.

I was crying. I hadn't noticed when it started but my face was wet and my nose was running and I wiped it with the back of my hand and turned the next page.

Red.

My little Red who pulled the ribbons from my hair.

My heart slammed so hard I felt it in my fingers and my teeth and behind my eyes all at once. She wrote to me. She sat in this room behind these boards and she wrote my name and I touched the ink where she'd written Red and goose-bumps ran up both my arms and down my back and across my chest because she was right there on the page talking to me and I wanted to read every word so badly my whole body ached with it.

Then the hair on the back of my neck stood up and my stomach dropped and I didn't know why. The cottage was quiet. The fire was still popping. Nothing had changed in the room but my body was telling me to move and I'd learned a long time ago not to argue with that feeling because every time I ignored it something terrible happened.

I went to the window and cracked a board enough to see out. The clearing was white. All white except for a trail of red cutting through the snow from the tree line to the cottage door. Blood. I could tell from the color even through the gap in the board.

The red cloak hung from the peg by the door. I grabbed it and pulled it around my shoulders before I even thought about why. Instinct.

I unbolted the door, shoved it open, stepped out.

My foot caught on something. I went down hard on my hands and knees on the doorstep. Cold hit my palms first, then the wet. I looked at my hands. Red. I was kneeling in blood.

My eyes went to the trees. The gray wolf stood at the edge of the clearing between two pines, lips pulled back from his teeth, muzzle dark and wet. Those yellow eyes locked on mine. He wasn't hiding. He wanted me to see him. He wanted me to know.

He turned. Ran into the forest. The trees swallowed him.

My whole body was shaking. I looked down at what I'd tripped on and my brain wouldn't let me understand what I was seeing. A body. Small enough to be a child. My heart was hammering so hard it hurt. My eyes filled up, everything went blurry. I wiped my face with bloody hands trying to see.

No. No no no no no.

I turned the body over.

Thomas. Emma's Thomas. His cap was gone. His hair stuck to his forehead with blood. His neck bent wrong. His eyes closed. He looked like he was sleeping except for the red soaking through his wool shirt and the angle of his neck that no sleeping child would ever have.

I screamed. Grabbed him, pulled him into my lap, held him against my chest. Screamed until my throat tore. He was cold. So cold and so small. His head lolled against my arm because there was nothing holding it up anymore. I was rocking him the way you rock a baby. He wasn't a baby. He was seven years old. He used to call me Auntie. Now he was dead on my doorstep, his blood soaking through grandmother's dress into my skin.

I pushed everything I had toward Dietrich. The blood. The body. The gray wolf's teeth. Thomas's face. The sound coming out of me that didn't sound like me. His shock hit me like a wall. Then his fury. Then he was running. I could feel his legs tearing through the snow, the wolf in him ripping through the underbrush. He was coming but he wasn't here yet. I was alone on the doorstep holding a dead child.

The vision I'd had years ago, before he was even born. A faceless boy with his neck bent wrong and blood in the dirt. I'd buried it the way I'd buried the hanging man. Told myself my sight lied. Told myself it wouldn't come true because I couldn't bear to believe it would. Thomas was born with the same curls and the same face and I'd pushed the knowing down so deep I'd almost convinced myself it wasn't real.

But it was.

I pressed my face against his hair. It smelled like

Emma's soap. She'd washed it that morning, probably. Combed it and smoothed it and sent him off to play without knowing she was sending him to die.

I looked up. Looked past Thomas's body to the snow beyond the doorstep.

The blood trail.

It didn't just lead to my doorstep. It led from the village, through the forest, past every deadfall and ravine, around every obstacle that had kept outsiders lost for decades. A straight, deliberate line of drag marks where something heavy had been pulled through the snow. Small boot prints, Thomas's prints, that cut off abruptly where the dragging began. Where he'd been grabbed. Where he'd been killed.

Erik hadn't just left bait. He'd drawn the villagers a map through woods they'd never been able to navigate. Every drop of Thomas's blood was a breadcrumb leading them straight to me.

A shout carried through the trees. Then another. Men's voices, harsh and overlapping, the sound of a crowd moving fast through the undergrowth. Through the trees I could see torchlight despite the daylight. The crack of boots on frozen ground. Metal catching the weak winter sun.

I looked down at Thomas in my arms. At the blood soaking my dress. At my hands red from cradling him.

They would see exactly what Erik wanted them to see. A witch with a dead boy in her arms.

The mob burst into the clearing.

Klaus led them — fifteen men or more, faces twisted

with the unified fury of a crowd that had already decided guilt. Jakob at his right side. The same Jakob who'd gotten Anna pregnant and then stood with his arms crossed while she drowned. Who'd pointed the finger. Who'd watched the water close over her head and gone home to eat his supper.

Behind them. Emma. Running, her face already crumpling, already seeing the shape in my arms. Heinrich beside her, his face carved from granite.

Emma reached me first. Her grief so profound it was killing her as she ran. She saw Thomas in my arms and I watched the last hope die in her eyes. I stood up cradling her son to give him to her.

"You," she whispered. Then louder, all the rage of a destroyed mother pouring out of her mouth: "YOU!"

Her hand cracked across my face hard enough to snap my head sideways. I tasted blood. Felt my lip split. I didn't let go of Thomas. Didn't drop him or push her away or try to defend myself.

"Emma, please. Thomas was ..." I started.

She slapped me again. Harder. Her palm connected with my cheekbone and stars exploded across my vision. "Don't speak. Don't you dare speak his name!"

"I didn't ..."

Another slap. My lip split further, blood running down my chin, dripping onto Thomas's shirt. I let her hit me. I let her pour it out. What were a few slaps compared to what she was feeling.

Heinrich grabbed Emma's arm and pulled her back. His

eyes devastated. Looking at his son in my arms. At the future that had been stolen.

"I found him like this," I managed, the words distorted by my split lip. "I swear to you, Heinrich. I found him on the doorstep ..."

"Liar!" Klaus shoved through the crowd, his face red with fury. "Look at her! Covered in the boy's blood! Caught in the act! Witch's sacrifice — blood-magic on an innocent child!"

"That's not true..."

"She killed him for her dark rites!" Klaus jabbed a finger at me. "Just like we warned everyone!"

"No!" The word came out as a sob. "Emma, please. You've known me for years. You know I loved Thomas. You know I would never ..."

But Emma wasn't listening. Couldn't listen through the grief that had swallowed her whole. She tore Thomas from my arms with a keening wail that broke something inside me too. Clutched him to her chest and collapsed in the snow, curling around his small body. Heinrich dropped beside her, his arms around both of them. His granite mask cracked as tears spilled down his cheeks.

The mob closed in.

Klaus's followers grabbed my arms. Rough hands. Angry hands. They yanked me to my feet with enough force that something in my shoulder popped. I stumbled, legs weak from kneeling, from shock, from grief.

Someone kicked my feet out from under me. I went down hard. Tasted snow. Tasted blood.

"Hang her!" Klaus's voice rose above Emma's keening, above the angry mutter of men who'd been convinced they were facing a monster. "String the witch up before she can curse us all!"

"Wait ..." I gasped, reaching for my power through the panic. "Please, just listen ..."

A boot caught me in the stomach. All the air rushed out and I curled around the pain, trying to breathe, trying to think. But all I could see was Thomas's face. All I could hear was Emma's wails.

I sent Dietrich everything — the terror, the grief, the certainty that I was about to die and felt Dietrich's answering fury blast through the connection like a wall of fire.

Klaus's men dragged me across the snow toward the big oak at the clearing's edge. Klaus had a rope in his hands. He threw one end over a thick branch with practiced ease. The noose dangled at the end.

"Please." I tried to summon the Forceweaving. But grief and shock had shattered my concentration. There was just emptiness where the force should be. "I didn't kill him. I didn't ..."

"Save your lies for the devil, witch." Klaus's voice came from behind me. I couldn't see him. I felt the rope go over the branch above my head and then his hands forced the noose over my face and down around my neck and yanked it tight from behind. The hemp bit into my skin, rough against the soft flesh under my jaw. My feet left the ground. Not all the way — just enough that my toes scraped the snow and my weight hung on the rope and I couldn't get a full breath.

I clawed at the noose with both hands. My fingers dug under the rope but it was too tight and my nails tore and I couldn't get air. My legs kicked and Jakob grabbed them and held them still and I couldn't move, couldn't breathe, couldn't do anything except hang there and choke while the sky went white above me and the trees tilted sideways.

My vision started to gray.

This was it. This was how I died. Hanged as a witch for a crime I didn't commit. Killed by the people I'd lived among my whole life.

And while I hung there with my toes scraping the snow and my lungs screaming for air I could see their faces. The men who'd eaten bread I'd baked. The men whose children I'd healed when fever came through the village. The men whose wives I'd sat with through labor, whose mothers I'd tended when they were too old to feed themselves. I knew every face in that clearing. I'd helped every single one of them at some point and they were watching me choke and not one of them was moving to stop it.

They'd done the same thing to Anna. Stood on the riverbank while she thrashed in the water. Counted to forty while she drowned. Gone home and eaten supper.

Sophia wrote about bread. She wrote about wildflowers

and grandmother's poultice and she was dead behind those boards and I hadn't finished reading her letter. She'd written my name. Red. My little Red. And I was going to die on a rope in the snow without knowing what came after.

I cracked.

The way the earth cracks before a volcano. The way a dam cracks before the flood. Deep and old and furious. It had been building since the cellar, since Klaus's hand on my throat, since Anna's body in the river, since Sophia's scratches on the door. Since every woman who'd ever been called witch and burned or drowned or hanged for the crime of being born different.

The Forceweaving didn't just surge. It detonated.

The blast ripped outward from my body in a wave that flattened everything in the clearing. Raw, uncontrolled. Every thread of power releasing at once.

Jakob flew off my legs. His body sailed through the air and hit the oak behind him with a crack that was definitely bone. He slid to the ground and his arm was bent wrong, elbow joint destroyed, white bone jutting through his sleeve.

The rope went slack. I dropped to the ground on my hands and knees, choking, gasping, tearing the noose from my neck with fingers that felt like someone else's. The hemp left burns that would scar. Air rushed into my lungs so fast it hurt.

Someone was screaming. Not from pain but from pure terror. One of the men who'd been thrown clear was crawling backward through the snow staring at me with his mouth hanging open and the whites of his eyes showing like a spooked horse. Another was on his knees crossing himself over and over so fast his hands blurred. A third was just standing there with piss running down his leg and his torch sizzling in the snow where he'd dropped it.

"Daemon," one of them whispered. Then louder, splintering: "DAEMON! Libera nos a malo, libera nos a malo, libera nos ..."

"Shut your mouth, Gregor!" Klaus roared from somewhere behind me. He was on the ground. The blast had thrown him back but he was already getting up.

I turned and threw the Forceweaving at him before he could stand. It hit him in the chest and launched him backward into the snow. He skidded ten feet and slammed against a fallen log and stayed down.

The clearing erupted. Men who could still stand ran in every direction. Some crashed into each other trying to get to the trees. One tripped over Jakob's body and went face first into the snow and scrambled up and kept running. The man who'd been praying in Latin hadn't moved, just kept crossing himself and muttering with his eyes squeezed shut like if he couldn't see me I couldn't see him.

I got to my feet. My legs were shaking. The rope burns on my neck throbbed. My hands were bloody from clawing at the noose.

But I could breathe. I could breathe and I was angry.

The fear was gone. The grieving was gone. The begging was done. The grief was still there. It would always be there, Thomas's small body, the smell of Emma's soap in his hair. But a fury had shifted beneath it. A fury that had been sleeping since the first time my power woke, since the first time I'd tasted what it felt like to push back instead of being pushed.

The Forceweaving crackled around my hands. Blue-gold threads visible in the morning air. The men who hadn't run yet froze where they stood. The praying stopped. Even the wind seemed to hold still.

"I am not a demon." I straightened my spine and let them look at me. Let them see the rope burns on my neck and the blood on my hands and the power sparking between my fingers. "I am a witch. I am a blood-keeper. And you are going to listen to me."

"I won't listen to ..." Klaus was pulling himself up against the log.

I threw a threading that hit the snow at his feet. The ground exploded upward and he fell back down.

"I am done," I roared, "being interrupted by men who think I don't matter."

The clearing went silent. Even the man with wet trousers stopped shaking.

"I didn't kill Thomas," I declared, and let it carry. "There is a wolf in this forest. A gray wolf. Larger than any natural animal. The same creature that killed my husband and six men sixteen years ago. The same creature that has been hunting in these woods longer than most of you have been alive."

“Lies ...” Klaus started.

I threw another threading. This one cracked the log he was leaning against clean in half. Both pieces fell away from him and he sat in the snow with nothing holding him up and nothing left on his face but fear.

“That wolf killed Thomas,” I continued. “Killed him somewhere in the forest and dragged his body to my doorstep to frame me. To bring you here. To turn you into weapons against me while he watches from the shadows.” I looked at each face in turn. “You were played. Every single one of you. Manipulated by a monster who knew exactly what you’d do when you found a dead child on a witch’s doorstep.”

“If this wolf exists,” Klaus managed through chattering teeth, “where is it now?”

Suddenly, a howl split the air. Deep. Resonant. Triumphant. The sound of a predator watching its trap close perfectly. The gray wolf stepped from the trees.

It was enormous in the daylight. Twice the size of any natural wolf. Silver-gray fur with darker markings across its shoulders. Yellow eyes burning with intelligence, with malice, with satisfaction.

Its muzzle was still dark with Thomas’s blood.

The mob saw it and the panic hit them like a wave. Men who’d been ready to hang me were now backing into each other, tripping over their own feet, grabbing at weapons they didn’t know how to use against something that big.

“That’s him,” I told them. My neck was burning from

the rope and my hands were bloody and I didn't care what they thought of me anymore. "That's the monster who killed Emma's son."

The gray wolf's lips pulled back from stained teeth. Almost a smile. Then it lunged at the mob.

Men scattered screaming. The gray wolf tore through the clearing, snapping at legs, driving them apart the way a herding dog splits a flock. It wasn't killing them. It was playing. Enjoying the panic, the noise, the chaos of grown men falling over themselves to run from the thing they should have been afraid of all along instead of stringing up a woman.

I was watching the gray wolf when the blow came.

Klaus hit me across the back of the head with a piece of the log I'd split in half. I went down face first in the snow and the world went bright white and then spotty and I could feel blood running warm down the back of my neck and into the collar of grandmother's dress. I tried to get up and my arms buckled and I went down again.

The gray wolf stopped.

I lifted my head from the snow and it was standing forty feet away and its nostrils were flaring and its whole body had gone rigid. My blood. Blood-keeper blood, open and flowing, the scent pouring off me in the cold air.

It forgot the mob. Forgot the game. Those yellow eyes fixed on me and it started walking toward me with that slow, deliberate stride I'd seen before. The stride of something that had stopped playing.

"See!" Klaus was shouting behind me, backing away, pointing at me and the wolf with a shaking hand. "See how the beast comes to her! She commands it! She called it here! The witch and the wolf are one!"

The gray wolf was twenty feet away. Fifteen. Its mouth was open and I could see Thomas's blood on its teeth and I tried to summon the Forceweaving but my head was splitting and the power was guttering and I couldn't hold the threads together.

Ten feet.

The black wolf hit it from the side.

It came out of the trees so fast the snow sprayed in a wall behind it. The black wolf slammed into the gray wolf's flank and they went rolling across the clearing in a tangle of teeth and claws and fur, black and gray. The gray wolf snarled, twisted, got its jaws around the black wolf's shoulder. The black wolf drove its teeth into the gray wolf's throat and they crashed through a snowbank and kept fighting.

The men should have run. Some did. The rest grabbed what they had, axes, pitchforks, torches, and went after both wolves. They didn't care which was which. Two monsters in their clearing and they wanted both dead. One of them buried an axe in the black wolf's left shoulder while it was locked with the gray wolf. Another drove a pitchfork into the gray wolf's flank. A torch came down on the black wolf's back and the fur singed and the smell of it filled the clearing.

The gray wolf ripped free. The axe wound and the pitchfork and the mob pressing in from every side had broken the fight apart. The gray wolf scrambled backward, bleeding from its throat and its flank, and bolted for the trees. It was gone in seconds. Swallowed by the forest.

The black wolf stood in the middle of the clearing with an axe wound in its shoulder and burns on its back and men closing in from three sides. It didn't attack. Its golden eyes tracked the tree line where the gray wolf had disappeared and I could feel Dietrich, the pull, the need to chase, to end it, to finish his father before he healed and came back. The men were nothing to him. The gray wolf was everything.

But the men were circling. Raising their weapons. Getting brave because one wolf was easier than two.

Kill them. I pushed it toward Dietrich with everything I had. *They tried to hang me. They're going to kill you. Kill them.*

The black wolf turned.

It happened fast. The man with the axe swung and the black wolf caught his arm in its jaws and I heard the bone go. The man with the pitchfork drove it forward and the black wolf twisted sideways and the tines missed and then its teeth were in the man's leg and he went down screaming. A third rushed from behind and the black wolf kicked backward with its hind legs and the man flew into a tree and didn't get up.

The remaining mob scattered. Running for the trees, dropping weapons, scrambling over each other. Klaus and his remaining followers ran deeper into the forest. The wrong direction. Away from the village path, toward the northern ridge.

The black wolf stood panting in the snow, sides heaving, golden eyes finding mine.

Go. I pushed myself up to my knees. My head was pounding and blood was still running down my neck but I was breathing and the Forceweaving was coming back, flickering between my fingers. *Go kill your father.*

The black wolf pinned me with its gaze for one more second. Then it turned and disappeared into the trees after the gray.

Emma and Heinrich hadn't moved. Still kneeling at the clearing's edge, still clutching Thomas between them.

I stumbled toward them on unsteady legs.

"Emma." I could hardly get it out. "Heinrich. There's another path. Through the eastern woods. It'll take you back to the village safely."

Emma looked at me. Her eyes red and swollen and utterly destroyed. "You — you didn't ..."

"I didn't," I confirmed. "Go. Before the fight moves this way. Take Thomas home. Bury him properly. Mourn him."

"The others ..." Heinrich's granite facade had cracked. "Klaus and his men went the wrong way ..."

"I know." I looked toward the northern ridge where they'd disappeared. I felt nothing — empty of pity, empty of concern. These were the men who'd drowned Anna. Who'd dragged me by the hair. Who'd put a noose around my neck and kicked me while I begged. "They chose their path. Let the forest decide what happens on it."

Heinrich stared at me. Then nodded once.

Emma took one step. Then stopped. Turned back with something new burning through the grief. Something old and dark and iron-hard.

"Promise me," she demanded, low and fierce. A mother's fury dressed in funeral black. "Promise me you'll make that beast pay for what it did to my boy."

I looked at Thomas. At his small still face pressed against her collarbone. At the blood dried dark on his clothes.

"Emma ..." I started.

"Don't." She cut me off. Tears ran fresh but her mouth was a hard flat line. "Don't tell me to grieve and move on. Don't tell me God will sort it out. I've prayed every night of my life and God let that creature rip my son apart." Her body shook. "So I'm not asking God. I'm asking you."

I held her gaze and felt what she wanted. "I promise," I declared. "I will hunt that creature down. And I will make it suffer in ways it didn't know a body could suffer. I will break it apart piece by piece until it's screaming for a death I won't give it. Until I'm good and ready. Until it's felt every single thing Thomas felt and worse." I bared my teeth. "For Thomas."

Emma's chin trembled. A sound came out of her that wasn't quite a sob and wasn't quite relief.

She reached out with one hand, the one not holding her

dead son, and gripped my wrist. Her fingers were ice cold and strong as rope. She squeezed once. Hard enough to bruise.

"On your life," she whispered. "Swear it on your life, Red."

"On my life." I didn't flinch. "I swear it."

She held on for one more heartbeat. Then let go.

She turned. Heinrich put his arm around her and they walked toward the eastern path. Toward safety. Toward home. Toward burying their child.

I watched them go until the trees took them. Then I turned toward the woods where the wolves had disappeared.

Chapter Twenty-Three

The wolves were tearing each other apart in the center of the clearing.

But this fight was different from the last one. I could feel it, Dietrich's strength, amplified by the mating, my Forceweaving running through his blood like liquid fire. The black wolf was faster than before. Harder. His jaws clamped down on the gray wolf's shoulder and I heard bone crack and Erik screamed, high and shocked, the sound of a predator discovering it was no longer the strongest thing in the forest.

The mating had worked.

Erik threw Dietrich off and lunged for his throat. The black wolf dodged — not desperately, but cleanly, with a speed that left Erik's jaws snapping at empty air. Then Dietrich drove forward and his teeth found the gray wolf's flank and tore, and the blood that sprayed across the snow was Erik's.

But Erik was cunning. He feinted left, spun right, and his claws raked across the axe wound one of Klaus's men had opened in Dietrich's shoulder. The black wolf staggered. Erik pressed the advantage — not with strength but with experience, with decades of knowing exactly where a wounded body would fail.

Pain. Dietrich's shoulder buckling. His determination burning through it. The wolf refusing to go down.

I couldn't just watch. I had Klaus's men to deal with first.

I turned my back on the wolves.

Klaus stood fifteen feet away. Axe gripped in both hands. His face twisted beyond recognition — hatred and terror and something unhinged burning in his eyes. He'd stayed behind while the others scattered.

"They're distracted," he observed, nodding toward the wolves. "Your demon is wounded. When he dies, I'm taking your head."

I looked at him. At this man who'd been the shadow over my entire life. Who'd drowned a girl for loving the wrong boy. Who'd whispered poison into every ear in the village until the whole town believed I was something evil. Who'd put a noose around my neck and pulled it tight and watched me choke.

"You can't even stand," Klaus taunted, raising the axe. "This ends now."

He swung.

I cracked open.

It wasn't Forceweaving. It was something older, something that lived in my blood, in the marrow of my bones, in the line of women who'd carried this gift for generations. Grandmother. Sophia. Every blood-keeper who'd ever been called witch and burned or drowned or hanged for the crime of being born different.

It surged through me like fire through dry wood. Wilder than the careful threading I'd been practicing, fiercer than the controlled blasts the grimoire described. Raw. Rage given form.

I caught the axe in midair, with something invisible that wrapped around the blade and held it frozen. Klaus's arms jerked to a stop. He stared at the axe motionless in the air, inches from my face.

"Anna was just seventeen," I stated, rising to my feet. The power held me steady, filled the hollowed-out spaces with something hot and ancient. "She loved the wrong boy. That was her only mistake and you drowned her."

"She committed a crime ..."

"She was a CHILD." I ripped the axe from his hands. It spun through the air and buried itself in a tree. Klaus stumbled forward, empty-handed, suddenly defenseless.

I reached out with the power and grabbed his body. Lifted him off the ground. His boots left the snow and he rose, jerking upward on invisible strings, no rope, no hands, nothing touching him. His body twisted and writhed, arms clawing at nothing, legs kicking against air that wouldn't let him go.

The vision.

The one from when I was ten years old. The man in the air who wasn't flying and wasn't falling. The invisible pressure. The face going red. It wasn't a nightmare. It was a promise.

"You held Anna under the water until she stopped breathing," I told him, and the words came out cold, nothing like the woman who'd been begging thirty seconds ago. "You watched a girl thrash and scream. And you went home and ate your supper. And came to me with your disgusting offer. Remember?"

"Let me down!" He was screaming now. All the bravado stripped away. A coward who'd only ever been brave with a mob at his back. "Please! Have mercy!"

"Did you show Anna mercy?" I asked.

The pressure built between my palms. This was not the threading. This was power that was older and wilder.

His face went red. Then purple. His eyes bulged and his mouth stretched open in a scream that never made it past his throat.

His head burst.

His body stayed suspended for one breath longer, still held by the invisible force. Then I released it and it dropped and hit the snow like something emptied out. Blood and worse soaking into the white ground.

The vision, fulfilled. More than twenty-eight years later.

I looked at what I'd done and felt nothing that resembled guilt.

The power should have been fading. Should have been running dry after the blast that levitated Klaus and the force that burst his skull. But it wasn't. It was growing, fed by the bond, fed by the mating, fed by revenge. Whatever ceiling had been containing my Forceweaving for weeks of training, the exhaustion, the collapse after every precise threading, it was gone. Shattered by what I'd done and not rebuilding. I could feel the difference in my bones. This wasn't the woman who'd bled from the nose after cracking a single boulder. This was beyond anything I'd done. Power the grimoire had warned about in passages I had not understood: *a blood-keeper reaching her full power*.

I'd reached it. And it was terrifying.

A sound behind me made me turn. Jakob was dragging himself through the snow, his shattered arm trailing behind him, leaving a smear of red where he crawled.

I followed him.

He heard me coming. Looked over his shoulder with eyes that were all white around the edges.

"Please," he gasped. "I didn't. I was just following Klaus ..."

"You got Anna pregnant," I corrected, walking slowly. He wasn't going anywhere. "You loved her in the dark and denied her in the daylight. And when they dragged her to the river, you stood with your arms crossed and watched."

"I didn't have a choice ..."

"She didn't have a choice." I caught his ankle with the Forceweaving and dragged him backward through the snow. He screamed. His broken arm caught on a root and the sound made the birds scatter. "She was carrying your child. When you refused to help her, she had to do something. And then you pointed the finger at her."

I dragged him to the creek. The water was shallow, four feet, maybe less, running dark beneath a crust of broken ice. Cold enough to stop a heart. Cold enough to steal every thought and replace it with the single screaming knowledge that you were going to die.

The way Anna had died.

I grabbed his hair in fist and forced his face into the water.

He thrashed. His good hand slapped at the frozen bank. His legs kicked. His body bucked with the desperate, animal strength of something that didn't want to drown. Bubbles rose from his submerged face, fast at first, frantic, then slower.

I held him there. And I counted.

One. For the night he'd told Anna he loved her.

Two. For the morning he'd denied it.

Three. For the finger he'd pointed.

Four. For the arms he'd crossed while she went under.

Five. For the bubbles that had risen from Anna's mouth while the village watched.

Six. For the silence that followed.

Seven. For the supper he'd eaten that night.

Eight. For the child that never drew breath because its father was a coward.

His legs stopped kicking.

I let go. His body slumped into the creek face down and the water ran around him and didn't care.

I stood and wiped my hands on my dress. For Anna. All of it.

The rest of them were still in the trees. I could hear them crashing through the undergrowth, trying to find a way home through woods they'd never learned because they'd always been too afraid to venture past the tree line. They sounded like cattle. Stupid and loud and bumping into everything.

I went after them.

I found them one by one. Behind boulders, behind logs, pressed flat against tree trunks like the bark would save them. I killed them the way you pull weeds out of a garden. No speeches. No explanations. They knew what they'd done and I wasn't interested in hearing them beg because Anna had begged and Sophia had begged and I had begged on my knees in front of Klaus and none of it had ever mattered to any of them.

My nose was bleeding by the third one. A steady stream running down my chin and dripping onto the snow and I kept going. My vision swam between kills and my legs were getting heavier and each time I used the Forceweaving it cost me something I couldn't get back. But Dietrich's strength was feeding mine through the connection and I drew on it without asking and felt his willingness pour through. Take what you need. Take everything. Just come back alive.

I came back alive. They didn't.

When the last one was done I stood in the silent forest with blood on my hands and blood on my face and blood on grandmother's dress and I breathed. My nose was still bleeding and my head was pounding from where Klaus had hit me and every muscle in my body felt wrung out.

Then something hit me and I stumbled. Dietrich had the gray wolf pinned. I could feel it — his jaws clamped on his father's throat, the gray wolf thrashing and twisting under him trying to break free and failing. He was winning. He was actually winning and I needed to get there before the fight turned again.

I ran.

The black wolf stood over the gray, jaws locked on his father's throat, not killing but containing. Erik thrashed and snarled but Dietrich held firm, the mating-strength visible in the way his muscles didn't shake, the way his grip didn't falter, the way his body absorbed Erik's desperate clawing without yielding an inch.

I felt the black wolf's awareness of me, my approach, my power, the blood on my hands. His fierce pride and his grief and his absolute trust that whatever I'd done in those trees, I'd done because it needed doing.

And beneath it — offered, not demanded, felt in a way words could never carry:

He was mine. If I wanted him.

I walked into the clearing.

The black wolf looked at me. Golden eyes bright with pain and exhaustion. It adjusted its grip and pressed the gray wolf flat against the snow until there was nowhere left to move.

"Make him shift," I ordered.

The black wolf bit down harder and the gray wolf howled and its body started to change. Dietrich was forcing it. His jaws commanding his father's body the way an alpha commands a lesser wolf. The gray fur rippled and pulled back and the bones cracked and reshaped and the massive body got smaller and smaller until what lay in the snow beneath the black wolf's jaws was just a man.

Old. White hair matted with blood. A face carved deep with lines that had nothing to do with laughter. Lean and scarred and wasted. But those eyes were the same, intelligent, calculating, burning with hatred even pinned and broken and beaten by his own son.

The black wolf released his throat and stepped back and positioned itself between Erik and the forest. Nowhere to run.

Erik tried to get up. Made it to his hands and knees with blood pouring from his throat and his flanks, steaming where it hit the cold air. His naked body shook. He looked at me. At the blood on my dress. At my hands red to the wrists. At the clearing behind me where Klaus's body lay in the snow with nothing above the neck.

I stood over him and waited for him to understand what he was looking at. A woman he'd hunted, standing upright. A man he'd used, headless in the snow. And his son, his own blood, choosing her.

"Sophia," I said. "Say her name."

He spat blood onto the snow between us. "Why should I."

"Because I'm telling you to." The Forceweaving crackled around my hands and the air between us got heavy with it. "Say her name."

His lips curled even now. Even naked and bleeding and beaten. Defiance was all he had left and he wore it like a crown. "Sophia."

"She was nineteen when you took her. You threatened to kill everyone she loved unless she walked into that forest and she believed you and she went." I crouched beside him because I wanted him to see my face while I said it. "She spent two years behind boarded windows while you forced yourself on her and drained her power. And then you killed her."

"That was an accident ..."

The Forceweaving wrapped around his right hand. I found the first bone in his index finger and I snapped it.

He screamed.

"That was for the first day," I told him. "Twenty-six more bones in that hand. Seven hundred and twenty-nine more days."

I broke the second bone. The third. Each one deliberate.

I was a healer and I knew the anatomy of the human hand the way I knew the herbs on grandmother's shelf. Every bone, every joint, every tendon and ligament mapped in my mind. I had used that knowledge my whole life to fix what was broken.

I used it now to break what was whole.

He screamed for the first eight. By the twelfth the screaming thinned to nothing. By the twentieth he'd stopped screaming and was making a thin keening sound that didn't sound human anymore. Good. He wasn't human. He'd never been human. Not where it counted.

"This is for every night you forced yourself on her," I told him while I worked. "Every scream she swallowed. Every mark you left on her skin."

I moved to the left hand. Started again.

I felt Dietrich standing guard behind me. He wasn't enjoying this. But he understood it. He accepted it. He knew what this was and he let me do it because it was mine to do.

When both hands were ruined and the fingers were pointing in directions fingers should never point I stood up.

"William," I said. "My husband. He laughed louder than anyone I ever knew and he brought me flowers from the forest and you tore him apart because he smelled like me."

Erik's glazed eyes found mine. "He was in my territory ..."

I pressed the Forceweaving into his ribs. Two cracked. His body convulsed.

"Thomas." I said it without shaking. I didn't recognize

the sound of myself. "Seven years old. You snapped his neck and left him on my doorstep like a gift."

"Necessary," Erik rasped. "To draw you out ..."

Two more ribs. He screamed but there was nothing left in the sound. Just air and pain.

"A child's murder was necessary," I repeated.

"Please ..." A bubble of blood on his lips. "Stop ..."

"Sophia said please. Every night for two years. Did you stop?"

He had no answer for that. There was no answer for that.

I stood over him and looked at what he was. This ruined broken thing with blood in his white hair and cruelty in every line of his face. He'd been a monster for so long he'd forgotten he'd ever been anything else. Maybe he hadn't. Maybe this was all he'd ever been.

"Sophia wrote in the grimoire," I told him. "Did you know that."

His eyes changed. Even through the pain and the blood and the ruin of his body something flickered in them. Interest. Hunger. The expectation that he'd mattered enough to fill her pages the way he'd filled her nightmares.

"She filled pages, Erik. Two years of writing. She wrote about the creek breaking in spring and grandmother's garden after the rain and a recipe for burn poultice because she was scared the knowledge would die with her. She wrote about wildflowers she could smell through the gaps in the boards. She wrote about bread from the village bakery that she said she could still remember if she concentrated hard enough."

I crouched beside him one last time.

"She wrote about bread, Erik. And not one word about you. Not your name. Not your face. Not a single thing you did to her in two years. You kept her in that cottage and she looked at you and decided you weren't worth the ink."

I watched it land. Watched something behind his eyes collapse that the broken bones and the cracked ribs hadn't been able to touch. He'd kept a woman for two years and she'd erased him while he was still in the room.

"This is for Sophia," I said. "For the two years you stole. For the songs she stopped singing. For the woman she was before you broke her."

I reached into his chest with the power. Found his heart. "This is for William. For the flowers he'll never bring me. For the mornings I woke up alone because you decided he didn't deserve to live."

I wrapped the force around the beating muscle and felt it pulse against my grip. Strong. Even now, even broken and begging, his heart beat strong.

"This is for Thomas. For a little boy who called me Auntie and never got to grow up."

I tightened. The heart stuttered and Erik's body arched off the ground and a sound came out of him that was beyond screaming.

"And this is for me. For every night I spent afraid. For the noose and the blood and the life you tried to steal."

I crushed it.

His gaze went wide. Then dark. Then empty.

His body shuddered once. Twice. Then it was still.

I stood over him and watched the life leave. Those eyes turned to glass. The old body collapsed as the last breath left it. Smaller than the wolf had been. Just a man now. Just meat and bone going cold in the snow.

Done.

I hit the snow on my knees and the cold soaked through grandmother's dress, the white linen heavy with Thomas's blood and my own and the blood of every man I'd killed today.

The black wolf was beside me before I finished falling. He shifted, quickly, the cracking muffled, the man emerging, and then Dietrich's arms were around me, his skin warm against my frozen body, his heartbeat slamming against my ribs and through his chest.

"I have you," he murmured against my hair. "It's done."

"Thomas." The word came out broken. "I saw it coming. Years ago. Before he was even born. I saw it and I told myself it was a lie and I ..."

"You couldn't have stopped it," he insisted fiercely, his arms tightening. "Erik was watching. Waiting. He would have found another way."

"A child," I whispered. "He killed a child to get to me."

His grief for the boy he'd never met, tangled with his grief for me and what this day had cost.

I looked at my hands. Red to the wrists. Klaus's blood. Jakob's. Erik's. The men in the forest.

The tears came. Not softly, in great, tearing sobs that shook my whole body. I cried for Thomas. For Anna. For Sophia under the birch tree. For William in pieces on the forest floor sixteen years ago. For the woman I'd been before today, the healer, the herb-woman, the quiet widow who'd lived a small life and asked for nothing except to be left alone.

That woman was dead. She'd died somewhere between the noose and the first kill. What walked out of that clearing was harder. Blood under her nails and a taste for violence that would live inside me forever.

Dietrich held me through all of it. Didn't try to stop the crying. Didn't tell me it would be all right. Just held me in the snow with the bond carrying his love into me in a steady current that asked for nothing.

When the sobs stopped, I sat in his arms and breathed and looked at what I'd made.

Blood on the snow. Blood on the trees. Blood on my hands and my dress and the ground in every direction. The clearing looked like something from a war.

But we were alive.

I pressed my ear against Dietrich's chest. His heartbeat — steady and strong, my Forceweaving still humming in his blood.

"It's over," I breathed.

His arms tightened. His lips found the top of my head.

"It's over," he confirmed.

Behind the cottage, under the birch tree, Sophia lay in frozen earth. Her monster was dead now. Twenty feet from her grave.

I hoped she knew. I hoped wherever she was, she could feel the weight lifting. The scratch marks on the door finally answered.

"We need to move," Dietrich murmured after a long time. "Before the cold takes us."

He was right. We were both bare, him from the shift, me soaked through with blood and snowmelt. He stood first. Pulled me up. We leaned on each other, two broken, bloody people holding each other upright the way we'd been doing since the night he'd carried me out of the forest.

We walked to the cottage. The door was still open, the fire still burning, the warmth reaching through the threshold.

I stopped in the doorway. Looked back one last time at the clearing. The snow. The bodies. The blood on everything, staining the world in a color I'd worn my whole life without understanding what it meant.

I stepped inside and closed the door.

They called me Red for the cloak I wore. Now they'd call me Red for the blood I spilled.

Chapter Twenty-Four

I woke in the bed with his arm across my waist and the fire burned down to embers. My body ached in places I didn't know could ache. The rope burns on my neck hurt badly. My skull felt hollow. Emptied out. Everything I'd been running on, power, rage, grief, burned through, and now there was just the space where it used to be.

Dietrich's heartbeat pulsed slow and steady against my spine. His breathing was shallow. The wolf in him working to stitch his body back together, knitting torn muscle and cracked ribs from the inside out. Slow. So much slower than it should have been. The axe wounds and pitchfork punctures and the gray wolf's teeth had taken everything he had.

I turned my head on the pillow and looked at him. His face was slack and bruised. Fever heat poured off his skin, the wolf's healing running overtime. The bandages I'd wrapped around his ribs before we'd collapsed into bed were already seeping.

I should change them. Should get up. Should do something useful.

Instead I lay there and listened to him breathe and stared at the ceiling and tried to feel something.

Nothing came.

Eventually I got up. Because the fire needed tending and the bandages needed changing and the blood on the floor needed scrubbing and the world didn't stop turning just because two people were lying in bed broken.

I built the fire. Heated water. Tore clean cloth from an old shift. Found what was left of grandmother's herbs, yarrow for bleeding, comfrey for bones, calendula for the wounds too deep to close on their own.

I unwrapped his bandages and cleaned each wound the way I'd cleaned a thousand wounds before. Packed the deepest ones with poultices. Wrapped them tight. He stirred but didn't wake — just made a low sound in his throat when I pressed too hard on the gash across his shoulder, and his pain spiked into me and settled.

I felt something else too. Underneath the pain. A hollow ache that had nothing to do with his body.

Erik.

His father was dead. The monster who'd haunted this forest for decades, who'd killed and caged women and destroyed his own son's chance at a life. Dead. And Dietrich grieved him anyway. Not the monster. The man Erik might have been once, before the hunger took hold. The father he never got to have.

I didn't say anything about it. Just cleaned his wounds and let my hands be gentle. Whatever I had left to give, I gave it.

When I finished, I pulled the furs over his chest and sat on the floor beside the bed with my back against the frame.

My hands were in my lap. I turned them over. Looked at them. The blood was still there despite the scrubbing. Caught in the creases. Under the nails. Brown now but I knew which stains belonged to whom. Klaus's blood on my right hand from where it had sprayed when his skull gave way. Jakob's from his hair, still caught under my nails from holding him under the water. My own from my nose — the price my body had paid for pushing the power past anything it was built to hold.

I'd killed men. In the flesh. With my hands and my power. I'd felt their bones break under invisible force. I'd watched the life drain from Erik's eyes while I crushed his heart inside his chest. I'd walked through a forest of bodies and meant every single second of it.

I waited for the guilt to come. The horror. The shame that a good woman should feel after taking lives.

It didn't come.

What came instead was Anna. Seventeen years old, thrashing under black water while Klaus held her down. Sophia in Erik's cottage for two years, her songs going quiet one by one. William walking into the forest with a smile, coming back in pieces. Thomas. Small and broken on my doorstep.

Every woman they'd hurt. Every child they'd taken.

The grimoire's words came back to me. Our purpose is not to hunt. Not to destroy. Only to witness and record.

Every woman who'd written in that book followed that rule. Watched the horror. Wrote it down. Hid what they were and prayed the hiding was enough.

I didn't hide. I didn't watch. I hunted the men who came for me and I destroyed them.

Maybe that didn't make me good. Maybe the women before me were better people than I'd ever be. Kinder. Softer. More willing to forgive the world for eating them alive.

But they were dead. And I was sitting on a floor with blood under my nails and a mate sleeping in the bed behind me and a forest that was finally quiet.

I could live with that.

Dietrich slept for two days.

I kept the fire going. Changed his bandages. Fed him broth when he surfaced enough to swallow. Watched the wolf healing do its work, wounds shrinking hour by hour, new skin spreading over torn flesh.

His dreams bled into mine. Dark and tangled. Erik's amber eyes. The gray wolf's teeth. Thomas's small body. The sound of his father's heart stopping under my power.

I didn't pull away from the dreams. Stayed with him through every one. Let him feel me there in the dark places.

On the second morning he woke properly. Sat up in bed and looked at me across the room. His color was better. The fever had broken sometime in the night. The worst wounds had closed to angry red scars.

"How long?" he rasped, his throat sounding like gravel.

"Two days."

He stared at me. Then at his hands. Then at the bandages wrapped around his ribs and shoulder.

"You stayed." Almost a question.

"Where else would I go?" I replied, crossing to sit on the edge of the bed.

His face softened. Deeper than a smile. He held out his hand and I took it. His fingers laced through mine.

"I felt him die," he admitted, keeping his eyes on the far wall. "The old bond. Parent and child. It snapped when you ..." He stopped. Swallowed. "I felt it snap."

"I know."

"He was a monster." Testing the shape of the words.

"Yes."

"I still felt it."

I squeezed his hand. "That's because you're not like him. You can grieve someone terrible and it doesn't make you weak. It makes you the human half."

"I'm not human," he whispered roughly.

"The part of you that grieves is."

He looked at me then. Everything he was feeling hit me at once, relief, sorrow, guilt, and underneath all of it his love for me. Still there. Still burning. Unchanged.

"You killed them all," he observed, pulling me closer. Not an accusation.

"Yes."

"How do you feel?"

I gave him the truth because I couldn't give him anything else. "Like I'd do it again. Every single one. For Anna. For Sophia. For William and Thomas." I paused. "Does that scare you?"

He tucked my head under his chin and wrapped his arms around me.

"It makes me glad you're on my side," he murmured against my hair.

On the fifth day, I went to the village.

Dietrich walked me to the tree line and stopped. I looked back at him, standing between two pines with his hands at his sides and his expression uncertain in a way I'd never seen before. He'd fought his father. He'd faced down a mob. But walking into a village where people lived ordinary lives and ate ordinary food and asked ordinary questions, that stopped him cold.

"You could come," I offered.

He shook his head slowly. "I've been watching that village from the trees half my life. I don't know how to walk down the street." He stepped closer, fingers curling around my hip. "Stay where I can scent you. If anything feels wrong, you come back."

I caught his face and pulled his mouth to mine. He resisted for half a breath, then his hands found my waist and dragged me against him. His teeth caught my lower lip. I made a sound against his mouth that I'd never admit to later. He kissed me like I was already gone and he was trying to memorize the taste.

I pulled back. His hands stayed on my waist.

"I won't be long."

I stepped out of the trees alone.

Smoke rose from chimneys in the gray morning air. The smell of wood fires and bread baking. Life going on the way it always did after terrible things.

Heinrich was splitting wood behind the smithy. He saw me and set the axe down slowly. Just stood there with sawdust in his hair and exhaustion carved into his face.

"Heinrich."

"Red." His eyes moved past me to the tree line, then back. A question he chose not to ask.

The front door of his house opened.

Emma's daughters appeared first. Lotte, the older one, had Heinrich's broad shoulders and Emma's dark eyes. She held her younger sister's hand. Margit was small and quiet, her face blotchy from crying that hadn't stopped in weeks.

They saw me and froze on the step.

"Auntie Red." Lotte's chin crumpled. She let go of Margit's hand and ran toward me hard enough to knock me back a step. Margit followed a second later, both of them pressing into me, arms tight around my waist.

I held them both. Lotte's shoulders shook against my

chest. Margit didn't make a sound, just gripped my cloak with both fists and wouldn't let go.

"I missed you." Lotte pulled back and wiped her nose on her sleeve. Her eyes were red and old in a way no child's should be.

"I missed you too." I brushed the hair from her face. "Both of you."

Heinrich crossed the yard and put a hand on each girl's shoulder. "Inside," he told them gently. "Let your mother talk to Red."

Lotte looked like she wanted to argue. Margit just tightened her grip on my cloak.

"I'll come see you before I go," I promised, squeezing Margit's hand. "I won't leave without saying goodbye."

Margit studied my face for a long moment. Then she nodded and let go. Heinrich steered them back through the door. He glanced at me once, then went back to his woodpile.

I stepped inside. Emma was at the kitchen table folding Thomas's clothes into a neat pile. Her hands moved slowly, smoothing each crease like it mattered, like getting the folds right was the only thing holding her together. She'd lost weight — her face hollow, her eyes swollen to slits, her hair hanging loose and unwashed. She wore a dark funeral dress, and Thomas's blanket was clutched against her chest.

She looked up. Her hands went still on a small wool shirt.

She looked at me. I looked at her. A lifetime of friendship and the absence of her son between us.

She walked toward me. I walked toward her. We met in the middle of the kitchen. Neither of us spoke. There was nothing to say. Emma opened her arms. I fell into them. She held me the way she'd held Thomas, fierce, desperate, her fingers digging into my back through the cloak. I held her the way I'd held him on the doorstep, gentle, broken, my face pressed against her shoulder while the tears came.

"I'm sorry," I sobbed against her shoulder. "I should have been here. I should have been here and I wasn't and I'm sorry ..."

"Shut up," Emma whispered fiercely, her arms tightening. "It wasn't your fault. It was never your fault."

She pulled back. Her hands came up to my face, cupping my chin the way she used to when we were girls and she wanted me to pay attention. Her eyes were ruined but the fire behind them was the same Emma I'd always known.

Her fingers found the rope burns on my neck. Traced them gently.

"They did this to you," she breathed, and the fury was aimed where it belonged, at the dead men who'd earned what they got.

"It doesn't matter now," I told her.

"It matters to me," she insisted, her teeth clenched. "Every one of them stood on that riverbank when they drowned Anna. Every one of them cheered while they strung you up."

"Did you keep your promise?" Emma pressed. "The wolf. The gray one."

"Every word of it," I replied, and something in me went hard without my permission. "I broke every bone in its hands so it could never hold another child. I crushed its ribs the way it crushed Thomas. And when I was done making it feel every second of what it had done ..." I held her eyes. "I stopped its heart."

Emma's breath left her in a rush. Her hand found Thomas's blanket and pressed it harder against her chest. When she looked at me again the grief was still there, would always be there, but underneath it, the first breath after holding one too long.

Her gaze drifted past me to the window. Her head tilted.

"There's something in the trees," she observed carefully. "Watching us."

I didn't turn around. I'd felt him shift the moment I stepped out of the tree line, the crack and reshape of bone rippling through me like a held breath released. He'd let me walk into the village alone. He hadn't let me walk in unguarded.

"I know." And I did.

She studied the window for a long moment. Whatever she saw, or thought she saw, she kept to herself. Her eyes came back to mine and there was a question in them she was too smart to ask and too kind to push.

"You're staying out there." Her eyes moved to the window and back. "In the forest."

"I'll visit," I promised. "But yes. I'm staying."

"With whatever's watching us from those pines," she added, and for one moment, just one, she sounded like the old Emma. Dry and flat and sharper than anyone gave her credit for.

"With whatever's watching us from those pines," I agreed, and my mouth twitched despite everything.

Emma gripped my hand. Squeezed hard enough to bruise.

"Come back," she whispered. "When you can. I'll make tea."

"I'll come back," I promised.

She let go. The door opened. Heinrich stepped inside and put his arm around her shoulders. He looked at me over Emma's head. Tired and honest and done pretending.

"Klaus wanted war," he acknowledged, shaking his head. "Wanted to burn witches and turn this village into his personal crusade. Fifteen men followed him into that forest." He paused. "None of them came back."

I held his gaze and waited.

"We're done," he continued. "The wolf is dead. Klaus is dead. That's the story. That's all anyone needs to hear."

"Peace," I offered.

"Survival," he corrected flatly. "I don't have the men or the energy for anything else." He folded his arms. "And you let Emma bring Thomas home. You could have, in that clearing, with what you can do, and you didn't."

"I would never hurt Emma."

"I know." He met my eyes. "That's why I'm standing here talking instead of reaching for that axe."

I held out my hand. He shook it. Firm. Quick.

"Go on now," Heinrich urged, stepping back. "Before people start coming out and asking questions I don't want to answer."

I turned toward the door. Lotte and Margit were already there, blocking the way out. Lotte's arms locked around my neck. Margit pressed her face into my shoulder.

"Take care of your mother for me," I told them, one hand on each head.

Lotte nodded. Her lip trembled but she held it.

Margit grabbed my cloak with both fists. "Come back soon."

"I will." I kissed her forehead. Then Lotte's. "I promise."

I loosened Margit's fingers from the wool and stepped past them before my face could betray me.

I turned back toward the trees. Walked across the snow alone. As I reached the tree line, a dark shape shifted between the pines, large, silent, falling into step beside me the way it had been falling into step beside me since the night I'd run into this forest with nothing but a stolen cloak and a prayer.

The black wolf walked beside me, his shoulder pressing

warm against my ribs, his head level with my chin. I rested my hand on the back of his neck and felt the coarse fur between my fingers and the steady pulse of his heartbeat underneath.

I looked back once. The village was already disappearing behind the trees, chimneys and rooftops shrinking to nothing, swallowed by the forest the way the forest swallowed everything.

It wasn't simple. It wasn't clean. But it was finished.

And that was enough.

Epilogue

Weeks passed.

The snow melted in slow retreats, pulling back from the clearing first, then the paths, then the deeper forest where the shadows held the cold longest. Green things pushed through the mud. Buds appeared on branches that had been bare since before I'd arrived in this cottage. The creek ran full and fast, swollen with meltwater.

We rebuilt what the fight had broken. Patched the wall where my Forceweaving had punched through. Replaced the shelf that had been shattered in the fight with Erik. The boards came down on the third day. Dietrich pried them off one by one while I stood in the clearing and watched. The nails screamed coming out, rusted deep after more than two decades. When the last one fell, light poured through grandmother's windows for the first time since Sophia had been alive. I stood inside and felt the sun on my face and my breath left me in a rush, a breath I hadn't known I was still holding.

We replanted grandmother's herb garden from seeds Dietrich had been storing in clay jars, he'd collected them years ago from the plants grandmother had left behind, keeping them viable without knowing if anyone would ever use them.

I thought about that sometimes. A man alone in a cottage, saving seeds for a garden he'd never plant. Keeping things alive on the chance that someday someone would come along who'd need them.

Dietrich traded furs with a peddler on the eastern road for supplies we couldn't make ourselves, salt, flour, and a new iron pot to replace the cracked one. The peddler didn't ask about the scars. Peddlers learned not to ask.

I trained every morning. The Forceweaving was different now, deeper, steadier, fed by the mating bond in ways I was still learning to understand. The threading came easier. The precision improved. I could hit a target the size of my palm from thirty feet and the power barely flickered. Whatever ceiling had been constraining me before the fight was gone, shattered by what I'd done in that clearing and not rebuilt.

I visited Sophia's grave every morning. Dietrich came with me sometimes. Sometimes I went alone. I'd sit beside the birch tree and talk to her, about the garden, about the training, about the way Dietrich looked at me when he thought I wasn't watching. Small things. Things she'd have wanted to hear.

The first crocus pushed through the mud on a morning in late March.

Purple and small and stubborn. Growing right in the middle of the path between the cottage and the woodpile where Dietrich's boots trampled everything flat. I crouched down and touched the petals with my fingertip. Thin as paper. Cold from the morning air.

Spring. I'd survived the winter.

I stood up too fast and the world tilted. I grabbed the doorframe. Waited for it to pass. It had been doing that for two weeks, dizzy spells in the morning, a rolling in my stomach that came and went. I'd told myself it was the bond settling deeper. The magic knitting two people together had to rearrange things.

That's what I told myself.

"You all right?" Dietrich called from inside. He'd already felt the dizziness — my sudden lurch, the spike of nausea.

"Fine. Stood up too quick."

I went around to the garden. The snow had melted in patches, leaving bare brown earth. I'd been clearing beds, turning soil, planning what to plant. The herb garden needed rebuilding from scratch. Winter had killed the rosemary and most of the sage. The thyme survived because thyme always survived.

I knelt in the dirt and started pulling dead stalks. The soil was cold and wet between my fingers.

The smell of the turned earth hit me and my stomach flipped. I sat back on my heels and breathed through my nose. The nausea had been worse this week. Yesterday the smell of the venison Dietrich was smoking made me run outside and retch into the bushes. His concern had poured into me so thick I could taste it.

I'd told him it was bad meat. He knew I was lying. But he didn't push. He never pushed.

I pressed my hand flat against my belly. Nothing. Just skin and muscle and the faint hum of the bond.

Two months. I'd missed my blood twice.

When William was alive, we'd tried for children. Two years of marriage. Two years of trying and disappointment and quiet grief and wondering which one of us was broken. He never blamed me.

After he died, I stopped thinking about it. Put that door away in the same dark place where I kept my dead. A woman alone didn't need to dream about children. A woman called witch definitely didn't.

I pulled my hand away. Stood up. Pushed the thought down.

The bond. It was just the bond.

But on the third morning after the crocus, my breasts ached so badly I couldn't sleep on my stomach.

I lay on my side staring at the wall while Dietrich slept behind me, his breath warm and steady against my neck. The bond pulsed between us. Quiet. Peaceful. He was dreaming about the forest, the green of it bleeding through the connection.

My breasts had never hurt like this. Not before my blood. Not from the bond. Not from anything.

I knew what it meant. Had known for days, maybe longer, the knowledge sitting patient and terrible at the bottom of my mind. Waiting for me to stop pretending and look down.

I looked down.

My hand found my belly in the dark. Flat still. Nothing to see. But a change lived on the inside. Small and new and impossible.

A child.

The word moved through me like a crack through ice. Every defense I'd built, every wall I'd put between myself and hope, cracking. Letting in light I hadn't felt since the last time I'd let myself want this badly.

I was thirty-eight. I'd tried for two years with a man I loved and my body had refused. And now, after the wolves and the war and the blood, now it decided to work. With a werewolf. With a bond no blood-keeper had ever survived long enough to test.

The grimoire held no record of it, a blood-keeper carrying a werewolf's child. The pages said nothing because it had never happened. Every blood-keeper who faced a werewolf bond before me died before the question could be asked.

I was the first. And I was terrified.

I didn't tell him that day. Or the next. Sat with the *maybe* of it the way I sat with visions, turning it over, feeling the shape, testing the edges for lies. Missed blood. Sore breasts. Nausea. All of it could be something else. The bond. Stress. Age.

But on the fifth day I woke before dawn and vomited so hard my ribs ached. And the nausea wasn't in my stomach. It was lower. Deeper. In a place I didn't have a word for.

That settled it.

He came back from patrol at dusk.

I was sitting on the porch in the red cloak. The evening air smelled like mud and new green things pushing through the forest floor. A woodpecker hammered somewhere in the birches. The sky was pink and gold above the tree line.

He came through the trees in human form. His hair was longer now, brushing his shoulders. The scars from the fight were white lines on brown skin. Faded. Almost gone.

He saw me on the porch and smiled. That real smile — the one that changed his whole face and made him look like someone who hadn't spent most of his life alone. His contentment washed over me. The quiet pleasure of coming home to someone. He still marveled at it. The wonder rolled through every time he walked out of the trees and saw me waiting.

"You're sitting outside," he observed, climbing the

porch steps and leaning down to kiss my forehead. His fingers caught a strand of hair that had come loose from my braid and tucked it behind my ear.

"Must be warm enough for it."

"Almost." I caught his hand before he could pull away.

He settled into the step beside me. Stretched his legs out.

"Something's different." He tilted his head, studying me. Not accusing. Careful. He'd been sensing the shift for days, the nausea, the dizziness, the way I'd been pulling away from certain smells. He'd been waiting for me to say it.

"You already know," I replied, watching his face. "Don't you."

He went still. The way he did when the wolf heard a sound the man needed a second to catch up to.

"I know things have changed," he admitted carefully. "Your scent is different. Has been for weeks. I didn't want to say anything until you were ready."

"What does it smell like?" I needed the wolf's confirmation because I still didn't trust my own body.

He brought my hand up and pressed his lips against my knuckles. "Like you. But more. Like there's a second scent underneath yours. One I've never smelled before." His brow creased.

"Nobody has," I told him, my throat tightening. "Because it's never happened before."

His hand stilled against mine.

"Talia." Just my name.

"I've missed my blood twice. My breasts hurt. I can't keep food down in the mornings." I looked straight at him. "You know what that means."

I felt it hit. The understanding broke over him like a wave.

Joy first. So sudden and fierce it nearly knocked the breath from me. His whole body flooded with it, nothing he could have hidden even if he'd tried.

Then fear.

Cold fear rising through the joy. Erik's amber eyes. The madness that had lived in the gray wolf. The violence passed from father to son in the blood.

"Dietrich." I caught his other hand. "Stop."

"What if it's ..." He couldn't finish. His fingers gripped mine too tight. I sensed his terror. Not of being a father. Of being his father's son.

"Look at me."

He looked. His eyes were wet. First time since he'd told me about Sophia's grave.

"You are not Erik," I stated, holding his face between my hands. "You watched over me for years and never asked for anything. You carried me through the snow when I couldn't walk. You let me choose you. Let me come to you. Never forced. Never demanded."

"The wolf ..." He stopped. Swallowed.

"The wolf is part of you. And you are good." I pulled him closer until our foreheads touched. "This child will know a father who is good. That's more than you ever had."

He broke. Not loudly. The tears came and he didn't try to stop them. His arms went around me and he buried his face against my neck and I held him on that small porch while the sky turned from gold to purple.

I felt him reassembling. Piece by piece. The fear didn't go away — it wouldn't for a long time. But the joy came back stronger. Pushing through the cracks.

"A child," he managed, rough against my neck. "Our child."

"Our child," I confirmed.

He pulled back. Looked at my belly. Put his hand there. Spread his fingers wide.

"Can you feel it?" I covered his hand with mine. "Through the bond?"

He closed his eyes. Concentrated. The bond between us opened wider. I felt him searching. Reaching.

"There." His eyes opened. Amber bright, the wolf looking out with wonder. "Something. Faint. Like an ember that just caught."

I laughed. First real laugh in weeks. It shook my whole body and made my sore breasts ache and I didn't care.

"An ember," I repeated. "That's our baby."

His hand stayed on my belly. His eyes stayed on my face. The bond between us was so wide open I could feel every layer of what moved through him. Joy first, bright and staggering, the kind that knocks the legs out from under you. Then fear, cold and sharp, threading through the joy like frost through new grass. Then something deeper than both. Something that had no name in any language I knew but lived in the place where the man and the wolf met and for once agreed on the same thing.

He pressed his forehead against my belly. Stayed there a long time, breathing.

"I used to think the wolf was a curse," he whispered into my skin. "A thing put in my blood to hunt and ruin and destroy. And now it's on its belly in my chest, whimpering at the sound of something the size of a heartbeat." His hands tightened on my hips. "You didn't just break the curse, Talia. You turned it into something worth carrying."

I put my hands in his hair. Held him there against my belly while the evening turned purple around us and the first stars appeared above the tree line.

"I'm going to be terrible at this," he warned.

"You'll be fine," I assured him. "I'll show you."

The echo of the first night — I'll show you — made something catch in both our chests. We felt the memory at the same time. His shaking hands. My patience. The tears and the tenderness and the beginning of everything.

"You always show me," he murmured, pressing his lips against my knuckles.

We sat on the porch while the stars came out. His hand on my belly. My head against his shoulder. The bond pulsating between us, carrying three heartbeats now instead of two.

That night I waited until he fell asleep.

The fire had burned low. Embers glowed orange in the hearth. His breathing was deep and even. His dreams drifted into mine — warm ones for once. Soft shapes. The feeling of something small held carefully in large hands.

I slipped out of bed. Pulled the red cloak around my shoulders. Lit a candle and set it on the table.

The grimoire was still under the bed where I'd shoved it. I pulled it out and opened it to the page I hadn't been able to finish.

Red.

My little Red who pulled the ribbons from my hair. Who crawled into Mama's bed and curled against her shoulder and slept with her thumb near her mouth. Who blushed at everything and laughed too loud and loved with her whole body, arms wide open, heart on the outside of her chest where anyone could reach it.

I did not leave you. I need you to know that. The note was a lie. I left to keep you safe because he said he would come for you and mama if I didn't, and I believed him. I would walk into a thousand cages for you. I would stay in every one.

You are braver than I was. Stronger. Mama saw it in you before any of us did. She called you Red but she meant fire. She meant the color that burns.

Live, little one. Live so loudly that I can hear you from wherever I am. Love someone who deserves the way you love, wide open, nothing held back, terrifying and beautiful and whole. Have the life I imagined for you on the nights when imagining was all I had.

I am not afraid. I was, for a long time. But I have Mama's garden and your laugh and the sound of the creek breaking free every spring, and those are enough. Those carry me through the dark places and out the other side.

Your Sophia.

I sat at the table and held the open grimoire against my chest and wept. Quiet and long and without shame. For the girl who kept her mother's garden alive inside her own head when everything else had been stripped away. For the woman who wrote about freedom from a cage and meant every word. For the aunt who loved me enough to walk through a door she knew would close behind her.

She had found it. Even there. Even in that prison with the boards on the windows and the bar on the door. She had found something Erik couldn't reach. Couldn't drain. Couldn't break.

I wiped my face. Looked at the blank pages waiting after hers.

The book had kept her from me until I was ready. Not until I was powerful enough. Not until I was safe enough. Until I was whole enough to receive what she'd left without being broken by it.

I understood now. That was what ready meant.

Blank pages. Cream-colored and rough at the edges. Left empty by the women who came before me. Waiting for the next blood-keeper to fill them.

I found a quill in the drawer. A pot of ink Dietrich had traded for with a peddler on the eastern road. I dipped the quill. Held it above the first blank page.

What do you write when you're the first?

The women before me wrote warnings. Survival guides. Instructions for daughters they'd never meet. Every entry in this book was written by someone who expected to die. Who was already dying. Who scribbled what they knew in borrowed time so the next woman might last a little longer.

I wasn't dying.

I was sitting at a table in a warm cottage with a man I loved sleeping in the next room and a child growing inside me that every generation before mine said was impossible. I had power in my blood and a wolf at my side and a future that stretched forward instead of closing down.

I put the quill to paper.

My name is Talia. They call me Red.

I am a blood-keeper. One in a line of women who carried the old blood and paid the price for it. My grandmother was a blood-keeper. Her mother before her. And back through the years to the first woman who tied a red thread around her wrist and said this is what I am.

I am not the last.

I wrote until my hand cramped around the quill and the ink pot ran low.

I set the quill down. Flexed my stiff fingers. Looked at the pages I'd filled.

It was a start.

Dietrich's hand landed on my shoulder. Warm. I hadn't heard him get up.

"Come to bed," he murmured, still half in a dream.

"I just finished." I closed the grimoire and pressed my palm flat against the leather cover. Felt all those women who'd written in it before me. Felt Sophia too. Her warmth running under everything else.

"What is it?" He leaned over my shoulder, looking at the closed book.

I looked up at him. His face soft with sleep.

"The beginning," I told him.

I took his hand and let him lead me back to bed.

I woke up kneeling at Sophia's grave.

The night wandering had always come from a place deeper than dreaming, a body moving while the self slept somewhere the bond couldn't reach. Dietrich wouldn't have felt me leave. Just the absence, when his arm found cold sheets instead of warm skin.

My knees were in the mud. My hands pressed flat against the frozen earth above Sophia's bones, fingers spread wide like I was trying to reach her through the dirt. My nightgown was soaked through with dew and my feet were bare and numb and the birch tree's white bark glowed like bone in the dark.

The night wandering. Again.

But the vision was already in me. Already moving behind my eyes.

A woman. Thin. Sick. I couldn't see her face. Just her hands — bony fingers wrapped around a small black key. Blood on her knuckles. Her own blood. Dripping slow and dark into the stones beneath her feet.

A shape stood behind her. Tall. Still. I couldn't see it clearly. Just the shape of it in the dark. Just the red where eyes should be.

It was afraid of her.

Then the vision shifted. The woman was somewhere else. A room full of candles that didn't move. She was kneeling. Touching something on the ground. Something cold. Her lips moved but I couldn't hear the words.

Her blood hit the floor and the thing in the dark flinched back like she'd thrown fire.

The vision broke apart. Scattered like ash.

I knelt in the mud, shaking. An owl called from the pines. The moon was low above the trees. Sophia's name carved into the bark above me, the letters deep and familiar under my fingers when I reached up to steady myself.

I didn't know who the woman was. Didn't know where or when. My sight never gave those details. Just pieces. Fragments that made no sense until it was too late to change anything.

But I knew what she was. Blood-keeper. I could feel the old blood in her the same way it lived in me.

Except hers was wrong somehow. Sick. Corrupted into something that hurt instead of healed.

Dietrich crashed through the underbrush. He dropped to his knees beside me and pulled me against his chest, his skin burning hot against my frozen body. His panic hit me first. Then relief, then fury at himself for not waking when I'd gotten out of bed.

"I'm here," I assured him, pressing my cheek against his collarbone. "I'm all right."

"You were gone." His arms tightened until I could feel his ribs. "The baby. The cold. You can't ..."

"I know." I let him lift me from the mud. Let him wrap me in his shirt. Let him rub warmth back into my hands while Sophia's grave sat quiet beside us.

The vision was already fading. The woman's hands. The black key. The blood on the stones. Going soft at the edges the way they always did.

I'd write it down tomorrow. Add it to the grimoire. Leave it for whoever came next.

For now, I let Dietrich lead me home with his arm around my waist and the baby still safe inside me, still burning like the ember he'd felt through the bond.

Outside the cottage, the forest was quiet. Snow melting into streams that ran fast and cold through the undergrowth. Green things pushing through dark earth toward the sun.

Spring had come.

Coming Next

TAMING BLUE: A TWISTED BLUEBEARD RETELLING

Once Upon a Monster, Book Two

He's a Sanguinarian.
She's a blood-keeper.
And now they're living under the same roof.

Acknowledgments

To my husband and kids. You lived with a woman who forgot to eat, forgot to sleep, and sat in the same chair so many hours a day for four months that she needed reading glasses by the end of it. I'd do it again.

To my beta readers. You read this book before it was ready and told me the truth. That's the only kind of feedback worth having.

To my ARC readers. You gave your time to a book that was still finding its shape. That kind of generosity doesn't get said enough.

To the two editors who took my money and wasted my time. You know who you are. I fixed it myself.

To my readers. I am nothing without you. I mean that. Every download, every page turn, every message telling me you couldn't put my books down. That is why I do this. That is the whole reason.

More monsters are coming.

Sephyrra

About the Author

Sephyrra watched Nightmare on Elm Street with her mom as a kid. She was terrified. But she didn't hate Freddy. That was the confusing part. Then came Beauty and the Beast, and when the Beast turned into a prince she felt cheated. She wanted him to stay the Beast. Then she saw Dracula take Lucy in werewolf form and that was it for her.

Villains over heroes. Creatures over men. She found her people on Tumblr, spent years writing the love stories no one was publishing, and eventually decided to publish them herself.

She writes dark romance and monster romance with plus size heroines over 35. The monster stays monster. The scenes don't fade to black.

Also by Sephyrra

Insatiable: A Horror Romance - Primal Sins Book 1

Drenched: A Horror Romance - Primal Sins Book 2

Devoured: A Horror Romance - Primal Sins Book 3

Bride Of The Haunted Manor

Upcoming Books

Touched: A Horror Romance - Primal Sins Book 4

This Soft Rotten Love

www.ingramcontent.com/pod-product-compliance
Lightning Source LLC
LaVergne TN
LVHW040214110826
845146LV00005B/1280

* 9 7 9 8 9 9 3 0 5 2 6 5 6 *